Fashioning the Future

by
KAY MOSER

FASHIONING THE FUTURE BY KAY MOSER
Published by Heritage Beacon Fiction
an imprint of Lighthouse Publishing of the Carolinas
2333 Barton Oaks Dr., Raleigh, NC 27614

ISBN: 978-1-946016-74-4
Copyright © 2019 by Kay Moser
Cover design by Elaina Lee
Interior design by AtriTex Technologies P Ltd

Available in print from your local bookstore, online, or from the publisher at:
ShopLPC.com

For more information on this book and the author visit: www.kaymoser.com

All rights reserved. Noncommercial interests may reproduce portions of this book without the express written permission of Lighthouse Publishing of the Carolinas, provided the text does not exceed 500 words. When reproducing text from this book, include the following credit line: "*Fashioning the Future* by Kay Moser published by Lighthouse Publishing of the Carolinas. Used by permission."

Commercial interests: No part of this publication may be reproduced in any form, stored in a retrieval system, or transmitted in any form by any means—electronic, photocopy, recording, or otherwise—without prior written permission of the publisher, except as provided by the United States of America copyright law.

This is a work of fiction. Names, characters, and incidents are all products of the author's imagination or are used for fictional purposes. Any mentioned brand names, places, and trademarks remain the property of their respective owners, bear no association with the author or the publisher, and are used for fictional purposes only.

Scripture quotations from The Authorized (King James) Version. Rights in the Authorized Version in the United Kingdom are vested in the Crown. Reproduced by permission of the Crown's patentee, Cambridge University Press.

Brought to you by the creative team at Lighthouse Publishing of the Carolinas (LPCBooks.com):
Eddie Jones, Ann Tatlock, Katie Vorreiter, Elaina Lee, Shonda Savage, Brian Cross

Library of Congress Cataloging-in-Publication Data
Moser, Kay.
Fashioning the Future / Kay Moser 1st ed.

Printed in the United States of America

Dedication

To the Hearties
for their unwavering support
of uplifting entertainment.
Thank you!

Acknowledgments

To God be the glory for the things He has done in my life and in my writing!

Thank you to the 75,000+ Hearties (the fans of "When Calls the Heart") for your support of my novels. Every time you choose faith-friendly, family-friendly entertainment—whether it be a novel, a movie or a television show—you are bettering the world. Onward, Hearties!

My gratitude for my readers is boundless! I will never know all your names, but you are invaluable players in my life. You receive the words I write and allow them to come to life in your imagination. My prayer is that my words will always lift you up, that they will inspire you as well as entertain you. You are God's beloved children. He made you worthy the moment He thought of you.

Thank you, Mother and Daddy, for teaching me godly values and perseverance. Thank you for always expressing your confidence in me. I miss you!

Novelists inevitably live in several worlds at a time. Their families and friends must extend a special grace—patience and unconditional love—to them. Thank you to Stan and Sue Moser, to Donna, Nancy, Mary, Christine, Jan, Chan, Andrea, and many more for extending that grace to me. I would be lost without you.

Thank you to the entire team of Lighthouse Publishing of the Carolinas (LPC) for your contributions to the publishing of the *Aspiring Hearts Series*. Special thanks to my editors, Ann Tatlock and Katie Vorreiter, for immeasurable patience, personal support, and professional guidance. Thank you to Diana Flegal, agent, for your efforts on my behalf.

Stacey Hitch of Trinity Social Media Marketing has been an invaluable partner and a treasured friend to me. Thank you, Stacey, for your vision, creativity, hard work, and prayers.

CHAPTER ONE

Sarah's spirits soared so high she felt she would surely float straight to the mountain top as she slipped her slender fingers into Lee's extended hand and allowed him to help her down from the buggy. For a thrilling moment, she stood cuddled up against him, her arm wrapped around his strong back as she pointed up to the iron-shaped slab of rock that covered the mountainside and jutted up to meet the early-morning sky.

"This is where I love to come at sunset. I climb up on the mesa and stare in awe at those rocks as the sun sets behind them."

"I can see why. They're gigantic, and it's easy to see where this mountain chain gets its name. Those rocks are shaped just like flatirons."

She turned him toward the valley where light was just appearing on the horizon. "And I've started most of my mornings here, watching the miracle of light returning to this vast valley, chasing the darkness away." She looked up into Lee's eyes. "But today is my happiest day here because you're with me."

"Thank God you're alive and here to enjoy it!" He cocooned her in his arms. "I don't know what I would have ... I simply couldn't have gone on living if you'd died in that canyon."

"But I didn't." She snuggled closer to him, taking great pleasure in the warm safety of his embrace. "I feel more alive than I ever have. The world looks twice as beautiful to me, and I'm filled with such hope. Oh, Lee, I can't believe you actually came!"

He stroked her head. "Did you think I could stay in Texas once I heard you were lost in the mountains?" He laughed softly. "My darling girl ... Don't you understand how much I love you?"

She pulled slightly away and looked up into his eyes. "I understand now. Oh, Lee! I have so much to say to you. Must you really go back to Riverford today?"

"Leaving you is the last thing on earth I want to do, my darling, but so many people are depending on me. General Gibbes can't carry the bank responsibilities alone. He's no banker! And August is the time when the sharecroppers need small loans to survive until the cotton is picked."

Sarah turned back toward the mountains. "When I'm here, it's so easy to forget Riverford exists. I look at these mountains. I feel this cool air. Can there really be a place where people—my people—hurry out to the humidity-laden cotton fields before dawn and sweat through the day, their backs bent, their fingers assaulted by the thorns as they pick? Can that misery exist at the same time as this beauty?" She looked up at him. "Should I be feeling such deep happiness while other people suffer?"

Lee stroked her cheek. "My amazing Sarah … It's impossible to decide whether you're more beautiful on the inside or the outside."

Sarah blushed and grabbed his hand. "Come on! I want to show you my favorite rock, the place I perch to watch the sunrise color the valley and greet the mountains. If we hurry, we can share that experience this one time." She began to run up the path, pulling Lee behind her.

They were laughing and out of breath when they reached the rock, but Sarah turned Lee toward the eastern plains. "Here it comes!" She pointed toward the shimmering, bright orange disk that was rising above the horizon.

He pulled her in front of him and wrapped his arms around her. "A new day beginning," he murmured in her ear. "And we're together."

Sarah watched the golden light march across the valley toward them, her pulse increasing with its approach. *Should I tell him? Is this the moment?* He was so close to her, she could feel his heart beating, feel his warm breath on her neck. When the sunlight finally touched their faces, she wiggled free and stepped back.

"Things have changed, Lee." She paused, grappling for the right words. His face filled with apprehension, so she hurried on. "These weeks have been like that sunlight." She pointed up toward the mountains. "See how it is transforming those massive rocks? That's the way it's been for me; I've been enlightened by my time away from you. But it was the dark hours when I was lost in that canyon, wondering if I would live to see you again … It was those hours that settled my mind." She took his hand and peered up into his face. "I love you, Lee. I don't want to go through life without you. I was devastated when I thought I was going to die and lose the chance to build a life with you. I confess that my determination to teach has not lessened one iota, but I cannot—I will not—go through my life without you."

Lee's face lit with joy as he grabbed her shoulders. "We'll find a way, Sarah, for you to go on teaching after we're married. Together we're stronger; don't you see that?"

"I see that my teaching career will never fulfill me completely. I need you, Lee. I love you."

"Marry me!"

Sarah nodded.

"Oh no, young lady!" Lee's eyes twinkled as he smiled down at her. "I won't settle for a nod; I want to hear words."

"Yes, I will marry you, Mr. Logan!" she shouted. "How's that?"

"Perfect!" He pulled her into his arms and kissed her.

Joy surged through her, and when his lips finally parted from hers, she murmured, "The mountains must surely be in full, glorious sunlight now."

"I wouldn't know. I can't take my eyes off you. *When* are you going to marry me?"

"I … I don't know. I'm determined to teach this year, and classes begin early next month."

"Of course you're going to teach! I wouldn't have it any other way, but how about a Christmas wedding? I would marry you today, Sarah, but if we wait until then, you will be halfway through your contract, and you will have proven how good a teacher you are."

Sarah looked up at him in wonder. "You're amazing, Lee Logan. I don't know of another man who would be so supportive of his future wife's profession."

"You don't know another man who gets to marry *you*! The truth is, I'm being selfish. I don't want you to be just another woman who sacrifices her dreams for marriage. I want you to be happy in our marriage."

"I will be."

"I'm a realist, Sarah. I can only do so much to make you happy. I know without a doubt that your calling is to help other young women break loose from society's restraints. You *must* fulfill that calling to have complete happiness."

Tears filled Sarah's eyes as she nodded, but Lee's lips took possession of hers and made her forget everything, even the massive, sky-reaching mountains.

As the sun continued to climb, they returned to the buggy, and Sarah showed Lee around Texado Park, the tent city that housed the Texas teachers who had come to Boulder, Colorado, for their first-ever Chautauqua. "Can you believe this summer school was all organized and readied in just six months?" She swept her arm around, indicating the two hundred tents lined up in rows.

"I can't believe you've been living in a tent for the last month! This place looks like an army camp. Are you sure you're safe here?"

"Of course. Right over there is the tent I share with Bert and Ella." She pointed to the green-and-white hipped tent. "Looks like it belongs in a carnival, doesn't it?"

Lee frowned as he shook his head. "Looks like there's nothing but a piece of canvas between you and whatever decides to wander down from the mountains behind it."

"Now, don't start worrying about me. I am perfectly safe as long as I'm here with the other teachers. It was that ill-advised hike into the mountains that got Bert and me into trouble. More specifically, it was Dr. Wickham's insistence that he knew the path that put our lives in danger."

"I'd like to talk to that man!" Lee clenched his fists.

"I'm just glad they finally found him. From what I've heard, he was in pretty bad shape. I'm sure he'll return to Boston as soon as he's able to travel. I don't know who will take over his classes—"

"As long as he's not here encouraging you to take dangerous hikes into the mountains, I'll be happy."

"Turn down this lane," Sarah directed. "I want to show you the auditorium before we go to the dining hall for breakfast. Oh, how I wish you didn't have to leave today! There's an outdoor band concert tonight, and Madame Makarova is performing soon. If only you could hear her play!"

"She's the Russian pianist who has befriended Christine?"

"Yes, and I can't tell you how much she's encouraged Christine to use her wonderful musical gifts. Let's stop here for a few minutes, Lee, and take a quick look at the auditorium. It's enormous and provides a place for the most amazing events."

Excited to share her new experiences with the man she loved, Sarah jumped out of the buggy. She linked her arm in his and pulled him past one of the soaring towers that anchored a corner of the huge wooden structure and into the open-sided building.

"Well, you weren't exaggerating its size!" Lee exclaimed as they left the bright morning light behind for the dimmer light of the interior. "Is there an event every evening?"

"Almost. We have an orchestra in residence, great solo players like Madame Makarova, choirs, lectures of all kinds, band performances—"

"Whoa!" Lee laughed as he held up a hand. "No wonder you're in no hurry to return to Riverford."

"Oh, Lee! You should have seen Christine playing on that stage last week. It was just a miracle to see her up there, finally able to utilize her great gifts. And so soon after—" Sarah's words halted.

"After Richard's death."

"Yes. She has so much more freedom here than she does in Riverford. I don't know how she'll ever be able to return to the restrictions of widowhood. She just has to continue her music. Can't you see a difference in her?"

"Of course I can. And Victoria's transformation is miraculous."

"She's been restored by this cooler climate, it's true, but there's so much more to it. The mountains have inspired her to paint again. There's no telling what the future holds for her. She's so talented!"

"Hayden needs to see her. He's still carrying around the image of her when she was so sick and he put her on the train." Lee turned to Sarah. "That's a major reason I'm returning to Riverford so soon; I want Hayden to be able to come here."

Sarah felt the prickle of coming tears. "I should have known." She reached her hand up to stroke his face. "You would be thinking of others. What a lucky woman I am to have you love me!"

"I'm the lucky one. We're going to have a wonderful life together, my love. I promise I'll do everything—"

Sarah gently placed her fingers over his lips. "I know you will. For the last three years, you've encouraged and supported me in my unusual—some would say outrageous—goals."

He took her in his arms and held her close. "We're entering a whole new age, Sarah. Not just you and I. The whole nation is. Our culture is on the brink of great changes. Even tradition-bound Riverford is in for change. Our generation must shoulder some of the responsibility of leadership. It's our time."

"You're right. I'm so glad I've had this experience here this summer because I've met so many dynamic, forward-looking women." She laughed as she pulled back and looked up into his face. "But none so dynamic as Victoria and Christine! I don't know exactly what's coming, but I sense that we'll see them both blossom in the next year. I can't imagine how Riverford is going to react when we return!"

"With shock." He grinned at her. "They're already reeling because recently widowed Christine dared break with decorum and bring Victoria to the mountains to heal."

"It's going to be a lively autumn. I don't want to leave here, but I really have missed you, and I can't wait to start my first semester of teaching."

"And I can't wait to get *you* back home. How long are you going to make me wait before I have you back in Riverford?"

"The Chautauqua ends in ten days. That's almost impossible to believe; it's whirled past."

"So, in about two weeks, I should be welcoming you back to Riverford." A loud sigh of exasperation escaped his lips. "Too long!" He pulled his watch from his vest pocket. "No time for breakfast, I'm afraid. I'll grab something at the station."

"Oh no!"

He grinned down at her. "I'd rather say my good-byes here in private anyway."

Sarah didn't wait for him to take her in his arms. She threw her arms around his neck and eagerly met his lips.

CHAPTER TWO

Fifteen minutes later, Sarah stood on the dining hall porch, watching Lee's buggy race down the steep hill as tears ran down her cheeks. Before he was even out of sight, a mob of giggling teachers surrounded her. "Who is he? What does he do for a living? Did he ask you to marry him?" Their questions crescendoed into a screech in Sarah's ears. She pushed through the excited women without answering and headed for the steep flight of steps.

Several followed her down the staircase, planning Sarah's wedding as they went, but she managed to ignore them until one loud voice rained an accusation down on her from the porch.

"So you're giving up your fine scheme to help the sharecroppers' daughters, Sarah Novak!" Claudia Kelly, the boisterous suffragette, taunted her. "I knew you wouldn't last. You got a taste of the high life from those wealthy friends of yours, and now you don't even remember how downtrodden women are in this country."

The enthusiastic babbling of the excited teachers halted when Sarah stopped in her tracks, slammed her fists onto her waist, and glared up at the woman. "Oh, I remember, Kelly! You see, that's where you and I are different. I will never forget the poor children because I nearly starved to death myself. I know poverty firsthand. You, however, have lived your entire life with a full belly. Your rebellion against the status quo is merely theoretical. Well, I won't be launching a theoretical skirmish against injustice when I return to Texas. I'll be waging all-out, hands-on war, and the man who just left here will be at my side."

As Sarah stalked away from the teachers, she heard their murmurs of disbelief. "You mean, she's going to teach? But she's got a man! What on earth is she thinking?"

The thought of Lee's leaving made her run uphill toward the auditorium and hurry to the eastern side of the hill. When she arrived, she saw a train just beginning to snake its way out of the valley spread below her. She threw herself down on one of the large rocks as tears brimmed over and differing emotions whiplashed her. *It will be weeks before I see him again! But he came. The minute he knew I was in trouble, he came.* She watched the train approach the first hill and turned around to take a quick look at the mighty mountains at her back. *I love it here. The beauty, the opportunity to learn, the freedom from Riverford. But oh, how I shall miss Lee!* When she turned back to the valley, his train straddled the top of the hill, glinting in the bright morning sun for just a moment, then quickly disappeared.

Before Sarah entered the crowded dining room, she hastily wiped away the tears that had flowed once Lee's train disappeared from view. Devoid of appetite but determined to eat something, she hastened through the serving line and settled at the nearest table.

"Sarah!" Her sister teachers Ella and Dorcas slid into the chairs around the table.

"How's Bert?" Ella asked as she wrung her hands. "I just know she'll never recover entirely."

"She's doing much better than we dared hope." Sarah tried to stop her friend's growing anxiety. "The cut on her head will take weeks to heal, but thankfully, her ankle isn't broken, just badly sprained. The doctor insists she stay in bed, but you know Bert. She's already demanding crutches, and she's determined to come back to class."

"So soon?" Dorcas' eyebrows shot up.

Sarah laughed as she shrugged. "You know Bert. She'll certainly try."

"Can we visit her?" Ella asked. "I just have to see that she's all right."

"I'd wait at least another day; the doctor really is trying to keep her quiet."

"Good luck with that," Dorcas exclaimed, then quickly changed the subject. "Have you heard about Professor Wickham?"

"Only that they found him. I'm relieved."

"Oh, the poor man!" Ella blurted out. "So dreadfully injured."

Dorcas snorted. "It's probably just his ego that's injured."

"Dorcas!" Ella exclaimed. "How can you say such an uncharitable thing? Poor Dr. Wickham is so injured he can't even come back and finish his classes. I don't know what will happen to the Chautauqua!"

Dorcas rolled her eyes. "Somehow we'll survive."

"Oh, there's Dr. Freitzig." Sarah pointed at the professor who was entering the dining room. "I've got to talk to him about today's exam. I can't possibly take it."

Laughing, Dorcas jerked her thumb toward Dr. Freitzig's back. "Go flutter your eyelashes at the man. He'll give you more time."

Sarah glared at her as she stood and took a last gulp of coffee before hurrying after the professor.

"I'm glad to see you looking so well." Dr. Freitzig's normally solemn eyes twinkled as he turned back from the faculty dining room. "No doubt you've come to talk about today's exam. I shall expect you to take it on Friday afternoon."

"Oh, thank you. I was just coming to ask you—"

"And I shall expect you to make an A on the exam, Miss Novak. We only have one more week of class, and I fully intend to send you back to Texas equipped to use the logic of science to lift children out of poverty. Science is the answer to the world's problems."

"Perhaps mixed with a bit of human charity?"

"*Hmmm* ..." He was clearly struggling to look annoyed. "Science is reason based and therefore much more reliable than emotion-based human charity. Science invents, improves; it creates labor-saving devices, discovers medications, increases food production—"

"Which someone has to put into the mouth of the needy."

Dr. Freitzig chuckled. "So you insist on a partnership, Miss Novak?"

"I do." Sarah emphatically nodded her head.

"So be it! Now, if you will excuse me, I must grab some breakfast before class time." He bowed slightly as he added, "But remember, Miss Novak. I expect you to make an A on your exam."

I hope! Sarah felt exhausted by the emotions of the morning as she turned away and hurried to her first class. By noontime, she was so tired she skipped lunch and returned to her tent for a desperately needed nap.

CHAPTER THREE

When Sarah awoke a full five hours later, she found that clouds were gathering around the peaks behind her tent. Determined to check on Bert's progress and eager to share the news of her engagement with Victoria and Christine, she hurriedly began the downhill walk to the sanitarium. Thunder began to rumble when she was halfway there, and a wind raced down from the mesa and lifted her skirt. She began to run, but the cold showers caught her, and when she arrived at Christine's rented cottage behind the sanitarium, she was soaking wet and shaking with cold.

"Sarah! Come in." Christine grabbed her arm and pulled her out of the pouring rain seconds after she knocked on the door. "Come over here. We've just lit the fire."

"You must get out of those soaking clothes," Victoria insisted as she stepped out of the shadows. "You're shivering!"

"Oh, I'm so glad you're both here!" Sarah exclaimed. "I have the most exciting news—"

"Not until you're good and dry," Christine interrupted. "Come into the bedroom. I'll lend you my robe. Frances is making tea for us, and Nancy is getting the girls up from their naps."

When Sarah returned to the sitting room a few minutes later, Victoria installed her in the chair closest to the fire, and Christine handed her a cup of tea.

"Drink up." Victoria impatiently tapped her foot. "Then start talking. We've been wondering all day ... Well, after all, you *did* leave at dawn with Lee. What happened?"

Sarah smiled mysteriously.

"Let Sarah drink her tea," Christine insisted.

"Forget decorum," Victoria ordered as she paced. "Gulp it down and start talking."

Sarah hurriedly drained the cup and glanced mischievously from one lady to the other.

"Talk!" Victoria insisted.

"We are engaged."

"How wonderful!" Christine exclaimed as she gathered Sarah into a hug.

Victoria remained silent, and Sarah was quick to untangle herself and stand to meet her mentor's gaze. "You don't approve, Victoria?"

"You are going to teach?"

"Of course. Lee is completely supportive of my career."

"But the school board won't be." Victoria shook her head.

Sarah's heart sank as she watched her. "You think I'm wrong, don't you?"

"No. I just think we have a new battle on our hands." She came to Sarah's side and took her hands in her own. "You love Lee. Christine and I have known that a long time. We want you to have love in your life, but we know how much you want to teach. We thought you had chosen teaching, at least for now."

"What changed your mind, Sarah?" Christine asked. "Was it Lee's racing up here to save you?"

"No. His actions have certainly shown me how much he loves me, but it was something Bert said when we were lost in the mountains and thought we were going to die."

"What did she say?" Victoria asked.

"She said to choose love. She said that love is the most important thing in a woman's life and that the professional women who insist they don't need or want love are lying."

Christine's eyes filled with tears. "She is right. Love is most important."

Sarah's heart wrenched as the memory of Richard's death raced through her mind. "Oh, Christine, I'm sorry! I've been so insensitive, so self-centered—"

"No," Christine murmured. "This is your time. You are a young woman in love with a fine young man."

"You're also an intelligent, educated woman ready to embark on a teaching career." Victoria's voice grew more heated as she talked. "And you shouldn't be required to choose between the two!"

"Victoria is right," Christine agreed. "It's time for tradition to change. You are a woman, of course, but you are also a talented person who can enable many needy children to rise in the world."

"It's time to ruffle society more vigorously!" Victoria met Christine's eyes. "And not just with Sarah's plans, Christine. You need to take your place in the music world."

"In time perhaps ... when the children don't need me so much. But what about you, Victoria? There's nothing holding you back right now."

A loud, exasperated sigh escaped Victoria's lips. "Just inspiration!" She clapped her hands together. "But today is Sarah's day!" She threw her arms around Sarah. "Did you set a date?"

"Maybe Christmas."

"Maybe?"

"I have to proceed cautiously if I want to keep my teaching job. And I do!"

"You and Lee are sacrificing for the future of other women," Victoria concluded. "And I must say, he's a remarkable young man to be willing to take on this challenge with you."

"He's wonderful!"

Victoria's laughter exploded and filled the room.

"Not exactly a surprising evaluation from a woman in love," Christine commented as she joined the laughter.

Heat surged through Sarah, and she knew she was blushing geranium red as she sprang to her feet. "Oh, you two!" She made her best attempt to look annoyed, but her traitorous mouth grinned. "Don't encourage me to dream about Lee. There's too much work ahead."

"I'm sure you'll have no trouble catching up," Christine encouraged.

"But something else has come up. Professor Morton has taken over Professor Wickham's classes, and he's asked a number of us to lecture for him. I did my best to beg off, but he knows I love

Wordsworth's poetry and has asked me to discuss it." Sarah shook her head. "I don't know what he's thinking. All the other teachers are older and more experienced than I am."

"But they haven't been studying Wordsworth as long as you have," Victoria said. "Age has nothing to do with the matter. Why shouldn't you teach?"

"I had hoped to start by teaching children! Oh, I've got so much to do. I better go; I want to stop in and visit with Bert."

"Do prepare yourself before you go in, Sarah," Christine advised. "Her head is bandaged, of course, but one side of her face is badly bruised."

Sarah hesitated outside Bert's door, uncertain whether to knock and risk waking her or just go in. Before she could decide, Bert called out, "I hope that's you, Dr. Reese. I have a few things to say to you!"

"I bet you do," Sarah murmured through a grin as she opened the door and peeked around it.

"Sarah!" Bert exclaimed. "Come over here and help me get out of this bed."

"I'll do nothing of the sort. You're supposed to be resting."

"Well, at least help me prop up. I refuse to lie flat on my back any longer."

Sarah hurried to the bedside and stacked the pillows behind Bert as the older teacher dragged herself into a seated position against the headboard.

"I'm glad you're here." Bert took command of the conversation at once in spite of the fact that she was grimacing with pain. "I want you to bring me my textbooks—"

"Bert! You must rest." Sarah tried not to stare at her friend's discolored face. "You don't need your books. I can just imagine what the doctor would say—"

"Good! Then we don't have to discuss him. He's the bossiest person I've ever met."

Sarah burst into laughter as she pulled a chair to the bedside. "Not counting yourself, you surely mean."

Bert dismissed the comment with a wave of a bruised hand. "I'm the principal of a school. I have to be bossy."

"And he's your doctor and, no doubt, knows he doesn't have a prayer of getting you well enough to return to Texas if he doesn't get tough with you."

"There! Now you've finally hit on the important matter. We only have a week and a half of classes left, and I'm not leaving Colorado without my science certification. I came all this way to earn it, and I plan to do so."

Sarah grew serious. "Bert, some things are just not possible. You and I know what a horrible ordeal you've been through—"

"May I remind you that you went through the same ordeal, and you're—"

"It's not the same." Sarah held up her hand as she interrupted. "I didn't fall off that ledge; I scooted down the hill on my backside. You've had a severe blow to your head, and your ankle—"

"Is not broken. Just sprained, so I'll have to hobble around Texado Park on crutches for a few days."

"What? Surely you don't think you're going back to class! The doctor said you'd need a wheelchair for several weeks as well as bed rest to heal your head."

"Nonsense! It's *my* head. I ought to know more than any man—I mean, any doctor—about my own head. I refuse to just lie here and lose my chance for that certification!"

"You don't have a choice."

"Who says?"

Sarah sighed, flung herself back in the chair, and studied Bert's battered face for a minute. "Okay. I understand your desire to finish the science course, but you must give yourself more time to heal. At least a few more days."

Bert didn't answer; instead, she folded her arms across her chest and scowled as she stared out the window.

"Bert?" Suspicion welled up in Sarah's mind. "What are you thinking?"

"You're right, of course, but I want to send a note to Professor Freitzig. I don't want him to think I'm giving up." She pointed toward a small table. "Give me some of that stationery, and I'll scribble something you can take to him."

Relieved, Sarah fetched the paper and supplied her own fountain pen.

A few moments later, Bert folded her brief note, stuck it in an envelope, and handed it to Sarah with a smile. "Well, I feel better about that now. Tell me what's going on with the other teachers."

CHAPTER FOUR

"Just drop us off here," Victoria directed the carriage driver as they reached the dining hall at Texado Park several evenings later.

"And after you take care of the horses, you must come enjoy the outdoor band concert," Christine added. "I am sure you will be welcome."

"Oh, I'm so glad you were able to come!" Sarah exclaimed as she ran toward them. "The band concert is going to be such fun. Lots of the new ragtime music, and afterward, we'll all gather around a campfire to sing."

"Sounds wonderful," Christine murmured as the driver helped her down. "So lovely to be out in the evening air."

Sarah's face turned sad. "I just wish Bert could be here; she loves our campfire gatherings. I can't bear to think of her stuck in that bed twiddling her thumbs on such a beautiful night."

Victoria's eyebrows shot up as she stepped down from the carriage step. "Should we tell her?"

"What?" Sarah asked. "What's going on?"

"I wouldn't worry about Bert tonight."

"Why not?" Sarah demanded.

Christine gave a little wave that was obviously intended to hush Victoria.

"Tell me! What's going on?"

"Bert has company this evening," Christine answered. "Now, we better make our way uphill to the bandstand. I am still slow moving in this high altitude, and we—"

Sarah refused to budge. "Who?"

Victoria grinned. "Just some friend of hers … a gentleman caller actually."

"Victoria!" Christine exclaimed. "That was supposed to be a secret." She turned to Sarah. "Dr. Freitzig is visiting Bert this evening."

"What?"

"I'm sure it's all school related." Victoria pretended nonchalance.

"Well, of course it is," Sarah retorted. "What else could it be?"

"What else indeed," Christine agreed. "Now, let's start the climb to the bandstand."

"And it's perfectly logical," Victoria said as she started walking, "that Bert would send for Christine to fix her hair and bring her a ruffled robe—"

"Ruffled?" Sarah broke in. "Did you say ruffled? Bert in ruffles?"

"Well, to be perfectly honest, she didn't ask for ruffles," Victoria admitted. "She just asked for something … something …"

"Feminine." Christine supplied the needed word.

"Good heavens!" Sarah exclaimed. "The world is surely coming to an end."

"I would not make too much of it, Sarah," Christine cautioned. "He was only bringing her books to her."

"He brought her books? Why would he do that?"

"Because she asked him to," Victoria answered. "You remember. You delivered the note yourself."

"That sneak! She's incorrigible. What are we going to do with her?"

"Absolutely nothing," Victoria answered. "She's a grown, independent woman who has a right to run her own life."

"But the doctor said—"

"But Bert decided. And that's an end to it."

"Victoria is right," Christine agreed as she linked arms with Sarah. "All we can do is try to temper her activities. Now, come on. I hear the band warming up. We better get up this hill."

Half an hour later as the sun began to set, the crowd was enjoying riotous ragtime music, but Victoria simply could not sit still and listen. The changing colors of the sky overhead had taken her attention prisoner.

"I'll be back," she whispered to Sarah before she rose and slipped away from her friends.

Her excitement built as she hurried downhill toward the large open field in front of the dining hall. "From there I can see straight up to that first rock," she murmured as she turned the corner of the two-storied building. "And I'll wager the sun is—oh, my word! Look at that!"

The sun was a fiery red disk perched atop the iron-shaped rock that covered the side of the mountain and jutted beyond its rounded top. At that moment, the point of the rock seemed to have snagged the sun, stopped its progress in the sky, and enabled it to send its radiant rings of orange and gold in a full circle. Its light shot straight up into the cloudless sky, creating a pointed crown for itself. Its warm color tinted the similarly shaped rocks on the string of mountains that lined the northern edge of the plains.

Victoria's pulse quickened as she held out her arms, clad in reflective white silk, and watched them glow with shades of peach. The fingers of her right hand twitched and shaped themselves to hold a paint brush as she thought of her palette, covered with glossy pools of fresh paint waiting to be stroked by her brush. As her eyes rose again to the sun-streaked sky around the rock, her whole body yearned to walk forward, to enter the painting she saw being enacted before her. Succumbing to her desire, she took the first steps toward that bright, mesmerizing disk. With each step she grew nearer, but the sun would no more wait for her than it would wait for any mortal. The rock released its hold, and the orange disk slowly slipped behind it into a world Victoria could not see. With each diminishing of the circle, her heart ached at the loss, but the sun gifted her with the ever-changing color and design of its sky-thrown beams.

"I shall meet you here tomorrow!" Victoria shouted when the top edge of the disk slipped behind the mountaintop.

"It'll be here." A deep male voice startled her. "I figure it'll be here long after we're gone to glory."

"Mountain Jack!" Victoria called out as she whirled around, for his voice was unmistakable.

He removed his battered felt hat and bent his long, lean frame into a quick bow. "Evening, Mrs. Hodges. Seems like you're mighty taken with our Rocky Mountain sunset."

"Indeed I am, and I intend to capture it in a sketchbook tomorrow evening."

He chuckled. "I'd pay a pretty penny to watch that, seeing as I ain't never seen nobody capture a sunset on anything."

Victoria joined him in his laughter. "You're right, of course. We painters can be a touch arrogant at times."

"A touch, you say?"

"Okay, okay! Outrageously arrogant. How's that?"

He grinned. "Okay for a starter." He dipped his chin and stared at the weedy ground for a few seconds. "Course, I figure if anyone can capture them colors ..." He raised his head and met her eyes. "Well ... I guess it's likely to be a Texas lady with sunset-colored hair."

Victoria found she enjoyed making this reticent man talk. "Have we Texas ladies unsettled your world this summer?"

"Well, let's just say you've ruffled it a bit."

"A bit?" She pursed her lips into a pout. "I'm disappointed."

"Well ... okay. A lot. Seems like I'm always hunting one of you down."

"And are you hunting me?"

"I am." Mountain Jack nervously shifted his hat from hand to hand. "That is ... well, that sweet Texas lady is worried 'bout you."

Victoria suppressed a laugh as she turned back to the camp. "That 'sweet Texas lady' would be Mrs. Boyd, of course. And what am I?"

"The fiery one," he answered, then ducked his head. "Course, a man can't live without fire."

"Why, Mountain Jack!"

True to her word, Victoria arrived at the entrance to Texado Park the next evening, eager to begin her attempt to catch the colors of a Rocky Mountain sunset. With a grumbling Frances following close behind, carrying Victoria's satchel of supplies, Victoria began the hike up the path that followed the rounded contours of the mesa until it disappeared at the base of the first gigantic rock.

"Just think, Frances!" Victoria was bubbling over with excitement. "We can come back tomorrow morning and follow this path all the way up to that rock."

"Oh no we can't! They's wild animals up there. Has you already forgotten how that wildcat nearly ate Miz Sarah up when she's lost in them mountains?"

Victoria paused to catch her breath and looked back at Frances. "We're not going at night. We'll be perfectly safe."

"We sure will 'cause we ain't goin' at all. Look at you! You's already outta breath. You gotta remember you's been sick, and you can't go climbin' no mountains."

"We just need to take our time and stop to rest now and then." Victoria turned back to the mountains and peered longingly up the enticing path. "What a view it must be from there!"

"Views like that's for folks like Mr. Mountain Jack. He got the lungs to get there. You ain't." She looked overhead at the coloring sky. "Besides, this here's a real fine view."

Victoria glanced skyward, then rushed forward. "And it's going to get better and very soon too. We must get in place."

"Seem to me the sunset gonna be ever'where. Ain't no gettin' away from it." Frances panted as she followed. "What's wrong with this place right here?"

"Sarah told me about a special rock halfway up that has the best view," Victoria called back between gasps for air. "She's going to meet us—" Victoria's words halted. "Oh, Frances! There she is. Just look at her silhouetted against the sky!" Victoria stepped off the path and plopped down on a small rock. "Quick! Give me my satchel."

"Yes'm. If it mean we's gonna stop here, I give you anything you want." She handed the worn, brown leather case to Victoria, who hurried to pull her supplies out.

"*Shh*. I don't want Sarah to know we're here until I've made a quick sketch." She flipped open a large sketch pad and, charcoal pencil in hand, began to draw.

As the sketch of Sarah standing on the rock, gazing out at the valley with the enormous flatiron-shaped rock of the first mountain behind her, grew on the page, Victoria's excitement increased. "Oh, she is magnificent!"

"Miz Sarah? Or that giant rock?" Frances asked as she leaned over Victoria's shoulder, watching her mistress' hand race back and forth across the paper.

"Sarah! The rock can't help but be what God made it to be, but Sarah has free choice. And just think what she's chosen. There she stands, a thousand miles from home, three years of constant toil away from her former life, holding her chin high, facing the light, staring out across the continent. She is the future, Frances. She is the twentieth century. She is the new woman!"

"If you say so, Miz Victoria. I don't for the life of me see how you sees such things." She glanced down at the drawing "But you's sure caught Miz Sarah on that paper."

Victoria reached for her box of pastel chalks. "And now to try to catch a bit of the sunset before it goes." She snatched up several colors and, balancing the pad on her lap, began to color the background behind her image of Sarah.

Their human voices, so alien in this wild place, were silenced by the coming grandeur of the vivid sunset. Victoria began to hear the birds of dusk calling each other home. She leaned forward, her own spirit yearning to join with the color and form in front of her, and without consciously choosing either one stick of chalk or another, she instinctively grabbed colors and swept them across the heavy paper, stacking them on top of each other, occasionally blending them with her fingertips.

Slowly the bright colors in the sky, the golds and oranges, changed to rose. Victoria turned to a fresh sheet of paper and swiveled to look up at the bright disk disappearing behind the massive, sharply etched edge of rock that jutted into the bright sky. She flung her previously chosen chalks into the box and snatched a new collection of rose, mauve, and purple. The birds quieted; darkness began to fall around them, but the vivid, ever-changing sky held her attention. The wind swirled down from the canyon, flapping her skirt and rustling the paper, but still she worked on, mesmerized by the colors that God could create.

Only when the sky began to turn leaden did Frances gently shake her shoulder. "Miz Victoria, it be dark, and here come Miz Sarah lookin' for us."

Victoria forced her eyes away from the top of the rock and sighed as she shifted her position.

"You's gonna catch cold in this here wind." The tone of Frances' voice changed from soft persuasion to fussing. "I ain't gonna be havin' you catch no cold."

Victoria felt a warm shawl being draped over her shoulders.

"Now that be enough for tonight," Frances insisted as she gently slid the pad from Victoria's lap. "We's gonna come back another time. That sun done gone back behind that mountain into a world we ain't never gonna see. Lawd only knows how many mountains be back there!"

Victoria looked up at Frances and smiled. "Oh, Frances! You are brilliant!"

"I is?"

"You are. There are indeed many mountains behind this one. This is, after all, the Front Range. Oh, Frances! Just think of all the vistas waiting to be painted. And I'm going to paint them!"

"They's way back there, way back where Miz Sarah done got lost. You can't go there."

Victoria sprang to her feet. "With Mountain Jack I can. And I will!"

"You will what?" Sarah called out as she approached them. "Are you okay? Why didn't you come meet me?"

"I did!" Victoria raced forward and hugged Sarah. "And I found my future. Oh, Sarah! I found my future."

"I don't understand."

"Neither does I!" Frances said. "Miz Sarah, you gotta talk to her. She think she goin' back into them mountains where the wildcats and bears is."

"What's this?" Sarah demanded, her voice laced with alarm.

"It's quite, quite wonderful!" Victoria's hands danced in the air. "I'm going to do a series of paintings of the mountains. There's nothing to worry about because I'm going to hire Mountain Jack to escort me to the best vistas."

Sarah clasped Victoria's hands and smiled. "Even in the dusk, I can see the sparkle in your eyes, the shine on your face. Oh, Victoria, this is good for you, isn't it?"

"Not if she freeze to death it ain't," Frances protested. "If she go climbing 'round on mountains, she gonna get sick again, and then what's Mr. Hayden gonna say? He gonna shoot me for sure 'cause I's supposed to be takin' care of her."

Sarah shook her head. "You're wrong, Frances. It's these mountains that have healed Miss Victoria's body, and now they will elevate her spirit."

"Thank God you understand, Sarah!" Victoria exclaimed.

"I do."

"What I understands is that we's gotta get down this path to the carriage 'fore it gets so dark we can't see nothing. Now you two come on." Frances stuffed Victoria's supplies into the satchel and began to herd them down the path. "There's the driver comin' up to look for us right now. He know it's too late for us to be up here."

"Okay, you win for now, Frances," Victoria conceded. "But I'll be back early in the morning. I want to catch the sunrise on those rocks, and I suspect the valley and the plains off to the east will be shimmering with color."

"Sunrise is very early this far north," Sarah warned. "Very early. The sun is completely up by six o'clock."

Victoria waved her hand disdainfully. "Then we will be here at five o'clock, won't we, Frances?"

Frances heaved a noisy sigh. "Yes'm. I figure we will. Ain't no arguin' with you."

CHAPTER FIVE

The early morning sky was an opaque, mourning-dove gray when Victoria, clad in her brown tweed bloomers and velvet-collared Eton jacket, climbed down from the buggy and hurried toward the mesa path in the crisp, cold air.

"It ain't fittin' for a lady to be climbin' mountains in the dark," Frances grumbled as she lagged behind, lugging Victoria's art satchel.

"This isn't Texas," Victoria called back. "There's no such thing as 'fitting' here."

"Well, it's too cold for you to be outside, and they's plenty of wild animals prowlin' this mountain, and I ain't wantin' to be they breakfast."

"They're more afraid of us than we are of them. Now stop your grumbling, Frances—"

"No, they ain't!" Frances dropped the satchel and pointed up the path. "They's a bear right up there. Quick, Miz Victoria! Run!" Frances turned back and ran toward the buggy.

Standing her ground, Victoria peered up the path into the thin fog that softened the distant trees. Slowly Frances' bear materialized, hurrying toward her, and Victoria laughed.

"Come back, Frances," she called. "It's just Mountain Jack." She retraced her steps, picked up the satchel Frances had dropped, and began climbing again. "We've no time to waste; the sunrise is beginning, and I must get into position." She veered off the path and, striding through knee-high grasses, hurried to a flat rock she had spotted the evening before.

All business, Victoria jerked a sketch pad and boxes of pastels from her bag and laid them out on the rock as skillfully as any experienced acolyte could prepare an altar. She knelt before the supplies, took up the pad and a pencil, and hastily sketched the barest outline of the mountain before her. Flipping through several pages, she made the same quick sketch. A look of resignation on her face, Frances settled in the grass behind her mistress just as Mountain Jack reached them.

"Morning, ma'am. I been expecting you."

Victoria nodded as she looked back over her shoulder at the horizon on the plains. The first line of color had appeared at what looked like the edge of the world. She turned back to the great slab of rock veneered onto the side of the mountain and grew still as she watched. Moments later, she reached for a single piece of chalk, and the frenzy began. As the sun peeped over the horizon behind her, then made its first tentative appearance, and finally began to rise, Victoria knelt in front of her "altar," her fingers flying across the pages. Color after color of chalk was snatched from the tray, each hue a vital instrument in the fingers of a human trying to duplicate God's creative grandeur. As Victoria worked to capture the color projected on the rock by the rising sun, she swiped through the pages of the sketchbook, trying to record the dynamic story unfolding before her.

Finally the sun cleared the horizon and turned the rock into a shimmering peach-colored flatiron that pierced the pale blue sky. The rock cast its commanding shadows westward across the fir-tree-covered mountain that held it.

"Stunning!" Victoria cried out as she worked. "Look at the shapes of those shadows."

Moments later, the tyrant named Time won the battle Victoria had been waging with it. The sun was sufficiently risen to reveal the reality of the rock—its charcoal color, its jagged crevices, its wind-hewn scars. Victoria sat back on her heels, a contented sigh escaping her lips.

"I ain't never seen anything like that." Mountain Jack's voice was solemn.

"Surely you've seen it many mornings, and how I envy you all your opportunities," Victoria answered.

"I ain't talking about the sunrise. I'm talking about what you just done on that paper. Ain't never seen nobody build them mountains on paper. Seen some photographs, but that ain't the same."

Victoria looked down at her paper-strewn altar with its tangle of colored chalk sticks. "They're only frantic sketches. The real art comes later when I try to capture that sunrise on canvas. When I'm home in Texas and cannot see—" Her voice choked as an unfamiliar grief washed over her. She looked up at him as tears stung her eyes. "I won't be here. I won't be able to see this—" She leapt to her feet. "If this spot holds such beauty, how much more is there back there?" She flung her arm toward the mountain range. "I must see it! You must show it to me."

"Now, Miz Victoria …" Frances held up her hands. "You gotta take care of yourself. You been mighty sick."

"I'm not sick now!" Victoria snapped. "I've never felt more vibrant, more alive than I do right this minute." She took a determined step toward Mountain Jack. "I mean what I just said. I want to employ you to take me into the mountains, to show me the majesty hidden back there. I intend to paint it!"

"Mr. Hayden ain't gonna like this," Frances warned. "He gonna—"

"Hayden will understand. You forget, Frances. I didn't meet my beloved husband in Texas. I met him in England on a cliff in Cornwall where I was painting the sea. He knows he married an artist." Victoria locked eyes with Mountain Jack. "Will you take me or not?"

He grinned down at her. "I'll take you, ma'am, 'cause I figure you'd just find somebody else if I didn't."

"Good!" Victoria held out her hand. "Then it's settled. We begin tomorrow at dawn. I want to see everything."

Mountain Jack shook her hand but did not release it. "Ain't nobody ever seen everything in them mountains, Mrs. Hodges. They're full of surprises. But we'll see more than enough to keep you painting all winter long."

"You gotta ask the doctor," Frances insisted as she began to gather up Victoria's art supplies. "But first we gotta get down off this cold mountain and get some hot tea and breakfast."

Mountain Jack finally released Victoria's hand. "I figure you'll be able to bully Mrs. Hodges into the breakfast, Frances, but I doubt you'll get her to ask a doctor or any other man for permission for anything."

A grin lit Victoria's face, but she quickly suppressed it. "Why, whatever do you mean by that comment, sir?" she drawled as she tried, but failed, to look innocent. "Will you join us for breakfast?"

"No thank you, ma'am. I figure I'm better off starting my day in the mountains."

"What? No room of chattering women for you?"

Mountain Jack grinned, then changed the subject. "Pick you up about eight o'clock in the morning. Ain't no need to start at dawn for what I got in mind."

"I'll be ready," Victoria assured him as she turned and started down the path.

"We'll be ready!" Frances called after her. "You ain't gonna go up into them mountains without me. No, ma'am, you sure ain't!"

"Be sure you bundle her up good, Frances," Mountain Jack directed. "It'll be cold the first couple of hours."

"Lawd have mercy! This here Colorado healed Miz Victoria, but it gonna kill me for sure."

"There you are!" Sarah called from the bare, dusty ground behind her tent as Victoria and Frances reached the edge of Texado Park. "Did you capture the sunrise?"

"Has any painter ever done so?" Laughing, Victoria hurried forward to hug Sarah.

"We sure gots us lots of paper with colors on it." Frances held the bulging satchel high. "And we's goin' up into the mountains early in the morning and die of the pneumonia."

"What's this?" Sarah's face was awash with concern as she glanced at Victoria.

"I employed Mountain Jack to take me further into the mountains to sketch. I want to capture every mountain, every canyon, every vista—"

"Why don't we start with breakfast?" Sarah interrupted her as she took her arm. "My classes begin in an hour, and Christine is bringing the girls up about ten for their—"

"What on earth happened over there?" Victoria pointed to the collapsed side of a nearby tent.

"We had what the locals call a chinook wind last night, and it hit the canvas side of that tent so hard it pulled the stake out of the ground."

"Lawd have mercy!" Frances swung her head from side to side. "Must've scared them ladies half to death."

"Needless to say, they had to abandon their tent and bunk with us," Sarah said.

Frances and Sarah continued chatting, but Victoria did not register their comments. Her attention had been caught by two teachers who began pulling a rope taut and hauling up the caved-in side of the tent. When they had it up to the required height, a younger teacher stepped forward, pushed a stake through a loop on the end of the rope and several inches into the ground. Then, much to Victoria's amazement, the young woman lifted a sledgehammer high over her head, and with one decisive downward stroke and deadly accuracy, she drove the stake into the ground. Victoria's heart pounded with excitement. *Imagine! A woman doing that ... and with such confidence.* Eager to capture the image to record on canvas, Victoria replayed the scene in her head. The triangular figure of the young teacher with her arms extended over her head. The wooden shaft of the sledgehammer elongating her further as it reached to the bright, blue sky. *This is a new breed of women. How exciting to think of their futures!*

"Victoria, are you all right?" Sarah's voice seemed far away to Victoria.

"Yes ... yes." Victoria's vague reply did no justice to the excitement she was actually feeling. The fingers of her right hand twitched as they yearned for a pencil.

"Are you sure?"

Driven by her need to record the scene, Victoria leaned over, snatched up a short stick, and drew in the sand the basic triangular shape she had just witnessed. She stood, and looking down the steep hillside, she peered at the town in the valley below, then raised her eyes to the horizon where a ribbon of mountains receded into the blur of the distance. Leaning over again, she added a small elongated oval for the town, a horizon line, and a simple sketch of the receding mountains.

"A painting?" Sarah joined Victoria and looked over her shoulder.

"She gotta eat first," Frances insisted. "We left that sanitarium in the pitch dark, and she ain't even had a cup of tea."

Victoria felt Sarah's hand on her arm. "We really do need to go to breakfast," she urged. "And you won't forget it." She pointed to the primitive drawing. "Not now."

A satisfied smile covered Victoria's energized face as she stood straight. "It feels so good to be creating again!"

"I wish I understood better what's going on in your mind. I guess I never will, but I'm so glad to see you happy and healthy."

CHAPTER SIX

After breakfast, Victoria settled under an apple tree and made quick sketches of the young teacher, her face strong with determination, holding the sledgehammer high over her head. Frances leaned against another tree, her eyes shut, her face lifted to the sun that dappled through the branches.

"My goodness, you must have left the sanitarium before dawn!" Christine exclaimed as she approached.

"*Shh!*" Victoria pointed to Frances. "Don't remind Frances; she was none too happy with me."

Christine settled on the bench next to Victoria. "May I see what you are sketching?"

Victoria tilted her sketchpad toward Christine. "I actually watched this young woman drive a stake into the ground this morning."

Christine's mouth fell open as she shook her head in amazement. "We would never have even tried such a thing."

"And we would have been condemned as unfeminine if we had."

Christine sighed as she leaned her back against the tree trunk. "I guess this is a good time for me to confess that I have no desire to return to Riverford. I do not want to veil myself again and recede from the world as a widow is required to do. Do you think I am awful, Victoria?"

"Absolutely not! I don't want the restrictions of Riverford either. I miss Hayden, but I don't miss the battle to be myself and the condemnation of my actions and attitudes. I want to stay here, wear my bloomers, explore these mountains, and paint." She turned to Christine. "And I want you to pursue your music. Christine, I really think you could and should perform publicly in the future. You are an artist! Artists are supposed to practice their art. And now that Richard—" Victoria stopped her effervescent flood of words. "I'm sorry. I shouldn't bring up your loss; it must make it so much harder to return to Riverford, knowing he won't be there to welcome you home."

Remorse for her careless words overwhelmed Victoria as she watched Christine's eyes fill with tears.

"I must eventually face that reality, of course." Christine's voice was low and weary. "Perhaps I could stay away a while longer ... give myself more time to heal."

"And more time to pursue your music." Victoria's voice grew encouraging. "We could stay even after the Chautauqua ends. Is Madame Makarova returning to New York at the end of the season? Perhaps she could stay into September. You two could continue—"

"There are other considerations." Christine held out a letter to Victoria.

Victoria hastily scanned it. "The boys ... of course."

"They will be coming home from camp around the first of September, and I want to spend time with them before they go back to school. As you can see from George's comments, they have not dealt with their father's death at all. A woman cannot quit being a mother just because she wants to practice her art."

"Why not have them come here?"

"They need to come home. They need to know they still have a home." Christine's face was grave as she struggled to her feet, wiped off her skirt, and grabbed her satchel of music. "I am going to go practice; Natalya will be rehearsing with the symphony this afternoon, and the piano will not be available."

"Shall we meet at noon for lunch?"

"I doubt I will be hungry." Christine's voice was listless. She shrugged, a wan smile on her face. "I guess I had better eat, though, so I will see you at noon." She raised her hand in a slight wave as she walked away.

Concerned for her friend, Victoria bit her lip and stared unseeingly at her sketch. Soon she heard a piano playing nearby and smiled as she listened to the tune. The words that were so emblematic of

Christine drifted through her head. *Lord, lift me up and let me stand, by faith on heaven's tableland. A higher ground than I have found. Lord, plant my feet on higher ground.*

"Oh, Christine!" Victoria exclaimed. "No one stands on higher ground than you do. If I could just *touch* the height you *stand* on, I would be so grateful."

"Lawdy, I 'most fell asleep in this warm sunshine." Frances shook herself and scrambled to her feet.

Victoria laughed up at her, then stood and brushed down her bloomers. "You didn't almost fall asleep, Frances. You were snoring like a big old Rocky Mountain bear."

Frances plopped her hands on her hips. "I don't do no snorin', Miss Victoria! You can be right sure Samuel'd tell me if I did."

"Maybe you were just breathing heavily," Victoria conceded as she gathered her supplies into her satchel. "I'm going up to the auditorium to listen to Christine play. Why don't you stay here and enjoy the sun a little more?"

"'Cause I needs me another cup of black coffee. This gettin' up 'fore dawn and traipsing 'round the mountains sure tires a body out."

"If you say so."

"I does, and I got something else to say about Miz Christine goin' home, too."

"Frances! You weren't asleep at all."

"I was playin' possum. But here what I got to say. When people got to face hard things, it help a lot if they knows they gonna get some relief down the road."

"Relief?"

"Miss Sarah say they gonna have this Chautauqua thing again next summer."

Victoria's mouth sprang wide with surprise. "And you think we should come back and that knowing we are coming back will help Christine."

"Yes'm, I does. And that ain't all. Miz Sarah say they's gonna build houses on this here land for the people that comes to the Chautauqua."

"And?"

"I thinks you oughta build one of them houses."

"Frances, you are a genius!"

The mighty sounds of Tchaikovsky filled the air and captured Victoria's attention. She whirled to look at the nearby auditorium. "Will you listen to that? Christine is playing her feelings."

"Sound like she be conquering them to me."

"Yes ... yes, she is. And I'm going to go listen to her play. This moment won't come again; I refuse to miss experiencing it. You go get yourself a cup of coffee and just relax."

"I's gonna get some coffee for me, and I's gonna bring you a pot of tea. Here ..." Frances handed the art satchel back to Victoria. "I think you gonna want this. You and Miz Christine seems to set each other's art to going."

Startled by Frances' insight, Victoria tilted her head and gazed deep into the servant's loving, wise eyes. "Yes," she murmured. "Yes, we do. And that's why this Chautauqua is such a gift. It allows us to be together, to be with others like Natalya and all the gifted people here."

"And to leave behind all the things that ain't really necessary."

Victoria's pulse pounded in her ears as excitement overwhelmed her. "You're right, Frances. We're freer here. Oh, Frances! We *are* going to build that house!"

Frances turned her toward the auditorium, and Victoria followed the glorious music flowing from Christine's fingers.

*   *   *   *   *

When she slipped into the massive auditorium, Victoria was transfixed by the sight of Christine. Her friend was dressed in the severe black dress of a widow, every inch of her skin covered except her white hands that flew across the keys and her fair face lifted toward the giant rafters far above her head. Sinking onto a bench that allowed her to see both Christine's hands and face, Victoria stared in wonder at the tiny figure, who was so obviously transported to another realm by the music she was making.

"Magnificent," Victoria murmured. "Such power in those tiny hands, such depth of feeling rising from that fragile body."

Victoria followed the line of Christine's gaze up to the rafters and found an intricate design of unfinished wood, a tracery worthy of a cathedral. She swept her eyes around the front of the auditorium, including the large, almost bare stage and the soaring walls of its backdrop. The single golden hue of unfinished wood created a soft backdrop for the startling spot of black. The shiny black concert grand piano captured her eye. Diminutive Christine, dressed in her widow's black, briefly melded into the massive instrument as if the two were one.

Christine paused a few seconds, her hands resting in her lap. Then quite suddenly her fingers reached for the keys, and her white hands began racing up and down the keyboard as they produced the sounds of a Chopin prelude. Clearly, she was not *part* of the instrument: she was its master. Without her, it was mute; with her, it commanded the vast auditorium. As Victoria watched in wonder, Christine's left hand flew into the air and descended on the bass keys in a series of rapid, rumbling chords. Unable to stop herself, Victoria snatched up her satchel and grabbed her sketchpad and pencil. To the bass chords Christine added treble chords. Raising both hands into the air, she repeatedly slammed them down onto the keys, creating rising volume and growing intensity. At the height of the drama of the piece, Victoria's eyes widened in amazement as Christine lifted her whole body from the piano stool, her tiny foot extended to the pedal, and dropped back down as her hands crashed into the chords and raced up the keyboard.

Victoria gasped. In that moment she saw a statement she must make to the world. Women possessed massive potential; they could change the world. They were rising and would no longer be denied the leadership roles they were fit for. "And I will not be denied my place in the art world!" she whispered fiercely. She loosed her hand on the whiteness of the sketch pad, capturing the moment when Christine had risen off the piano stool—both hands raised with fingers splayed—poised to pound the waiting keys and lift her audience into ecstasy.

Lost in the music and the movement of her hand across the pad, Victoria did not hear Frances approach, did not know that the servant carried a loaded wooden tray until she heard a thud and felt the bench quiver. Her eyes flicked to her right as her eyebrows flew upward. Before her, she saw an ornate sterling teapot surrounded by thick white mugs and a tin pan of cornbread.

"What's this?" She looked up at Frances and was startled to find her scowling.

"This be the best I can find in this here place." Frustrated, Frances raised her voice. "And I had to climb the hill to Miz Sarah's tent to get that teapot. These things here—" She pointed to the heavy crockery. "They calls these things 'mugs,' and they be all they got to drink outta, and"—Frances paused for effect as she pointed derisively—"that be what they calls 'cornbread.'"

From the stage, Christine burst out laughing as she rose from the piano stool. "What? No French pastries, Frances?" she asked as she descended the steps to the auditorium floor.

"Not even a biscuit! They ain't gonna have nothing 'til dinnertime—only they calls it lunch."

"But they do have tea." Christine smiled as she reached them. "Thank you for carrying this heavy tray up the hill—Oh, Victoria!" Her tone changed to amazement as her eyes fell on the sketchpad.

Victoria placed the sketch of Christine on the bench in front of her. Reaching into her satchel, she pulled out her sketch of the young teacher pounding the stake into the ground and added it.

"They are magnificent!" Christine exclaimed. "What power they portray."

"The power of women, power the world needs but refuses to access." Victoria added her drawing of Sarah on the mountainside.

Christine covered her lips with her long, tapered fingers as she gasped. "Victoria! You've captured our girl perfectly ... so strong, so determined, so proud. Just look at her!" She met Victoria's eyes. "She's quite a lady now."

Victoria's eyes stung with surprising tears as she nodded her agreement.

Silence fell on the cavernous auditorium as Christine picked up and studied first one sketch and then another. "You know," she finally said, "together these three paintings make quite a statement."

"I hope so because I know now that these three sketches are the beginning of a collection I intend to paint and show at a major New York gallery."

"Your first show! Yes, it's time, but ..." She picked up the drawing of Sarah and, stepping back several paces, held it up for Victoria to see. "Not a collection of mountain scenes. These paintings are about the strength of women. 'New century ... New woman.' Give your first show that title, Victoria, because it's women like you who are ushering in the new woman."

Victoria drew in a quick, audible breath. "You're right! 'New century ... New woman.' Oh, I like that! But I hope you're including yourself as a new woman, Christine."

Christine pinched her lips together and stared up at the rough-hewn rafters high above her as tears filled her eyes. "Yes!" she finally gasped as she pointed toward the grand piano. "Now that I've played on that stage, I cannot go back to the quiet domesticity of a widow."

Victoria raced to her side and hugged her.

"Riverford ain't seen nothing yet!" Frances exclaimed.

"Heaven help us," Christine groaned. "We must soon return to Riverford with all of its stifling traditions. How will we *ever* please everybody and continue in our art?"

"We won't." Victoria's answer was simple and decisive. "We'll take care of our loved ones, of course, but we *will* practice our art as professionals and let the gossips of Riverford chatter away."

Christine gazed back at the stage and out the open sides of the auditorium at the towering mountains. She sighed. "And we will try to remember this brief reprieve and let these few weeks support us through the coming years."

"No." Victoria felt a smile curving her lips. "These weeks of reprieve will only need to support us for the next ten months or so. After that ..."

Christine cocked her head. "What?"

"They're selling lots here at Texado Park and encouraging us Texans to build cottages before next summer."

"They are?"

Victoria's smile widened. "They are."

"Oh, Victoria! Are you going to ... You are! You are going to build a cottage here at Texado Park. What does Hayden think of this plan?"

"I haven't told him yet."

CHAPTER SEVEN

On Saturday morning, Victoria sat quite still, watching a squirrel cavort in the sanitarium garden. He arched his back into a hump worthy of a miniature camel, then suddenly sprang upward, forward, flying through the air until his claws dug into the bark of a fir tree. Looking back over his shoulder, he sent an insolent, cocky glance Victoria's way as he swished his tail. "*Magnifico!*" she called out as she laughed. His fussing call filled the air as he scampered pell-mell up to the top of the tree. As Victoria threw back her head to watch his progress, she felt her loosened red hair streaming down her back. How comforting the morning sun felt on her arched neck! How glorious to feel cool air in August!

"We found her!" Christine called out as she and Sarah exited the sanitarium door. "We should have known you would be outside on such a beautiful day, Victoria. Are you working, or may we sit with you for a while?"

"Come sit. I've been watching a saucy squirrel."

"Sarah and I both have letters to share. If we pool our information, we shall certainly know what's going on in Riverford."

Victoria grimaced. "Do we want to know?" She stood and gave Sarah a welcoming hug. "I hope you're going to spend the day with us."

"I wish I could," Sarah answered as she settled next to Christine on a garden bench. "I just came down to visit Bert, but I've got to study. I'm so far behind!"

"What a week this has been!" Victoria exclaimed. "Think about it. Just a week ago today, you and Bert went up into the mountains for a fun day with the other teachers and ended up lost."

Sarah shuddered. "I won't forget last Saturday night as long as I live. Lost in the mountains, Bert badly injured from her fall, no food or fire, wild animals … Thank God for Mountain Jack's dog! Without him, I wouldn't be sitting here talking to you and Bert wouldn't be recuperating upstairs."

"It's too horrible to relive," Christine muttered. "Victoria and I were up all night praying and pacing the floor."

"But you were saved." Victoria cut off their negative memories by slamming her hand down on the arm of her chair. "And Lee came all the way from Texas to find you, and you're engaged to be married."

"Yes." Christine picked up the more positive strain of conversation. "We just visited Bert, and the doctor says she'll be recovered enough to leave with the other teachers in a week or so."

"Oh, the Chautauqua can't possibly be ending so soon!" Sarah wailed. "Only one more week of classes, and then we teachers will all disperse to the far corners of Texas. How I shall miss everyone and the camaraderie of like-minded women!"

"Nevertheless, we need to make our own plans." Victoria held up a letter. "Hayden writes that he'll arrive here on August twenty-fifth and plans to escort us all home on September seventh. Clearly, our departure date will have to be adjusted since Christine's boys are coming home on September seventh."

Christine shook her head. "That doesn't mean you have to leave the cool air, Victoria. You must stay here as long as you can."

"I must go home earlier too," Sarah said, "to prepare to teach. So I can escort Christine and the girls home."

"That settles it!" Christine declared. "Victoria, you are staying here, and you and Hayden can have a much-deserved vacation, just the two of you." She turned to Sarah. "What news of Riverford do you have, dear?"

"A letter from Mother and …" Sarah turned bright red. "A letter from Lee that he wrote on the train and posted in Amarillo."

Victoria and Christine exchanged a knowing look. "Just tell us the news from your mother," Christine suggested.

"She describes my brother Josef's wedding to Anuska Sykora." Sarah looked down at her lap.

"And you wish you could have been there?" Victoria asked.

"I wish that Josef had wanted me there ... but he didn't, and that's that." Sarah sighed, then sat up straight and struggled to change her tone. "On a happier note, I also received a letter from Lavinia. She and Reverend Neville have set October thirtieth as their wedding date. She asked me to be her maid of honor."

"How nice ..." Christine's voice faded.

Victoria sighed. "It seems like just yesterday that Lavinia and Sarah presented their paper on Wordsworth to the Riverford Literary Society. My, how things have changed for the shy, scholarly Lavinia!" She laughed. "The Riverford ladies must be gossiping nonstop. Christine, you and I must host a bridal shower for Lavinia."

Christine's face contorted, and she quickly covered it with her hands as a quiet sob escaped her lips.

Victoria was furious with herself. "Oh, my dear friend!" She raced to Christine's side and wrapped her arms around her. "How insensitive of me! Here we are chattering away about weddings and happy days ahead and—"

"As you should!" Christine insisted. "Your world need not stop just because mine has."

Victoria knelt in front of Christine and, pulling her friend's hands down from her wet cheeks, tried to encourage her. "Your world hasn't stopped entirely. Your boys are coming home. Ceci and Juli desperately love you and need you. You have your music. I know, I know. It's not enough to make up for the loss of Richard. Nothing will ever do that. You'll miss him from now until the moment you see him again, but your world's not empty. It's just not full."

"If only I could remain suspended here in this bubble of time and place! Here, where I am not forced to acknowledge the fact that he is gone. I would give up everything I own if I could just bring the boys and Father here and—" Christine's words were choked off by another sob.

"But you can't do that," Victoria concluded as she sat back on her heels. "This place has been a gift to us all. We've been restored by the beauty here, inspired by the companionship of other seeking minds, buffered from the difficulties of Riverford. But soon we'll all have to go home."

"Is it still my home? I feel like I have become two different people, the widow and mother in Riverford and the musician in Colorado. Only the first of those women will be welcome in Riverford; the musician must disappear."

"No!" Victoria sprang to her feet. "Christine, do you remember when I first moved to Riverford and missed England so much I didn't think I could stay in spite of my love for Hayden? Do you remember visiting me in my garden right after the Italian fountain had been installed?"

Christine nodded as she dabbed at her eyes with her lace-edged handkerchief.

"And what did you counsel me to do to make myself feel at home in Riverford?"

"To plant an English garden around the statue."

"And to throw caution to the wind and bring as much of European culture to Riverford as I could. In other words, you advised me to bring my two lives together to create a new one. And that's exactly what you're going to do this year. That's what you *must* do, or you will suffocate."

"Fashion a new identity for myself ..."

Sarah moved to Christine's side and put her arm around her friend's shoulders. "We're all fashioning a new future in our own ways, Christine. I'm beginning a teaching career that most of Riverford disapproves of. They'll disapprove even more once I become a married woman and continue to teach. Victoria will be preparing her first public showing of her art."

"And you, Christine, will be redefining widowhood and motherhood by adding the life of a female musician," Victoria added.

"It seems almost impossible ..."

"But it isn't!" Victoria was startled by the hardness of her tone and struggled to soften it. "Opportunities for women are beginning to open up. The door into the male-dominated world of the arts has been cracked open on the East Coast by brave women like Natalya Makarova. We're going to crack it open in Texas."

Christine, her eyes brightening, looked up at her friend. "Inch by inch," she murmured.

"Exactly." Victoria nodded. "Those inches will soon make the first foot." She looked over at Sarah and grinned. "And you and I, Christine, are not going to let the younger generation have all the fun of battering down the doors of stifling tradition!"

"Thank goodness!" Sarah exclaimed. "Because I don't think we know how to do it." She grabbed Christine's hands. "We have to do it together."

Victoria turned back to her chair, snatched up a letter, and waved it in the air. "But we'll gladly accept any support a male wants to offer. This is a letter from Antonio Santoro. Listen to this!"

"'My dearest Victoria, I gladly accept your invitation to spend Christmas at your home in Texas before I begin a tour of the southern states after the New Year. Tell the talented Mrs. Boyd that she must clear her calendar entirely for we shall make music every day. With you to gaze upon, *carissima*, and Mrs. Boyd to concertize with, my life will be *bellisima*. I shall be in heaven itself. *Deo gratia!* Tell Hayden there will be no need for his presence and boring games of chess. What man worth the name needs the presence of another man and a chessboard when he is blessed to have two such enchanting women at his side?'"

Sarah burst out laughing. "He hasn't changed a bit!"

"No," Victoria agreed. "Antonio is *always* the Latin lover."

"Is he really coming?" A hopeful smile grew on Christine's face. "Oh, how I've missed making music with him."

"It's been three long years since he first visited us."

"And helped you jolt Riverford out of its mid-century traditions with your art and books and fashions." Sarah laughed heartily.

"Not to mention her elegant parties and musicales," Christine added.

"And electric lights on Christmas trees!" Sarah exclaimed. "What a shock that was!"

"In other words," Victoria summed up Riverford's response to her, "all my outlandish, foreign ways."

"Now you sound like Edith Bellows," Sarah commented.

"Oh, it's too beautiful a day to think of my less-than-welcoming next-door neighbor," Victoria insisted. "Let's live it to the fullest!"

Sarah sighed as she stood. "I have a long afternoon of study ahead of me."

"But that's your way of living. You love your books," Christine encouraged.

"And you're going to meet us for the concert tonight," Victoria added.

"Yes, you must!" Christine exclaimed. "Madame Makarova will be conducting Tchaikovsky's First Symphony, and it will be Victoria's first time to watch her."

"I wouldn't miss it." Sarah kissed both of them on the cheek. "After all, we're not likely to hear Tchaikovsky in Riverford anytime soon." She waved as she left. "See you tonight in the auditorium."

CHAPTER EIGHT

My most unique concert experience ever. Those were the words that played around in Victoria's mind, tossing like lively waves in sparkling sunlight as she sat on a bench, dead center in the cavernous wooden auditorium of Texado Park. *Yes, that's how I'll describe tonight in my letter to Hayden.* A twinge of longing for her husband plummeted her exuberance until four-year-old Juli Boyd threw herself sideways into Victoria's lap, looked up at her, and demanded, "Where's the archester?"

"Or-ches-tra!" Distress raced across six-year-old Ceci's face as she corrected her sister. "Sit up straight like Mama said. Everyone is looking at you."

Juli jumped up onto the bench and gazed around the half-full hall. "No, they're not! They're all talking to other people."

"Mama!" Ceci hissed in a stage whisper. "Make her behave. It's so embarrassing!"

Christine leaned across Ceci and pulled Juli down. "Juli, please remember that you insisted on coming in spite of the late hour. I expect you to make me proud."

"Yes!" Ceci insisted. "Remember who you are. What would Daddy think?"

"Daddy is with Jesus," Juli retorted.

Victoria watched a wave of disapproving faces turn toward them and felt a surge of sympathy for Christine. "Ah, here comes the bass player, Juli." She pointed to the stage. "See the man with what looks like a giant violin. Do you think you could draw him?"

"I'm sure she could." Christine joined Victoria's efforts to distract the child. "She could draw all the orchestra members if only she had a better view. It is too bad she cannot sit with Nancy at the *back* of the auditorium where the benches are higher and people have the *best* view."

"Yes." Victoria picked up the clue. "If only she could see better ... An artist must always position herself where she can see her subject from the best perspective. I don't suppose you would consider allowing her to join Nancy?"

"Oh ... no." Christine gravely shook her head. "A little girl needs to be with her mother on an occasion as grand as this one."

"But I'm an artist like Miss Victoria!" Juli slid off the bench, stumbled across Ceci, and grabbed at her mother's skirts. "I have to go up high where Nancy is."

Christine cocked her head as she looked at Victoria. "What do you think? Would it be too scandalous to let her go?"

Victoria rose with great dignity, pretending to be affronted. "My dear Christine, nothing is too scandalous in the cause of great art. Juli *must* be allowed the best view of her subject."

"I suppose you are right," Christine agreed as she stood, her black silk skirt swirling around her ankles. "I will take her to the heights of the auditorium." She held out her hand to Juli, who promptly jumped up and down with glee.

"I look forward to seeing your masterpieces tomorrow," Victoria called as the little girl skipped away.

Yes, my most unique concert experience ... It had been strange enough to ride in an open carriage in the bright sunshine of a late summer's evening toward the majestic mountains. It had been stranger still to drive through a tent city and arrive at a gigantic auditorium, so newly built, its unpainted clapboards still held their golden hue and emitted the scent of fresh-cut wood. All around them, hundreds of people from different lifestyles converged into a colorful mosaic. The trains had brought the crowds of concertgoers from Denver, the ladies all dressed in their finest evening clothes. *What a stark contrast they are to the bareness of this auditorium,* Victoria thought. She glanced over at the section reserved for the teachers. *And what a contrast to the simple black skirts and white shirtwaists of the teachers.* She looked down at the green silk and ivory lace of her own dress and smiled. Frances had certainly believed Victoria would regain her health, her active life, when she added this dress to the trunk.

"Where's Christine?" Sarah joined Victoria on the bench and snapped her attention back to the present.

"She's delivering Juli to Nancy." Victoria rose and hugged Sarah. "Where have you been?"

Sarah held up her class notebook. "Sitting outside memorizing some science facts."

"Juli wouldn't behave herself!" Ceci's face was indignant. "I knew she wouldn't."

"You must remember that your sister is only four years old," Sarah said as she slipped past Victoria and sat between her and Ceci.

"But this is our first real concert ever!" Ceci protested. "Look!" She pointed to the stage. "A whole orchestra with violins and horns and ..."

Victoria's attention drifted away from the little girl's enthusiasm and focused so intently on the stage she hardly noticed when Christine rejoined them. The whole orchestra had assembled now; the fifteen resident players of the Chautauqua from the Kansas City Orchestra had been joined by another ten or so from Denver. All male. All dressed in their formal black tuxedos. Victoria was intrigued by the contrast of neutral colors. The black and white of the orchestra so different from the honey-colored, wooden stage and back wall. The rich, mahogany tones of the string instruments and the silvers and brasses of the horns. A possible painting was nudging its way into her creative spirit. "A pleasing palette," she murmured, "but no contrast to—" Her words stopped as her eyes caught a flash of color moving onto the stage. Seconds later, the auditorium filled with an under-rumbling of polite applause that failed to cover their startled comments. "Look at that dress!" "Oh! Isn't she just the most elegant ..." "Hardly a conductor's attire, surely..."

Madame Makarova, her full cobalt satin skirt trailing after her, glided to the center of the stage and bowed rather than curtsied. The electric lights glanced off the shimmering blue-crystal beads decorating the shoulder-revealing bodice of her dress. Her curly black hair was swept up and secured by a sparkling diamond clip. She was stunning!

Christine stood, her ivory-gloved hands applauding, and Ceci threw her treasured decorum to the wind and climbed up to stand on the bench so she could see.

"Isn't she magnificent?" Sarah exclaimed.

"Wait … just wait until you see her conduct," Christine answered as Madame turned her back on the audience and walked to the raised podium.

"A woman conductor!" Victoria was shocked by her own words. She had known Madame Makarova, the woman she had come to know as simply Natalya, would conduct tonight, but she had never visualized this moment. And now, Natalya was actually raising the baton into the air, and the men of the orchestra were focusing intently on her. *Waiting to be led by a woman!* As the thought flew through her head, Victoria felt like she would burst with joy.

Victoria's eyes, her mind, her artistic sensibilities were so riveted to the woman standing dead center on the stage, she had dismissed the presence of the audience of nearly a thousand. The moment had become more than a historically important event; it had become a painting, a permanent record of a door being flung open for women.

Christine reached over and gently pulled Victoria down onto the bench just as Madame Makarova swept the baton straight down and the mighty opening chords of Beethoven's Fifth Symphony boomed through the stark, perfectly plain auditorium. The heat of unfettered excitement infused Victoria; she straightened her spine, raised her chin, and narrowed her eyes with determination. It was happening! Another impossibly high wall vaulted over, another iron door battered down, another new frontier conquered. The fingers on Victoria's right hand began to sketch on her lap. Sarah smiled, opened her class notebook to a clean sheet, slipped it onto Victoria's lap, and placed a pencil in her mentor's hand.

During the pause after the first movement of the symphony, Victoria slipped into the aisle and quietly made her way to the side of the rounded stage where she spent the *andante* movement attempting to capture the poignant expressions on Natalya's face. She also made several quick sketches of the male players, their hands engaged in the playing of their instruments, but their eyes focused on Natalya, who loomed over them.

"It has been quite a night," Christine whispered as the carriage carried them past the towering mountains that guarded the gates of Texado Park. She pointed to Nancy whose chin had lowered to her chest in sleep as Ceci and Juli both snoozed in her arms. "I knew they would be asleep by the third movement of the symphony." She smiled at Victoria. "I believe you found the fourth painting of your collection tonight."

Victoria nodded, then threw her head back against the seat and gazed up at the stars in the inky sky. "I keep seeing the future," she murmured. "The future of women who are liberated from their historic definitions, liberated from the idea that they are mindless and controlled by their emotions. I see the arts enhanced by female participation, female input. I am so bold, I even see a better nation, a kinder people. Do you think I'm insane to be so hopeful?"

"No. Not insane ... a bit impatient, perhaps."

Victoria laughed quietly. "A bit?"

"Not every woman will choose to grab onto the opportunities that are coming. You must remember that, or you will be disappointed."

"Most of our generation won't grab on; I know that. It is Sarah's generation we're fighting for."

"Yes, we are fighting for the future." Christine sighed. "The truth is most women are not as blessed as we are. For most, life is a daily struggle to feed their children. I am in awe of them; millions of them have traveled across an ocean and settled in a new land where nothing is familiar, not even the language."

"And they *will* keep coming." Victoria pointed to the stars overhead. "As many as the stars. More even."

"How can we help so many?"

"By helping as many Sarahs as we can find, by daring to break down barriers for them and enabling, encouraging them to march through."

"And we start at home. Our job is Riverford."

Victoria laughed. "Heaven help us!"

CHAPTER NINE

On Monday afternoon, Christine sat on a shady bench outside the auditorium waiting for Natalya. As she listened to the sad call of the mourning doves who had nested in the Moorish towers of the structure, her spirits began to sink. "You must not think of your loss," she chastised herself. The official quiet hour period of early afternoon had begun, and the rows of tents stretching up the hillside held the camp's dozing residents. She smiled as she thought of Ceci and Juli sprawled on a quilt on a wooden floor, their limbs limp, their angelic faces happy while Nancy dozed close by in a rocker. What a morning they had all had! Folk dance classes, which exuberant Juli adored and reflective Ceci tolerated. Arts and crafts class, where Ceci had happily cut out the prescribed pieces of paper to create a collage of the mountains, but Juli had jerked her chin up, her lips pinched with disapproval, and tossed her blonde curls over her shoulder.

"It's not real art!" Juli had condemned the craft outright as she pulled her sketchbook and pencil from the satchel Nancy held. "I only do real art."

Christine sighed but smiled at the memory as she murmured, "If I did not distinctly remember the pains of giving birth to that child, I would believe Victoria had brought her into the world."

Christine thought of her friend, who at this very moment was sketching or painting high in the mountains. A quiet laugh bubbled through her lips at the thought of Mountain Jack, who had found himself enthralled by Victoria's desire to paint every mountain she could reach.

"Poor man. He has lost control of his own life. I wonder if he will ever want to see another Texas lady coming." She thought about that a minute, then nodded her head. "He will want to see Victoria. For all his gruff, limited speech, his devotion to her is obvious. It's a good thing Hayden is coming soon."

A mourning dove called from the tower, its haunting sadness descending on Christine. *But Richard is not coming. Richard will never come again.*

The thought slammed into her, stealing her very breath. Tears stung her eyes as she covered her face with her hands *Oh, dear God! He is dead. What am I doing here, so content, so alive?* She opened her eyes and scanned the tent city on the hillside, the tents' striped roofs and sides waving in the sunny breeze. Her gaze traveled up the mesa and stopped at the sight of the gigantic rocks. Confusion took her prisoner, and the resulting anxiety loosened her tongue. "Such different worlds I live in. I don't know which is real! How can the darkness of his death, the searing pain of his absence exist alongside the bright, cool world of these mountains? They cannot both be true!"

"They can." Natalya's heavily accented voice announced her presence. "They are." She joined Christine on the bench. "Listen. Listen, Christine. What do you hear?"

"I hear that pathetic dove up in that barren tower calling for its mate. How it must be scanning the skies, longing for union with its mate." Christine fumbled in the sleeve of her black dress, seeking the black-edged handkerchief of a widow to dry her tears.

Natalya pointed to an apple tree close by. "What do you see?"

"A tree with birds—sparrows, I think—flitting around." She pressed the handkerchief to her eyes. "What difference does it make?"

"What kind of sounds are they making?"

Christine sighed. "Cheerful. So happy to be alive."

"The lone dove sings of its sadness while the sparrows chatter their joy. Both at the same time." Natalya clasped Christine's arm, her grip gently reassuring. "You are allowed to live in both worlds, my dear friend. Everyone does, for that is the human condition."

"I've never experienced this overlapping of the two before. When Mother died, my world went dark. Then Richard proposed, and my world dazzled with light so bright it could not be increased, I thought. Then my son was born ..."

"And you experienced happiness you never knew existed. Yes, I know about this joy."

Christine peered into Natalya's eyes, her face earnest. "But one can experience both at the same time? Is this all right? To have hours of happiness so soon after Richard's death. Is this ... is this ..."

"Proper? Is that the word you seek?"

"I suppose it is." As Christine dropped her gaze to her lap, she felt Natalya's grip on her arm tighten.

"I will tell you what is improper," Natalya declared as she withdrew her hand and stiffened her spine. "It is improper to refuse our loving God's gifts, not to embrace the joys God sends us as consolations." She sighed loudly. "No doubt, the ladies of Texas would not agree. I assure you the ladies of New York do not."

A faint smile lifted Christine's lips. "Perhaps, Natalya, we musicians are just strange."

"Not strange. More perceptive perhaps. But what we are is God's gift too. I will not feel unworthy because I am not like others. I think it is quite possible they have never explored their minds."

"If Sarah were here, she would be calling you a Thoreau."

Natalya drew back in alarm. "What is this thing—a Thoreau? I'm a Russian immigrant. I don't know this English word."

Christine laughed. "Thoreau was a famous American writer who insisted that some people march to a different drummer."

"Ah ... We have such a writer. His name is Leo Tolstoy. I wonder if Sarah knows about him."

"I very much doubt it, but she would be delighted to learn."

"This writer still lives, and he loves music. Did you know he sat next to Tchaikovsky at the debut of his first string quartet? It is said that he cried when he heard the beautiful, melancholic *andante cantabile*. Just think, the great Tolstoy, moved to tears by one's composition."

"I am ashamed to admit I know less about Russian literature than I do about Russian music."

"But just think what I do not know about this great country that is now my home! Even my English is inadequate." She grabbed Christine's hand and pulled her to her feet as she herself rose. "But we both have the privilege of learning, especially here at this meeting they call a Chautauqua. Next summer I shall ask Sarah to tutor me."

"Next summer?"

"Yes! Next summer. You will return, of course. We will all meet again here at the base of these Rocky Mountains. I shall study all things American. Victoria will paint to her heart's content."

"And I could continue to study the Russian composers, and Sarah could study—" Christine laughed. "As usual, Victoria is far ahead of us!"

"What do you mean?"

"She is already planning to build one of the first cottages here at Texado Park."

"There! You see. We shall all meet here next summer to share our knowledge, our lives. Here, in this beauty, we shall create more beauty."

"Such a dream would certainly make the winter months easier."

"It is not a dream. It is real, and so is the fact that you are going to play with the chamber orchestra tomorrow evening."

"What?" Christine's eyebrows raised in alarm. "Play with the chamber orchestra? Have you gone mad?"

Natalya chuckled. "There are many who would tell you I've always been a little mad. But you are ready to play in public, Christine, and we are beginning the last week of this Chautauqua. The public deserves to hear you, and you have no right to withhold your God-given talent from them. More importantly, you *deserve* to play."

"Natalya, there are compelling reasons why I cannot play in public!"

Natalya softened her voice as she took both of Christine's hands in her own and held them, fingers splayed, out in the dappled light of the orchard. "Look at these amazing hands God has given you. Such long, slender fingers. I am envious. They were created to play the piano. You were created to play the piano. You, Christine, with your extraordinary sensibilities."

"My hands do not alter the compelling reasons for me to remain modestly in the background."

"I don't think your beloved Richard would agree. He would urge you to abandon the conventions of society, to live every precious moment of life that God gives you."

"But I am not prepared. I have not planned and practiced—"

"Nonsense! I want you to begin our program with two of Chopin's preludes. You could play those in your sleep. Then you will join the other players in Schubert's quintet, the one they call 'The Trout.' You know that well too."

"But I have not rehearsed with the other players!" Christine jerked her hands away and began to wring them.

"You will this afternoon and also in the morning. I played through the piece with them after supper last evening."

"So they expect to play with you. They will never accept me!"

Natalya drew herself up to her full height. "They will do as I say. I am the conductor!"

"Natalya, I have never played in a concert, only in musicales in homes. A much smaller audience. I cannot walk across that stage in that enormous auditorium—"

"This chamber music concert is merely a local event. Many of the teachers will come, of course. Perhaps a few will come up from Boulder ..." She shrugged. "But really, we cannot expect an audience of more than several hundred."

"Several hundred!"

Natalya placed a reassuring hand on Christine's shoulder. "Naturally, you feel some stage fright, my dear friend, but beginning in this small way is best."

Christine grimaced. "It may seem small to you ... But should I be beginning at all? Oh! I must think about this ... I must consult Victoria."

Natalya burst out laughing. "It's settled then. You will play! We both know what Victoria will say."

Christine sighed as she nodded. "Indeed we do. Perhaps if I wear a short veil, it would not be too—"

Natalya held up a commanding hand. "Stop! I forbid you to worry about tradition until you step off the train in Riverford."

Christine crossed her arms over her chest and hugged herself as she looked up at the wailing doves. "I can hardly bear to think about that."

"Then don't! All we have is the present. Let us use it." Natalya slipped her hand around Christine's elbow and urged her forward toward the auditorium.

CHAPTER TEN

Eager to relax on the mesa and wait for the cool mountain breeze to drift down from the mountains, Sarah escaped the noise of the dining hall as quickly as possible. Her makeup assignments were complete, and she felt free, at last, to reflect on the life-changing events of the last week.

"Could it really have been just a week ago today that Mountain Jack brought Bert and me down from the mountain?" She shuddered at the memory of Bert's bloodied head, their fear-filled night alone in the canyon. "Oh thank you, God, for saving us!" She paused to look back at the valley, at the goldening of the land as the sun began to set. The beauty of the light turned her memory to the joy of finding Lee waiting for her when they brought her down from the canyon. *It was like God brought Lee here just in time to hear about my change of heart, my resetting of my values.* She reached the rock where she had told Lee of her love and they had agreed to marry. *Marriage!* The old anxieties reared their heads again. Could she really remain in her teaching position if she married? Would the school board fire her?

Sarah pulled Lee's letter from her pocket at she settled on the rock. She hadn't allowed herself to open it when it arrived in the noon mail. There had just been too many curious teachers around. But now ... She carefully unsealed it and read.

My darling Sarah,

Another hot, busy, lonely day is ending here in Riverford. I feel like I'm sleepwalking through these days as I await your return. They're so empty without you! Oh, I know I'm making a difference at the bank, but how impossible it is to fill Richard's shoes, and how hard it is to concentrate.

My mind wanders continuously to you, and I ache to see you, to hear your voice, and yes—to hold you in my arms. Tell me you are coming home soon!

Lavinia and Mother chatter day and night about Lavinia's wedding this fall, but I can only think of Christmas, the time when we'll finally become one. I know you continue to worry about your teaching position, and it's true that the school board election has heated up. General Gibbes is now being opposed by Tom Lynch, the man who hated Richard so much and tried to force Christine to sell the bank. Nevertheless, I believe the General will win. He must win!

When are you coming home? See how I keep returning to the same theme. I am being selfish, I know. I should be encouraging you to stay up there and enjoy yourself a while. But I miss you too much!

God bless you, my love,
Lee

Sarah clasped the letter to her bosom, which ached with a yearning she could only describe as a sad joy. "I miss him so!" she told the tall, honey-colored grasses that had begun to wave in the chinook wind that flowed down out of Bluebell Canyon. "Everything, my priorities, my desires … They have all changed since I faced death a week ago. Think of it! Only a week …"

Sarah shivered and pulled her shawl closer around her neck as she thought. *When am I going home? Oh, how I wish I could be in two places at once!* She thought of the crammed activity schedule of this last week of the Chautauqua and was shocked to realize that one week from today the teachers would begin leaving. The tents would remain up another week, but the trains back to Texas would start leaving, and every day more teachers would go. How she wanted to board the first train to leave!

But what about Christine and Victoria? They both would benefit from staying longer. Victoria's health would be better and her artwork would continue. Christine needed to avoid the sadness of Riverford for as long as possible.

So many new hopes … so many fledgling new beginnings that must be nurtured—not cut short. Sarah's stomach began to churn as her breathing became shallow. She looked out at the valley and saw that it had fallen into purpled shadow, but when she turned to gaze up at the mountains, she was greeted by bright, lively sunlight bouncing off the rocks. "That's just how I feel," she confessed to the waving grasses. "Torn between an ending and a beginning. This amazing season of growth and adventure is ending, but I'm so excited about the next season of my life. About Lee ... about us. There's an 'us' now. Think of that!"

CHAPTER ELEVEN

Gratitude filled Christine's heart as she slowly inhaled the cooler, rain-cleansed air that had followed the blistering heat of early afternoon. As she practiced with the quintet in the auditorium shortly after lunch, she had wondered at times if she would faint from the combination of heat, nerves, and the exertion of playing. She had certainly wondered if she would be so drained she would not be able to play that evening. But the blessed rain had come when the heat of the plains grew intense enough to war with the cool air of the mountains. The phenomenon was strange but delightful to the Texans who were accustomed to no such relief on August afternoons back home. Christine considered the rain a divine gift, for she had been enabled to nap, and she now returned to Texado Park with renewed strength to face the ordeal of her first public performance.

The carriage quickly left the trees of the town behind and began the climb up the steep, bare hill that lay at the foot of the mountains. Christine clasped her music tightly as she glanced up at the fast-moving gray clouds and wondered if the change in weather would decrease or increase attendance at the chamber music concert. Guilt swept through her as she realized she was hoping people would stay home.

Natalya was awaiting her at the auditorium where there was the inevitable general bustle of preparation for a concert: benches were being straightened, the sawdust floor was being raked, the string players were creating a cacophonous sound as they practiced different measures of music. "Ah, Christine, there you are. I want to play through the Schubert quintet before anyone arrives." She strode to the piano and began untying the cover that protected it. "How are you feeling?"

"Nervous ... excited ... so glad for the cooler air."

"You don't mind playing through the Schubert now?"

"Oh no! I need all the rehearsal I can get." Christine hurried to help Natalya. "Thank goodness we covered the piano well. That was quite a windy rain."

"Yes. What refreshes us does not refresh a piano!" Natalya turned to the string players and raised her voice. "That's enough tuning, gentlemen. I want us to practice the *andante* movement of the Schubert. We should just have time before the audience begins arriving." She strode to the podium and opened her music as Christine slipped onto the piano stool. "From the beginning now ..." Natalya raised both hands, baton in the right. "Remember, I want a crisp, definitive sound on that first note."

Half an hour later, Christine, eager for a quiet moment alone, slipped through the arriving crowd and walked away from the auditorium. Above her, the clouds were just beginning to clear, and when her eyes sought the crest of the mountains, she found it mostly obscured in a light fog that was tinted with the lavender-mauve tones of a fading sunset. Sadness mingled with her anxiety, and she sighed as she nervously smoothed her black silk skirt. *Oh, Richard! What am I doing? I cannot walk out on a stage and play for an audience of strangers. Well ... I can, but should I? It seems so—* She was distracted by a white light shining in a widening break in the clouds. Slowly the gap opened, and the moon glided into view. A soft laugh escaped Christine's lips as she placed her hand on her heart. "Oh, look at that! The moon was there all the time. Just temporarily obscured by the clouds." As she stood and watched the gap widen and the moon begin to reign over the darkness, her nerves settled. "How absurd I am being. This evening is not about me. I am just one of five players, and I will not even be the only woman on stage. Natalya will be the focus."

"Christine, are you all right?" Sarah's voice was gentle as she approached Christine. "Why are you out here?"

"Just settling my nerves and worrying one last time that I am not behaving properly." Shrugging her shoulders, she turned toward Sarah. "Have you ever seen anyone behaving so absurdly?"

"I don't think you're absurd. Just very conscientious."

Christine pointed up to the moon. "Just look at that moon."

"How beautiful!"

"And so very capable of reminding me of my place. It is lighting half the world and will light the other half soon. I am just here in this place and in this hour of history to bring a bit of joy to a small group of music lovers."

Sarah hugged her. "I'm glad to see that you've found your peace again, but Natalya is fast losing hers. She's been looking for you."

"Oh dear. We must go." Christine took Sarah's arm and turned back to the auditorium.

"I think—I think I should—should warn you." Sarah stumbled over her words. "The audience is sizable."

Christine stopped. "How sizable?"

"Well ..."

Christine wrung her hands.

"But your biggest fans are seated right up front," Sarah added. "Ceci is beside herself with excitement!"

"And Juli? Is she behaving?"

Sarah laughed. "She's behaving like Juli."

Christine groaned. "Poor Victoria! She must be so annoyed. And those sitting around them—"

"Stop worrying. The minute you walk onto that stage, both of the girls will be transfixed. Just play *for us*, Christine, your little private audience sitting down front."

"Yes! That is what I will do." She hugged Sarah. "I will just pretend I am home playing for you." She hurried forward. "We must go!"

When Christine walked onto the stage with the male string players, a murmur of shock wafted across the audience, and Victoria realized she had left out an important component of her painting of Christine on stage. The audience! All around her, she heard whispered comments that ran the gamut of possible response—surprise, shock, delight, disapproval. It suddenly occurred to her that she must add an audience to her painting of Christine on stage. *What was I thinking? Christine isn't an amateur performer who has sneaked onto a bare, unguarded concert stage to try out the grand piano.* Victoria looked around her at the faces of this evening's audience as Christine began the gently lyrical opening measures of Chopin's Prelude No. 15. *I must capture the audience reacting to her.* As Christine repeated the bass chords, striking them as regularly as a pendulum swinging, Victoria studied the faces around her. She saw mild interest from most, a few male eyelids slowly sinking, and studied attention from a few teachers. The hypnotic bass chords continued, but the treble rose in volume and intensity. The audience momentarily became more alert, but were lulled back into comfortable complacency by the sweet melody at the end of the piece.

Christine launched into the thunderous opening of Chopin's "Revolutionary Etude." Nodding heads jerked up, eyes popped open, delicate female hands covered startled, gaping mouths. The teachers leaned forward, their faces suddenly lit with excitement. All around her, Victoria saw people's faces register their uninhibited responses to a tiny woman taking command of the massive grand piano and filling the cavernous hall with the sounds, the emotions of war-torn Poland. Victoria saw shock, disbelief, disapproval, delight, and sheer joy on faces. *And that's exactly how I shall paint it! With Christine leaning forward, her hands above the keys, poised to strike again, the audience responding.*

Once the audience became part of the future painting, Victoria yearned for her sketchpad, but she had to settle for memorizing faces in the crowd that expressed differing reactions. As her eyes roved, one face stopped her examination—an eager face broadcasting the listener's intense interest and approval of Christine's performance. A male face. A well-dressed man. Victoria watched as he pulled out a fountain pen and a notebook from his coat pocket. As Christine moved on to the haunting sounds of Prelude No. 4, the man began to write.

Who is he? Victoria's curiosity kept her eyes glued to the man.

When Christine finished the prelude and stood to bow, the audience applauded enthusiastically. The man Victoria was watching jumped to his feet and shouted "Brava!" Soon, others joined him.

Clearly surprised by the audience's reaction, Christine bowed again and hurried off the stage, but shouts of "Encore!" filled the auditorium. A moment later, Natalya led Christine back to the piano, and the audience took their seats. Christine paused, concentrating intensely on the ivory keys, then plunged into the dramatic opening of Chopin's fast-paced Prelude No. 24. Victoria's heart raced with excitement as she watched the members of the audience move to the edges of their seats. The man with the notebook had actually risen to his feet and was leaning forward, his face full of intense emotion. When Christine played the last chord, the man grinned as he clapped vigorously. While Christine took her bow and the thunderous applause continued, the man slipped up the aisle and exited the auditorium. *A newspaperman!* A thrill ran through Victoria. *Christine is about to receive her first review!*

Juli grabbed Victoria's hand and brought her attention back to the children. She glanced over at Ceci. In her excitement, the six-year-old was standing on the bench to get a better view of her mother.

Deafening applause jerked Victoria's attention back to the stage. Christine was standing next to the piano, her face shining with delight. Slowly she descended into an elegant curtsy and bowed her head. She held the pose a moment as the applause thundered more loudly. Then she straightened and walked off the stage.

"Can I move now?" Juli demanded.

"Yes, yes, of course," Victoria answered as she slipped the child off her lap and joined the others who were standing and applauding around her. She looked over to see Ceci's reaction, and the child was gone.

"Where's Ceci?" she shouted to Sarah.

Sarah pointed toward the stage.

The little girl was standing at the foot of the stage, her clapping hands raised above her head, tears flowing down her cheeks. Victoria shifted Juli toward Sarah and went down to shepherd Ceci back to her seat, but the applause continued and Ceci was immovable. Victoria sank onto the empty first row bench and watched the child. Natalya led Christine back onstage, then stood back while Christine took a second bow. Victoria's right hand clenched around the absent pencil she yearned for. *How could I have missed the necessity of this painting in the collection? A young girl inspired by a woman breaking through the barriers. And the woman is her mother!*

With the greatest of difficulty, Victoria finally persuaded Ceci to return to their seats, but Ceci would not sit down. Once again she climbed up on the bench and stood when she saw Christine take the stage with the four male players of the quintet. Once the group had seated themselves, Madame Makarova entered and was applauded as she bowed slightly, then turned to conduct.

Ceci leaned over and whispered far too loudly, "Mommy has to play with those men now." She shook her head, her face pinched with disapproval. "It won't be as good as when Mommy plays by herself."

Several concertgoers around them laughed, and the man behind leaned forward and commented, "Somehow we'll just have to muddle through their male mediocrity."

Ceci turned around, smiled at him, and nodded her head vigorously.

Victoria was saved from bursting into a laugh by the beginning of the quintet.

CHAPTER TWELVE

The next morning, Victoria snatched the Denver paper off her breakfast tray the minute Frances carried it into the room and snapped open the successive pages so violently she ripped a few.

"All the big news supposed to be on the front page," Frances suggested. "That's where they talks 'bout worrisome stuff like the war in Cuba and such."

"*Hmmm* ..." Victoria nodded as she finally found the arts section. "I'm interested in an entirely different war."

"You mean they's another one?"

"Aha!" Victoria jumped to her feet as she exclaimed, "I *knew* he was a reporter!"

"Lawd have mercy, Miz Victoria," Frances exclaimed as she stepped back to save Victoria's breakfast tray. "You's gonna knock the teapot over."

"Just look, Frances." Victoria stuck the folded-back newspaper under Frances' nose. "A review of the concert last night." She hurried over to the window to see the print better. "Now ... does he mention Christine?" She mumbled the words of the opening sentences as she scanned the article. Three sentences in, her heart started racing as her eyes galloped over the review. "Listen to this, Frances! 'Amazingly talented pianist, Mrs. Richard Boyd of Riverford, Texas, happily startled the audience with her superb performance of Chopin's "Revolutionary Etude." Why is this pianist not regularly performing in the great halls of America? Let it be known henceforth that it was the *Denver Post* that first discovered her rare talent. Had the Chautauqua at Boulder begun its first season by giving music lovers only the unparalleled piano virtuoso, Natalya Makarova, we would have been thoroughly awed. But no! That accomplishment has now been further embellished by a second gift—the exquisite playing of Mrs. Boyd.'"

"Well, I'll be!" Frances declared. "He seem mighty impressed with Miz Christine."

"Mighty impressed!" Victoria snatched a shawl off her chair and charged toward the door.

"Where you goin'?" Frances cried.

"To Miss Christine's cottage, of course," Victoria called back over her shoulder.

"But you ain't even touched your—" Frances started to protest, then set the breakfast tray down and hurried after her. "Wait for me! I wants to be there when she hear."

Christine's heart lurched into a gallop. She stared up at Victoria, who was reading the critic's comments aloud to her for the second time.

"Now what do you say to that?" Victoria demanded.

"We must not ... we should not make too much of this," Christine stuttered. "After all, this is just one man's opinion, and he is obviously just being kind."

"Kind? Christine! Critics are *not* kind. They don't get paid to be kind."

Unable to sit still, Christine jumped up and began tidying the small sitting room.

"Do you realize what has happened?" Victoria demanded. "The music critic of the *Denver Post* has coupled your name with Natalya's."

"Oh no!" Christine stopped in her tracks. "No ... not really."

"He called you the second music gift of the new Boulder Chautauqua. He definitely coupled your name with Natalya's."

"Well ... he has overstepped reason in doing so." Christine abandoned her organization of Juli's art supplies. "Now to important matters." She hurried across the room as she struggled for composure. "I must hurry the girls along, or they will be late to their lessons at Texado Park."

"Fine!" Victoria smiled as she rapidly folded the paper. "But I promise you, Christine, that you have not heard the last of this." She turned to Frances. "Go get ten copies of this morning's paper from the front desk."

Christine stopped in her tracks. "Whatever for?"

"I'm sending this article to the Galveston, Dallas, and Ft. Worth papers."

"Oh no! You must not do that, Victoria. They will merely laugh."

"They will not! You just wait; you'll see when you talk to Natalya that this is the beginning of your professional career."

Christine hurried to Victoria's side and took hold of her arm. "You are dreaming, Victoria. All you are going to do is cause the most awful scandal in Riverford."

"Good! Riverford needs shaking up. Heaven only knows how many talented women they have suffocated. Not to mention the sharecroppers and colored folk they won't give a chance."

"Victoria, I am a widow! A recent widow who has to return to her home in a few days and confront … whatever it is I must confront. Oh! I need time to think. You must give me time to think!"

Victoria wrapped her arms around her friend. "Yes, I see that. But while you're thinking of this fall and your return to Riverford, don't forget that Ceci and Juli are forced to grow up in that stifling town, and they're both very talented little girls."

"Who are going to be late to their classes." Christine turned and started toward the door again. "I will think about all of this later, I promise."

"May I at least send the article to General Gibbes? He'll be so proud of you."

"Yes, of course, if you must. Just … just tell him. Oh! I do not know what to tell him or anyone else for that matter. I just know we must not draw attention to my performance. After all, I will probably never play in public again."

Victoria crossed her arms and impatiently tapped her foot. "And it probably won't be hot in Texas next summer either."

When Christine entered the dining hall for lunch later that day, she was ambushed by eager teachers offering their congratulations. As she demurred and tried to brush away their compliments, she was keenly aware that Ceci stood at her side proudly beaming up at her. Juli, on the other hand, was pretending to jump rope in the middle of the dining hall and putting quite a few diners at risk of collision.

"Allow me to rescue you from this madness." Christine heard Natalya's voice over the hubbub. "I have a table over in the corner."

"Gladly, as soon as I grab Juli," Christine responded as she pointed toward the child.

"I'll go get her," Ceci groaned as she hurried away.

"We're so proud of you!" Several more teachers raced up and hugged Christine.

"Thank you." Christine smiled at the gaggle of well-wishers as she slowly pulled away from them. "Truly, you are making too much of this. It is really nothing—"

Juli crashed into her skirts. "Did you see me, Mommy? I was jumping rope without a rope!"

"We saw you!" Ceci answered for her mother.

"The review is far from nothing, Christine," Natalya said as she grabbed Juli's hand and pulled her toward the corner. "When the *Denver Post* gives a so-called amateur any notice at all—and they gave you a stunning approval—such a review cannot be ignored."

"Surely it is just a fluke, a personal opinion of one writer."

"Not just any writer! Mr. Penn's reviews are often picked up by the New York papers."

"Well, it's all very complimentary, but surely fleeting."

"What's 'fleeting' mean?" Juli demanded.

"Not lasting long," Christine answered as she seated the four-year-old and scooted her chair close to the table.

"Like bubbles?" Juli asked.

"Yes, like bubbles. Now sit up straight, dear."

"But the newspaperman won't forget you, Mother," Ceci insisted as she took a seat across the square table from her mother. "Not after he wrote all those wonderful words and even published them in the newspaper."

"You're right, Ceci," Natalya agreed. "He won't forget your mother because we won't let him. He will be back this Saturday for our last concert. You can count on it."

"And I've no doubt he will be quite impressed with the orchestra and especially with you, Natalya."

"He will be impressed with you, Christine. Of that I intend to make sure."

"What on earth are you saying?"

"That you will be a featured player on the program."

"But it's too late," Christine protested. "The program is already set. Besides, I have caused quite enough stir already. I just have to hope that no one in Riverford hears of my indiscretion."

"Indiscretion?" Natalya's eyes widened with shock. "Since when is a talented pianist performing for the delight of an audience an indiscretion?"

"When the pianist is a recent—" Christine cast a worried look at her daughters and cut her words off. "I cannot play again."

"But why not, Mommy?" Ceci leaned across the table, her eyes wide with distress.

"Well, dear. I am a widow now, and—"

"But it's not your fault Daddy got sick and went to see Jesus!" Juli blurted out.

"I know, dear, but there are certain traditions … What I mean to say is that certain behaviors are expected from a widow."

"But we came to Colorado when you weren't supposed to," Juli protested. "I know 'cause I heard mean ole Miz Bellows say—"

Christine placed her fingers over Juli's mouth. "Don't speak disrespectfully of your elders, Juli. Coming here was different because I broke the rules to help Miss Victoria."

Juli shook her head and dislodged her mother's quietening fingers. "Why can't you do something that helps *you*?"

"Yes." Ceci's lips quivered as she began to cry. "Why can't you, Mommy? Why do you have to let those hateful women stop you?"

"Well … sometimes it's better to …"

Christine's heart wrenched when a low sob escaped Ceci's mouth. "When I'm big, will they stop me? Will they keep me from playing the piano on the big stage?"

"No!" Christine's heartbreak turned to fury as sudden heat flushed her throat and cheeks. Reaching across the table, she grabbed her daughter's hand. "No one is ever going to stop you! I will not let them."

"But if they can stop you ..." Ceci's tears began to flow freely.

Christine looked to Natalya for help.

Her friend's face was stern. "Your daughters will stand on *our* shoulders, my dear Christine, or they will not stand any taller than they do now. We are fashioning their future."

Christine stared at Natalya as the truth of her words sank in. "Then we'd better aim high!" Christine retorted. "For their sakes, we better not be controlled by the irrational." She stood and hurried around the table to gather Ceci into her arms. "I shall play, my darling girl, so that you can play."

*   *   *   *   *   *

Sarah could not stop her tears from flowing as she sat in the auditorium surrounded by almost a thousand concertgoers who had come to hear Madame Natalya Makarova play but were now transfixed by the stirring performance of a diminutive, blonde-haired woman from Texas.

"Who is she?" a well-dressed woman behind Sarah asked.

"Some unknown talent Madame Makarova discovered," the answer came.

"Amazing!"

"*Shh!*" others protested.

"But who *is* she?" The woman persisted.

I could tell you, Sarah thought, *but you would never believe me. She is selfless love and hard-earned courage bound together.*

The sound of the piano swept Sarah back in time to the desperate day when Christine had entered her life as an angel of mercy. Once again, Sarah was the helpless six-year-old daughter of a sharecropper. She felt the heat of that stifling August day, the nausea of hunger in her emaciated body, the panic of watching her mother collapse. Once again, she experienced the flurry of wide skirts as Mrs. Christine Boyd swept into the church vestibule and revived Sarah's mother. *She saw the need; she acted. That is who Christine is.* Sarah returned her thoughts to the stage in front of her. And now Christine had taken the stage to play in public, in spite of the inevitable criticism she would receive in Riverford. She saw the need to widen and heighten the canon of acceptable female behavior. Sarah glanced at Ceci, who stood in the center aisle, transfixed by the example of her mother on stage sharing her talent. *A decade from now, I will be watching Ceci play on a concert stage. I know it!* A thrill ran through Sarah at the thought.

She turned her eyes to Victoria and found her friend sitting tall, leaning forward, her face glowing with joy. *She looks like a fine china doll,* Sarah thought, but she knew that the striking red hair and translucent white skin were not the woman. Victoria was elegantly camouflaged iron, strength created out of personal suffering. And daring. Yes, Victoria was definitely daring. Sarah smiled through her tears. *She dared to believe in me, and here I sit! And tomorrow this Chautauqua ends, and it is my turn to exert myself to lift others, to enable them to choose better lives for themselves.* Sarah bowed her head, closed her eyes, and allowed the music to carry her to a vision of future challenge. To pictures of young faces raised in delight as they gained new knowledge and thus new power. To the altar at St. Paul's Episcopal Church and to Lee, standing tall, smiling down at her, his warm brown eyes melting with love.

When Victoria sprang to her feet, clapping wildly, Sarah realized she was the only one left seated. All around her the audience stood, their hands crashing together, enthusiastic smiles on the men's faces and tears on the ladies' cheeks. Sarah jumped up, wiped her own face with her fingers, and joined the salute to her friend. Christine seemed stunned by the reaction of the audience as she rose from the piano. She smiled, then placed her hand over her heart and curtsied. She immediately left the stage, but the audience would not quit applauding, and Natalya led her back for a second bow.

Cries of "Encore!" filled the auditorium as the clapping continued. Sarah's spirits soared as she joined her voice in the plea for more.

CHAPTER THIRTEEN

Victoria wore a tan suede ankle-length skirt as she sat in front of the dressing table mirror in her sanitarium room for the last time. She had coupled the western skirt with an ivory silk blouse featuring billowing sleeves and a floppy bow at the neck. "Now there's a picture of contrast," she said to Frances as she examined her reflection. "Thick, fuzzy suede from Colorado and delicate, shiny silk from Paris." She studied the red curls cascading over her shoulders. "Need a new style for the new me. Something Hayden will notice the minute he steps down from the train."

"Mr. Hayden ain't gonna be lookin' at your hairdo. And he ain't gonna be lookin' at them clothes either."

Victoria swiveled on the bench to look at Frances. "What *will* he see, Frances? I mean, beyond my body."

"That you's stronger than you ever been, and that be sayin' a lot. He gonna see the sparkle in your eyes." Frances glanced down at her mistress' hands. "Then he gonna see all them stains on your fingers and know you been painting. That gonna tell him all he needs to know. If you's paintin', well, then you's goin' strong."

"And I'll be going stronger with him here." Victoria turned back to the mirror and simply gathered her curls up on top of her head into a fluffy pile. "Oh, how I have missed that man! I couldn't allow myself to say much …"

"No, ma'am. Not with poor Miz Boyd missin' Mr. Boyd so much."

"I hope that Hayden's coming won't be too … too painful for her."

Frances sighed. "I figure she gonna have a much worse time of it when she get off the train in Riverford. But you shouldn't be thinkin' on that. Mr. Hayden be alive, and you gotta grab every minute the good Lord give you two."

"I intend to." Victoria plopped a wide-brimmed straw hat on her head and tilted it to a jaunty angle. "There! That'll have to do." She hurried to the window and noted with delight that the early morning fog had receded to the base of the mountains. Directly overhead, the sky was cornflower blue. "Just what I wanted for Hayden. Sunshine! He'll experience Boulder at its best. The golden plains topped with a bright blue sky and the drama of the mountains jumping straight up from those plains."

"Mr. Hayden ain't gonna see nothing but you."

Victoria grinned.

"I got all your things loaded on the wagon to take to the hotel. You sure you gotta go to the station by yourself?"

"Positive." Victoria turned and winked at Frances.

"Well, it ain't proper, but I guess we's doin' things the Colorado way now."

"We are indeed."

"I's just gonna have to trust the driver to take care of you."

"Right. Now go on, Frances. I'll be leaving in a couple of minutes."

"What 'bout this vase of flowers? We takin' it?"

Victoria looked at the stately spire of blue delphiniums. "No, we'll leave them for the next patient." She walked to the vase. "All but one, that is." She broke a blossom-clustered stem off and stuck it in the ribbon band of her hat.

Frances grinned. "That be just the color of your eyes. I wish I could see Mr. Hayden's face when he first see you."

"I'm going by myself." Victoria pointed to the door. "Go!"

"I's goin'. I'll have everything ready when ya'll get to the hotel."

"It may be a while. I want to show Mr. Hayden around first."

Frances paused, her hand on the doorknob. "We see what Mr. Hayden gotta say 'bout that. Lot more likely I's gonna be the one out lookin' 'round."

"Frances!"

"Well, he ain't seen you in over a month. He ain't gonna want me or nobody else 'round that hotel suite."

Victoria laughed. "Good-bye, Frances!"

Victoria impatiently waited a full five minutes more until she was certain Frances would have reached the servants' entrance and couldn't see her. Then she rushed out the door, down to the front lobby, and out onto the portico. Just as she had ordered, a livery boy had a small buggy waiting for her. After he helped her up onto the seat, she took the reins and clucked the horse into motion. "Here I come, Hayden!" she called. "And I feel more like myself than I have since we married and left Europe."

When Hayden stepped off the train a half an hour later, Victoria was standing on the platform ready to throw her arms around his neck. She watched with amusement as he scanned the crowd, apparently looking for an entourage of greater size or grander dress. As his eyes panned the crowded platform a second time, she removed her hat, allowing the sun to splash across her red curls, and Hayden's eyes stopped as his mouth fell open in amazement.

He bolted toward her and swept her off her feet and into his arms.

"Did you forget what your wife looks like?" Victoria demanded as she laughed at him.

"You are transformed," he declared as he lowered her to the wooden platform and stroked her head. "Where is that pale, emaciated lady I carried onto the train in Fort Worth?"

"Gone! Forever gone. I banished her."

"Good riddance. I like this one much better." He leaned down and kissed her longingly as the crowd swirled around them.

"Hayden!" She laughed as she pushed him away. "What *will* people think?"

"That I adore you. That I've missed you beyond description. That I'm desperate to be alone with you." He took her arm. "Let's go!"

"Where?"

"Anywhere. Just so there's absolutely no one else around." He hurried her forward.

"Are you abandoning your luggage?"

Hayden stopped. "Blast!" He looked back over his shoulder at the rows of suitcases and trunks on the platform. "I could." He turned back to her. "I would ... for you."

She winked at him. "You're likely to have more of me over the next ten days if you bathe and change clothes occasionally."

"We'll send the driver back for them while we snuggle in the carriage."

"There is no driver ... only me."

"That settles it!" Hayden exclaimed. "Don't move. I only have two cases to grab." He darted off, then turned back and pointed at her. "Don't move!"

She saluted and blew him a kiss.

A few minutes later, Victoria took the reins and started the horse off at a fast clip. "I should have known you would come alone," Hayden said. "How far's the hotel?"

"Not far ... but it is in the opposite direction."

"What? Where are you taking me, woman? I have plans for you."

"You are being kidnapped, or should I say 'man-napped' by a wild red-haired woman."

Hayden grabbed her arm. "Victoria, I didn't come all this way for a tour of the mountains."

She leaned into him as the horse trotted on and gave him a smacking kiss on the cheek. "Good! Because you're not going to get one."

"But—"

"Patience, dear lover. All will be well, and I promise you that you will be thoroughly satisfied."

Hayden whipped his head from side to side, looking at the fast disappearing town, then peered straight ahead. "Is that a canyon?"

"It is. An isolated canyon with soaring fir trees that have dropped their needles for centuries and produced the softest beds." Victoria grinned at him. "Beds quite hidden by their drooping boughs ..."

His eyes twinkled as he struggled to arrange his face in a serious pose. "Ah ... Such a phenomenon demands study. It's the least we can do for science."

"I thought so!" Victoria agreed gaily.

CHAPTER FOURTEEN

A light fog on a gentle breeze drifted around them as Sarah climbed the mesa with Victoria and Christine for the last time. The fog seemed intent on cocooning the women as long as possible, providing protection from the jarring of the coming events of the day. It mercifully blocked their view of Texado Park below and prevented their seeing the tearing down of the tents and the removal of furniture and other items that had marked their life-changing time at the foot of the mountains. Christine paused and looked up the path to the base of the first rock, which drifted in and out of view as the fog swirled around it. "I feel like I am wandering in the lap of a loving mother I cannot see," she said.

"A strong mother who has held us wisely," Victoria added. "Letting us grow as she nurtured and protected us."

"Oh! I cannot bear to see this magical time end." Christine covered her mouth as she unsuccessfully tried to stifle a sob.

Victoria threw her arms around her friend. "Neither can I! These weeks have transformed me. I'm not going back to Texas as the same woman who left, and I'm not talking about my health. I'm talking about purpose."

"Purpose ... yes, that is what I shall miss." Christine's face crumpled. "Without Richard ..."

Grief tinged with a bit of guilt rose in Sarah. *In my own eagerness to return to Lee, I have set aside Christine's loss, her inevitable surge of fresh grief when she returns.*

"I have no cure for grief to offer you, my dear friend," Victoria said. "Just a balm to lessen the pain. The girls—"

"Yes, of course!" Christine jerked herself upright. "I must not allow myself to become maudlin. I have the girls to consider. And the boys are coming home. Why, before I know it, they will both be young men. I must look ahead to their college ... to their preparation for professions. I must ... I must ... Oh, Victoria! I must help them confront their father's death." Christine's lips quivered, but she pursed them together as she turned suddenly to Sarah. "And I must not forget the positives." Her struggle to change her tone was obvious to Sarah. "Why, Sarah will begin teaching, and ... and just think of the joys ahead as we plan her wedding."

Sarah's chest felt heavy; her throat tightened. *What, oh what can I say to comfort her?* Some lines from Wordsworth's "Tintern Abbey," which she had so recently taught, floated into her mind, and she began to quietly quote them. "'Let the moon shine on thee in thy solitary walk; and let the misty mountain winds be free to blow against thee; and in after years, when these wild ecstasies shall be matured into a sober pleasure, when thy mind shall be a mansion for all lovely things, thy memory be as a dwelling place for all sweet sounds and harmonies—'" Sarah's voice cracked and she could not go on.

Victoria grabbed Sarah's hands and, with tears in her eyes, finished the lines. "'Oh! Then, if solitude, or fear, or pain, or grief, should be thy portion, with what healing thoughts of tender joy wilt thou remember ...'" She changed the next line. "Wilt thou remember these glorious, healing days at the foot of the Rocky Mountains."

"And our experiences of art and music," Sarah added. "And friendship. So many new friends, but more important, such a deepening of our friendship."

Christine took Victoria's hand and thus created an unbroken line of three. "And we will be comforted by God's active presence in our lives. Here you are, Sarah, safe and sound when you might well have died in the mountains. And Victoria, you are returned to vibrant health."

"And you, my dear Christine, have found purpose and renewed strength. It's true that you will have to face Richard's death again, but I believe you'll find that your grief is less raw now. You will see the boys through their grief and off to school again. You will set the girls on their paths of development and learning. And … you will find your future holds the music you love, however you wish to embrace it."

The breeze carried the sound of a tapping hammer to Sarah's ears, and she turned toward the valley that held Texado Park. "Victoria's right, but I could do without the sound of our little village being dismantled."

Victoria laughed. "That, my dear friends, is the sound of the beginning of a new house—our house."

"So soon?" Sarah asked.

"Why wait?" Victoria shrugged her shoulders. "Winter comes on early here."

"So Hayden agreed?" Christine asked.

"He even chose the lot." Victoria pointed down the slope to a spot just outside the gates to Texado Park. "We bought two acres just outside the entrance, so we could have a garden."

Quiet laughter bubbled from Christine's lips. "My dear Victoria, you are one of a kind. You really do believe we will all return next summer."

"I do!" Victoria slid her eyes toward Sarah. "Although a certain young schoolteacher may be late due to an extended honeymoon."

* * * * *

"I want to stay with Miss Victoria!" Juli stomped her foot on the wooden platform of the Boulder train station the next morning, and to Christine's horror, she plopped down on the dusty boards and crossed her arms.

"You can't. Get up!" Ceci grabbed her little sister's arm and began tugging on it.

"No!" Juli shouted. "I don't want to go to Texas. I want to stay with Miss Victoria!"

Christine's melancholy was instantly covered over with irritation as she left the adults behind and hurried across the platform. "Stand up, Juli, and brush off your dress."

Juli squinted up at her in the bright sunlight but did not move.

"Mommy said to get up!" Ceci's voice became shrill as she grabbed both her sister's arms.

"No!" Juli wrenched an arm free and hit her sister. "No, I hate Texas!" She began to sob. "I hate it. It hurts me!"

Christine drew in a sudden, shocked breath as she realized that Juli was not simply throwing a tantrum. "Stop, Ceci. Leave her alone."

"But everyone's staring at her, Mommy. It's so embarrassing! You should have sent her onto the train with Nancy."

"I will handle this. Turn loose of your sister and go say good-bye to Miss Victoria."

As Ceci huffed her indignation, turned on her heel, and marched off, Christine reached down and gathered Juli into her arms. "Now, tell me why you are crying, darling."

Several more sobs escaped Juli's lips before she finally managed to say. "It's sad in Texas. Everybody cries, and Daddy won't be there." She drew away and looked up into her mother's face. "I want to see Daddy!"

Sudden tears scalded Christine's eyes. Unable to trust her voice, she hugged Juli to her and fought for control of her emotions.

"Christine?" Victoria hurried toward her. "Are you all right?"

Christine frantically wiped her wet face with her gloved hand but still could not trust herself to speak.

"Mommy and I are sad," Juli explained as she turned her tear-stained face to Victoria. "'Cause Daddy won't be in Texas. Can I stay in Colorado with you?"

Victoria sank down on one knee and took the little girl's hand. "I think, Juli, that you need to go back to Texas to take care of your mother. You see, she *has* to go back. Your brothers are coming home."

"I don't care." Juli shrugged her shoulders. "They'll just go back to school anyway."

"What about your grandfather? He's there all alone."

"Why can't we bring him here? He'd like it here in the mountains."

"Your grandfather has to run the bank and take care of all your mother's land. Many, many people depend on him to keep things going so they can raise their crops and feed their families."

Juli concentrated on Victoria's words a minute, then turned her face to her mother's. "Does Grandpa help poor children like Daddy used to?"

Christine nodded. "Yes, darling, and it is a big, big job."

Juli sighed as she snatched her hand free and crossed her arms in frustration. "I guess we better go help him."

"Good girl." Victoria hugged her. "And I'll be back home in two weeks, and you and I will paint and paint all fall. We're going to be so busy we won't have time to be sad. Right?"

Juli nodded vigorously, then escaped Victoria's arms and started running toward her sister.

"It's much harder for her than I realized." Christine sighed.

"She'll be fine if we keep her busy. It's you I'm concerned about, Christine. I feel like jumping on that train and going home with you."

Christine shook her head. "I would never allow it. Poor Hayden has spent the summer in the heat helping Father keep the bank locally controlled, not to mention managing the store as well as Richard's farms on top of his own. How exhausted he looked when he arrived day before yesterday! He needs rest and private time with you."

"I know." Victoria nodded as she leaned closer to her friend and lowered her voice. "Between you and me, I'm hoping Hayden will fall as much in love with these magnificent mountains as I have."

Christine smiled. "He will. Be sure you cherish these next days with your husband, Victoria." Christine's voice grew wistful. "Love him. Create memories to sustain you—"

Victoria's eyes filled with tears. "I'm so sorry you have to—"

"All aboard!" The conductor's sharp, loud voice drowned out her words.

"You'll be in my prayers; you can count on that," Victoria promised. "I know it's almost impossible on the train, especially with the children, but try to rest."

Christine took her friend's arm and began her walk to the steaming train. "Nancy will take care of the girls. My only concern is making the change of trains in Ft. Worth. That station is absolute havoc."

"Let Sarah take charge of that. She can handle it."

Christine watched as Sarah hustled the girls aboard. "Yes, she can handle just about anything now. She's so grown up!"

"Time to get you aboard," Hayden called out as he walked toward her and led her to the steps.

"Good-bye, dear friend. Thank you for rescuing me." Victoria raised her voice as the train whistle blew.

"It turned out to be a blessing to me," Christine called down from the platform. She raised her eyes to the mountains looming over the town. "Yes, yes. A profound blessing to us all."

CHAPTER FIFTEEN

"How far are we from Fort Worth?" Christine asked the conductor as he passed through the car.

"About an hour out, ma'am." He glanced at her black veil carefully arranged on the seat next to her. "Been a long night for you, ain't it?"

"Yes ... yes, it has." She glanced across the aisle where Juli lay curled up in Nancy's arms and Ceci was stretched out on the seat. "I want to thank you again for allowing my servant to stay with the girls overnight."

The conductor avoided her eyes as he shifted uncomfortably. "I ain't got nothing against the coloreds, ma'am. As long as the other passengers don't complain ... well, I just figured a lady in mourning ... well, you probably needed the help, and it ain't like she's been eating with the passengers or anything."

A flame of anger ignited in Christine's exhausted mind, forcing her to struggle to control her tongue. In the end, she simply nodded, but after the conductor moved on, she slammed her fist down on the seat as she muttered, "When, when will we grow up and move beyond this stupid prejudice? Isn't life difficult enough—" She quickly pressed her finger to her lips to stop her words. *I am just so tired. Nearly twenty-four hours on this train, and the girls so restless yesterday. Thank God they've slept through the night, even if I have been tortured by dreams.* She resolutely turned her face to the window and studied the flat steaming land that stretched for miles before disappearing into the hazy horizon.

"It must have rained last night," she murmured as she picked up a fan and stirred the stifling, humid air. "Already so hot." She leaned her head back against the seat, her mind full of worry. How would they ever make their way through the Fort Worth terminal? And once they did, the next stop would be Riverford. Her spirits sank lower. *No Richard waiting … How will I go on? What can I say to the boys to comfort them …*

"You must not allow yourself to think of such things," Christine ordered herself. She stood, and fighting the sway of the train car to keep her balance, she stepped out into the aisle. A few steps brought her to Sarah's seat, and when Sarah glanced up in surprise, Christine said, "I am going to freshen up before we wake the girls." And she walked on before Sarah could comment.

Sarah returned to her daydream. She was not thinking of the Fort Worth train station and the difficulty of the transfer at all. That was simply an ordeal to hurry through so she could finally reach Riverford. She smiled as she imagined the scene. She would step down the last step into Lee's arms, and the girls would squeeze past her and race over to General Gibbes with Nancy right behind them, fussing for them to slow down. Undoubtedly, Sam would be waiting in the Hodges buggy to take the luggage home. *I wonder if Mama will be there … Oh, I hope Lee brings her!* Sarah sighed with contentment. Then she remembered Christine, and her heart skipped a beat. *How difficult this will be for her. And she's already worrying about the Fort Worth transfer.*

"Well, at least I can arrange that right now and relieve her mind," Sarah muttered as she rose from her seat and walked to the back of the car to find Zebediah, the porter she had befriended the previous day.

"Don't you be worryin' 'bout a thing," Zebediah said when she mentioned Fort Worth. "I already got a plan all worked up. Right 'fore the train come to a stop and everybody start movin' 'round, I gonna take you up to the head of the car. I gonna grab us the first boys that waitin' to carry bags, and I gonna tell them what to do. I gonna take care of you ladies, miss. You just relax your mind."

Sarah smiled as she sighed with relief. "I really appreciate your help."

Half an hour later, the train began to slow, and they heard one short blast of its whistle. The girls scrambled toward the window on their side and began to point and chatter excitedly. Zebediah hurried up the aisle and said to Sarah, "If you just come right this way, Miss. We be in the Fort Worth terminal in about two minutes."

"I'll be back for you as soon as we have everything arranged," Sarah assured Christine, then followed Zebediah.

"I hope it ain't gonna be too noisy for you out here on the platform, but I knows those baggage boys. They's always fightin' each other for the first customer. If we's standin' out here, a couple of them gonna jump on 'fore this here train even stop."

"Really?"

"Yes, ma'am. Now don't you be givin' them no money 'til they gets you settled on the Riverford train. Can't trust them boys no further than you can throw 'em."

As the train entered the station, Sarah saw boys running toward the slowing cars.

"Here they come!" Zebediah waved the boys forward. "Over here, boys. Gotcha some business sure thing."

Two of the biggest boys soon caught the railing and swung themselves up to the platform, and Zebediah wasted no time giving them their orders. "You boys gonna be looking for three trunks. They gonna have the name 'BOYD' on them. Just like this here paper." He thrust a scrap of paper, on which he had printed the letters B-O-Y-D, into the hand of the bigger boy. "You bring 'em back to this car after we's stopped. Then you wait for this lady to come out. You's gonna take her and her friend and they servants and they little girls to the Riverford train. And you gonna get paid right handsome for doing it. You got that?"

"Got it, Zebediah!" the older boy yelled before both boys swung back to the ground and raced off toward the end of the train.

Zebediah laughed. "Those boys be searching them baggage cars 'fore this train good and stopped."

Sarah pulled a quarter out of her skirt pocket and pressed it into the porter's hand. "You've been so kind to us, Zebediah—" With a deafening sound, the iron wheels squealed as they dragged along the rails when the engineer applied the brakes, and Sarah's words were drowned out. She tried to yell above the sound. "I want you to know how much—" The whistle shrieked.

"Oh, I can't take no money from you, Miss," Zebediah shouted back. "Why, that gentleman that put ya'll on the train back in Boulder already paid me real handsome."

He gave the coin back to her. "You keep your money, Miss."

"But this is my way of thanking you personally. It's not much, but it's money I've saved."

"You want to thank me, I tell you what you do. You's gonna be a schoolteacher, ain't you?"

Sarah nodded.

"Then maybe you can help a colored child. You know, one that ain't gonna be goin' to no school. Maybe you can teach him to read."

Sarah felt the sting of tears as a lump rose in her throat. "I'll do that," she choked out, then swallowed hard. "I promise you, Zebediah."

"God bless you, Miss." He smiled down at her. Steam swirled around them as the train jolted to a stop. "Well, we's here. You best get back to your friends and get them all ready—"

"Sarah!"

Sarah whipped her head toward the crowded platform.

"Sarah!" She heard her name called again as she frantically searched the crowd.

"You gotta get back to your friends, Miss," Zebediah insisted, "'fore them passengers start leavin' this car. They ain't gonna be in no mood to wait."

"But I heard someone calling me!" She scanned the crowd again. "I did!"

"Sarah!"

Her eyes flew to the source of the sound, and she gasped as she excitedly waved her hand in the air. "Lee! Oh look, Zebediah, it's Lee!"

Zebediah's hearty laugh boomed out. "And here I's tryin' to take care of you when you's got you a young man!"

"But I didn't know he was coming!" Sarah waved wildly at Lee.

"Well, he know which car you's on now, so let's get you back to your friends 'fore you get trampled."

Sarah waved one more time, and with her heart thumping wildly, she darted back into the car and wove her way down the aisle. "Lee's here!" she shouted to Christine before she reached her.

Sarah watched as a smile flashed across her friend's exhausted face.

Finally, she reached Christine and the girls. "Lee's here, and Zebediah's already sent some boys for the trunks."

"Thanks be to God," Christine said.

"Mr. Logan!" Juli shouted.

Sarah wheeled around, saw Lee hurrying down the aisle, and flew to meet him.

"He's going to kiss Miss Sarah!" Juli squealed. "I want to see!"

Sarah felt Lee's strong arms encircle her and heard his deep voice demand, "Well, am I going to get to kiss you?"

"Yes!" Sarah flung her head back, and her spirits soared as she felt his lips briefly meet hers.

"Yay! He's kissing Miss Sarah!" Excited clapping and little-girl giggles exploded behind them.

"More later." Lee winked at her as he released her and led her down the aisle to the girls.

"You kissed Miss Sarah!" Juli shouted as she jumped up and down.

"I sure did." Lee swung her up and held her over his head for a few seconds. "What are you going to do about it?"

"Nothing!" Juli giggled as Lee lowered her to the floor.

"Good, because we need to get organized and hurry across the station to the Riverford train."

"I have all my things packed," Ceci announced primly.

"Good girl." Lee patted her on the head as he leaned into the compartment, took Christine's hand, and kissed it. "The General is waiting for you in Riverford, dear Christine. In fact, the whole town is eager to have you home."

"I cannot tell you how relieved I am to see you."

"Nothing to worry about. Let's get everyone and your luggage outside. We'll be settled on the Riverford train in no time."

Sarah's heart swelled with pride as she watched Lee organize everyone. When he tucked Christine's hand into the crook of his arm and led their little procession through the crowded terminal, trusting her to bring up the rear, Sarah was pleased. Obviously, he defined their relationship as the partnership she wanted.

CHAPTER SIXTEEN

Without warning, the train lurched ahead, its whistle shrieking, as it began its journey to Riverford. Christine fought back a wave of desperation close to panic as she closed her eyes and struggled to find peace in prayer. Every positive thought she drummed up was countered by the swaying of the car, the incessant clacking of its heavy wheels on the rails, the stifling heat that threatened to suffocate her. Another shriek of the train whistle sent a shock through her exhausted nerves, and her eyes flew open. Directly across from her, she saw the girls eagerly watching out the window as the train moved through the suburbs of Fort Worth. She saw Sarah one row up, snuggled close to Lee, her face tilted up as she listened eagerly. *What joy she must be feeling! Her life ahead of her ... her love beside her, strong and ... alive.* A sob escaped Christine's lips, and as she pressed her hand to her mouth, she blessed the racket the train was making. "You must not dilute their happiness!" she warned herself.

Nancy slid into the seat beside her and pressed a cool, damp cloth to her cheek. "Wash your face with this, Miz Christine. This train hot enough to make the Devil feel at home, but when we get outta the city, we be able to open the windows."

"Yes, thank you, Nancy." Christine's lips trembled. "The heat is ... I mean, it has been such a long ..." Christine dissolved into tears, and Nancy gathered her into her arms.

"You go on and cry now, Miz Christine. Ain't nobody gonna notice. Better to get them tears out 'fore we get back to Riverford."

Christine's mind flew to their impending arrival, her father standing tall on the platform, doing his best to mask his concern for her. She shuddered at the thought of breaking down and adding to his anxiety. *Best to cry now.* She allowed her tears to flow quietly into the damp cloth, and when she was cried out, she leaned against the pillow Nancy arranged and dozed.

"Mommy! Wake up. We're almost home." Ceci's excited voice broke into her slumber. "The porter said only half an hour more."

"How long's half an hour?" Juli demanded as she climbed into Christine's lap.

"It's from when the long hand on the clock goes from twelve to six. Everybody knows that!" Ceci's voice was filled with disgust.

"That's too long!" Juli wailed. "I'm hungry. Let's ask Nancy for an apple."

"I don't want one." Ceci shook herself free of Juli's grasp.

"Why not?"

"I'm not hungry! Go away. I want to have a *tête-à-tête* with Mommy."

Juli's eyes widened. "What does one of those taste like?"

"You don't eat it, silly! It's a talk. A talk with no little sister around." Ceci proudly lifted her chin and scowled down at Juli. "It's a French word."

"Actually it is several French words." Christine took control of the growing fight. "Where did you learn that expression, Ceci?"

"From Madame Makarova. She speaks French all the time, and I'm going to speak it too. It's sophisticated, and I'm gonna be sophisticated from now on."

"What's 'fisticated, Mommy?" Juli scrambled back onto the seat so she could scoot past her sister and poke her face into Christine's. "Is Miss Victoria 'fisticated?"

Christine felt her face relax into a smile as she looked into the eager eyes of her vivacious little girl. "Yes," she murmured as she stroked the blonde hair away from Juli's flushed face. "Miss Victoria is sophisticated."

"Are you?" Juli demanded.

"Of course she is!" Ceci retorted. "Don't you remember how she played the piano on the big stage in front of all those people?"

Christine closed her eyes. Images of mountains and the large auditorium, accompanied by memories of Natalya's and Victoria's faces floated through her mind. Was it all a dream? It seemed so far away ... so long ago.

The train's sharp whistle snapped her back to the present. "We'll have to wait until we get home to talk about sophistication," she said as she planted a kiss on Juli's cheek. "And we are nearly there. Go get your apple from Nancy and watch for Riverford out the window." She pushed Juli away, and the little girl forgot her questions in the excitement of her new activity.

Ceci climbed onto the seat and snuggled against her. "I don't want to go back to Riverford, Mama. It isn't home anymore. Daddy's not there."

Her statement felt like a blow to Christine's abdomen. "Riverford will be what we make of it, my darling, and I am going to need your help to make it a happy place for us. Remember, your brothers are coming home."

Ceci nodded. "But they won't be there long."

"No, not long." Christine thought of all the changes that the boys would have to assimilate in their two-week stay. She shuddered at the thought of taking them to their father's grave, and her spirits plummeted.

"Ten minutes 'til Riverford!" The porter called out as he passed down the aisle. "Just ten minutes, folks."

Christine began to drape her long black widow's veil over her head and down her shoulders.

"No!" Ceci cried as she lifted the veil back off her mother's face. "No, Mommy!"

"No?"

Ceci scooted to the floor and, leaning into her mother's lap, peered up into her face. "You said we could make Riverford a happy place. That veil isn't happy. Our music is happy, Mommy. Let's just have our music."

Christine looked down into the earnest upturned face and took her veil off. "No more veil. Now, go help Nancy gather up things, please."

As Ceci hurried away, Christine turned her face to the window. *She's right.* The train rounded a bend, and she saw the Riverford station in the distance. "I am not ready," she whispered. "I am so very tired. Help me, Lord."

Whistle screeching, wheels grinding, steam blasting through the open windows of the car, the train finally jolted to a halt at Riverford. Christine's journey was over. A new journey, a challenging journey was beginning. When she looked across the aisle, she saw Lee jump up and hold out his hand to Sarah. *No Richard will hold out his hand to me ...* The thought stung her, but before she had time to think more, the girls raced across the aisle and, leaning past her, eagerly waved out the window.

"Grandpa!" Juli squealed. "We're home!" She scrambled over Christine's feet and pushed Ceci onto the seat as she rushed back into the aisle.

"Stop her!" Christine commanded Ceci. "Make her wait, or she will get hurt."

"I got her," Nancy yelled over the commotion in the car. "She ain't goin' nowhere."

Lee took over and began ordering things. "Nancy, you take the girls. Sarah, you gather up everything. I'll send a boy back to help you carry it off." Then he leaned toward Christine and held out his hand. "I'll take Christine." He raised his voice and ordered all the passengers. "Make way, everyone!"

Christine stuffed the black veil into her carpet bag and allowed Lee to lead her to the end of the car. When she stepped down from the train onto the soil of Riverford, her father gathered her into his strong arms. "Welcome home, daughter!" His gruff voice suggested the emotion he was struggling to suppress. "This has been an empty town without you."

"Oh, Father!" Christine whispered into his ear. "I feel so incapable, so weak—"

"But you are not weak." He pushed her slightly back and with kind eyes looked down into her tense face. "You are strength incarnate, my child. Look what you have accomplished."

Christine felt a gentle hand on her shoulder, followed by a soothing female voice. "I could never have saved Victoria the way you did, Christine. Not on my best day, and certainly not when my grief was raw."

Grateful tears sprang to Christine's eyes as she turned. "Lavinia!"

"And I could never ratchet up my courage enough to perform on a stage before an immense audience." The Reverend John Neville reached for Christine's hands, raised them to his lips, and kissed them. "We are so proud of you, dear Christine."

"I am so grateful to you both for coming out in this heat."

Christine felt her father straighten his elderly bones, and she knew he had become the general again. "Time to move out! Miss Lavinia, if you will kindly escort Christine and the children home, I will be much obliged. Neville, you stay here with me, and we will see to it that the baggage is properly delivered."

"No need for you to stay out in this heat, sir. I can take care of the baggage," John Neville made the mistake of saying.

General Gibbes glared at him. "It has been a hallmark of my service, sir, that I am the last man off the field of every campaign."

Christine felt a wave of amusement push aside her sadder feelings as she struggled not to smile. "Come, Lavinia." She held out her hand. "Let us leave the field to the soldiers and seek the shade of a porch."

Lavinia wrapped her arm in Christine's. "Josie has iced lemonade waiting for you at home," she promised as she led Christine to the carriage where Nancy had corralled the girls. "If you aren't too tired, I want to hear all about Victoria."

"Will you and Lee join us?" Christine called to Sarah, but when she saw Lee's reluctant expression, she hastened to add, "But perhaps Sarah feels an obligation to check on Hodges House."

Lee grinned at Christine. "Duty before pleasure."

"How fortunate that sometimes they can be accomplished simultaneously." Christine gave him a knowing smile.

CHAPTER SEVENTEEN

"I'm dying to see Mama," Sarah said as Lee drove his buggy up the driveway of Hodges House. "I was hoping she would be at the station."

"She wanted to come, but I persuaded her to wait until this evening when it's cooler. I'll drive you out to the farm then." Lee looked toward the darkening western skies. "With a little luck, we'll have had a cooling storm come through by then."

Sarah fanned her face as he pulled back on the reins to stop the horse at the edge of the front verandah. "It does seem steamier than I remember late August being."

"You've been in the dry mountain air, my darling. It's back to reality now."

Sarah smiled at him. "My *new* reality."

"*Our* new reality." He squeezed her hand before jumping down to help her from the carriage.

Moments later, she crossed the threshold of the grand Hodges House. "It's so strange to be entering this empty house. Only yesterday I left Victoria and Hayden in Colorado." Sarah turned to Lee. "It feels so lonely."

"I have a solution for that." Lee pulled her to him and eagerly pressed his lips to hers.

Forgetting entirely that she was standing in the foyer of Hodges House—or indeed any house—Sarah raised her arms, wrapped them around his neck, and sank into his embrace.

"Well, really!" An indignant, caustic voice shattered Sarah's bliss. "So this is the way you thank Mrs. Hodges for picking you up out of the gutter."

Sarah sprang back from Lee's embrace, and whirling around, she found Mrs. Bellows standing in the doorway. "I—I just ... I mean *we* just arrived!" Sarah exclaimed.

"I know that!" Mrs. Bellows staggered forward. "I've been watching this house like a hawk. I'm determined to speak to Mrs. Hodges the minute she shows her face in Riverford again." She whirled around, scanning the main hall. "Where is she? I insist she come out at once!" Mrs. Bellows lost her balance and grabbed the large circular marble-topped table in the center of the entrance to steady herself.

Hurrying forward, Lee took her arm. "Mrs. Hodges is in Colorado enjoying a vacation with her husband."

"I should think *she* has vacationed enough!" Mrs. Bellows jerked her arm from Lee's hold and turned on Sarah. "Are you telling me that she made poor Christine come home by herself? That woman has no heart! To think that poor, grieving Christine left the loving support of Riverford to take that woman to ... to ..." Mrs. Bellows' words ground to a halt as her face openly displayed her confusion. "Where *did* she take her?"

Sarah's heart sank as she realized why Mrs. Bellows' behavior was so bizarre. "To Colorado." Sarah made her voice as soothing as she could. "And now we must get you home, Mrs. Bellows. You're not feeling well."

"I feel fine!" Mrs. Bellows shouted as she staggered toward the door. "I must go help poor Christine. She has been abandoned! I see it clearly now." Her voice became shrill as her agitation increased. "Poor Christine's been abandoned! Oh, how she must be suffering!" Mrs. Bellows began to sob.

"She isn't suffering, Mrs. Bellows." Sarah hurried after her. "I just left her—"

"What do you know about the pain of abandonment?" Mrs. Bellows sneered as she turned on Sarah. "You're young. You think this man—" She pointed at Lee. "You think he'll love you forever, but he won't. He's just like all the rest. He'll use you, and when you don't give him what he wants, he'll throw you away like trash." Mrs. Bellows clutched Sarah's arm as she wailed. "He hates me now. He loved me once, but he hates me!"

"What's going on, Sarah?" Lee demanded.

"Mrs. Bellows has been—" She gave Lee a meaningful look. "She's taken too much of her medicine."

"I'm going to get Mr. Bellows." Lee strode toward the door.

"No! That will only make things worse. He will ..." Sarah couldn't bring herself to speak the words.

"I best take her home like we always does." Delphie stepped out of the shadows of the back hall. "I take her out the back door so as nobody see her, and I get her home to Ada. She know how to do for her when she like this." Delphie took a firm hold on Mrs. Bellows' arm. "I's gonna take care of you, Miz Bellows," she cooed. "I's gonna take you home where you can rest. You's just havin' one of your bad headaches, but you's gonna be just fine."

"Delphie? Is that you, Delphie?" Mrs. Bellows cocked her head. "Where am I?" A look of panic flashed across her face. "Oh, no, no! I've done it again, and he'll have me locked away!"

"No, ma'am. He ain't ever gonna know. I's gonna take you home now." Delphie began to walk Mrs. Bellows down the hall. "We gonna go out the back door. Ain't nobody gonna see you. Ever' thing gonna be just fine."

Sarah dropped her head into her hands and shook it.

"You've never told me she was this bad off," Lee said. "Why haven't you told me?"

"Victoria and Christine have been trying to help her for years."

"But why haven't you told me?" Lee demanded.

"What would you have done? Told Mr. Bellows?"

"Of course. She needs help."

"Mr. Bellows will lock her up in an asylum. He can do that, you know." Sarah glared at Lee. "He's her husband. Under the law, he can do exactly that!"

"No wonder marriage hasn't looked very attractive to you, if this is what you've been watching. Does Hayden know about this?"

"He does. He and Victoria have tried for several years to get her to go to a sanitarium, but she's too afraid. She doesn't drink for months at a time, but then her life just becomes too painful. Mr. Bellows blows up at her, and—"

"Do you think I could ever treat you—"

"No!" Sarah rushed into his arms. "I do *not* think that. But I wonder, Lee, if you have any idea what most women put up with in marriage."

"Probably not." Lee looked grim. "But I swear you'll never put up with anything that would drive you to drink."

"I'm certain of that."

A crash of thunder shook the house. "I better get to the bank." Lee gave her a quick kiss. "You get some rest, and I'll pick you up about seven to drive you out to—"

A second boom drowned out his words. "Go!" Sarah laughed as she pushed him toward the door. "See you tonight."

"You take this here veil of Miss Victoria's," Delphie insisted as she pressed Victoria's gardening veil into Sarah's hand. "Them woods is gonna be buzzin' with bugs after this rain."

"Good idea," Lee agreed. "And take some gloves too."

Sarah laughed at both of them. "I did grow up on a farm. Remember?"

"That farm ain't in the woods." Delphie pulled a pair of old cotton gloves out of her apron pocket. "These here gloves is what Miss Victoria calls 'retired.' That mean we can't get 'em clean no matter how we scrubs 'em."

"Looks like you're all decked out." Lee held out his arm to Sarah. "May I have the honor, Miss Novak?"

Sarah shifted the package she was taking to her mother to the other hand and took his arm.

"Don't you be keepin' her out too late, Mr. Lee." Delphie gave her best imitation of her mother Frances' stern tone. "She gotta think 'bout her reputation. Besides, she ain't had 'nough rest this afternoon."

"I promise to have her back by ten, Delphie," Lee called back as they crossed the verandah to the *porte cochere* and Lee's waiting buggy.

The afternoon rain had lowered the temperature but raised the humidity considerably, and Sarah's starched white shirtwaist wilted before she and Lee had reached the edge of town. "I'm thankful the rain cooled the air, but did it have to leave all this moisture behind?" Sarah complained as she lifted her dampened sleeves off her arms.

"That's Texas in late August." Lee released the tension on the reins to let the horse choose its own pace as it pulled the buggy up the hill away from the river and the town. "Colorado has spoiled you."

"Definitely. Those crisp, cool nights are pure heaven. I never thought I'd ever wear a thick shawl in August."

"You miss it already, don't you?"

"Of course." She snuggled closer to him. "But you're here, and you matter the most."

He shifted the reins to one hand and put his arm around her. "How do you feel about a delayed honeymoon in Colorado next June?"

"Ecstatic!"

Lee laughed. "A Christmas wedding with a June honeymoon. I guess that's what happens when you marry a teacher."

Sarah bit her lip as her chest tightened with worry.

Lee pulled away from her and peered into her face. "You're not saying anything. What's wrong?"

"It just occurred to me that the school board might fire me the minute we take our vows."

"Not likely. General Gibbes is sure to be on the board by then. And I wouldn't imagine they'd have an easy time finding a replacement at midterm, would they?"

"No, I suppose not. Too inconvenient for them." She relaxed against his side.

"Better put on that veil," Lee advised as they entered the woods.

They both fell silent as the buggy entered the half mile of pine trees and moss-draped oaks that separated the town from the cleared cotton fields beyond. The shady reprieve from a day's sun, which Sarah had often eagerly sought in her daily walks between the farm and the town, was a different experience after the afternoon's storms. The damp breeze dislodged raindrops from the needles of the pines, the cicadas screeched in the oak trees, great swarms of gnats and mosquitoes surrounded them, and the night birds exchanged calls. By the time they exited the dismal place, Sarah and Lee were both soaked.

"Okay?" Lee asked as he swatted away a swarm of mosquitoes.

"Fine." Sarah peeled back the veil and peered up at the cloud cover that blocked the stars. "There should be a full moon tonight. I wish we could see it."

"Over there." Lee pointed to a blurred light. "Too many clouds in the way, I'm afraid." He ignored the trotting horse long enough to lean down and kiss her. "We don't really need a full moon, do we?" he murmured.

"No, sir!" Sarah grinned at him. "Are you going to ask Pa for my hand this evening?"

"Naw!" Lee's tone was teasing as he straightened and gave his attention to the road.

"Why not?" Sarah demanded.

"Don't have to. He'll be glad to get rid of you."

"Lee!" Sarah's exclamation was tinged with the expected playful outrage, but her heart began to ache at the truth of what he'd said. "You're right," she quietly agreed as her head bowed. "He'll be glad."

Lee pulled back on the reins and stopped the horse at the hilltop that overlooked the Novak farm. He turned to her and, placing his hand under her chin, forced her to raise her head and meet his eyes. "Your father, like many a man of his generation, is a fool when it comes to the worth of his daughter. But what's important, Sarah, is that I recognize your value. You're more than any man could ever hope for, much more than I deserve. That's why I came out here to see your father the minute I returned from Colorado."

"You did?"

"I did. I couldn't wait to seal whatever bargain *he* might think we had to make. As far as I was concerned, you had promised yourself to me on that mountain the morning I left Colorado, and your promise was all that mattered."

"But you went to see him anyway."

"Of course. I wanted us to begin married life with his blessing, so I asked for your hand in marriage, and he gave it to me."

Sarah gritted her teeth at the thought that her pa still thought he owned her enough to give her away, but she nodded. "You did the right thing. In spite of the fact that he and I have been estranged, he is still my father."

"And always will be." Lee brushed his lips across hers. "But I'm going to be your husband."

Sarah grinned at him. "So you think you're going to control me!"

"I've got more brains than that." He slapped the reins. "Let's go see your mother."

As they descended the hill, Sarah pointed to a lantern sitting on the porch. "She's waiting for us. Oh, I can't wait to hug her! All those weeks I was in Colorado, she was on my mind, and the thought of her back here working in the heat ..."

"Her joy comes from knowing that you're free of a farm wife's drudgery. She's so very proud of you, Sarah."

"I know." Tears stung Sarah's eyes. "I must never let her down. Not after all she's done."

Lee took her hand and squeezed it. "You won't." He pointed toward the house, and Sarah's heart soared when she saw her mother waving from the porch.

The minute Lee pulled the horse to a halt, Sarah jumped out and threw her arms around her mother's neck.

"Oh, honey! How I missed you!" her mother exclaimed.

"Not a day went by I didn't wish you were with me in Boulder. Oh, Mama! You should see the mountains. They're enormous and the most beautiful thing you've ever seen. And the Chautauqua was heavenly. To be with all those other teachers and to get to study under the professors. And you should have heard Christine play on that stage. Mama, there were a thousand people at her second concert. And Victoria—"

"Stop!" Her mother held up her hand as she laughed. "I want to hear every detail, but not scrambled together and heaped on top of each other." She untangled herself and stepped toward Lee, her arms outstretched. "Welcome, Son!" she exclaimed as she embraced him.

A thrill of joy shot through Sarah when she heard those words come from her mother's lips. Then she saw her pa walking out of the shadows on his way back from the barn. "So you finally come home," was all he said.

"Yes, sir."

"When you getting married?"

"Christmas. After the end of the first semester."

His loud sigh of exasperation filled the awkward silence. "If you had any sense at all, you'd marry this man while he still wants you."

"I'll always want Sarah," Lee insisted.

"Well, I've given you my advice, Daughter. Going to bed now."

"But Sarah just arrived," Jana protested. "Surely you want to hear about all her adventures. Why, she's seen—"

"Rather sleep. Got to get up early to work." Pa passed them by and went into the house.

Sarah forced herself not to respond.

"Oh, honey!" her mother exclaimed as she turned to Sarah. "I'm so sorry—"

"Don't be, Mama. I didn't expect any more from him."

"You got any of that cool blackberry cider you gave me last time I visited?" Lee diplomatically changed the subject.

"Sure do. Been keeping a jug of it in the spring house for days now."

"Well, let's get inside," Lee suggested. "Sarah's brought you a present all the way from Colorado."

"A present? Oh my!"

CHAPTER EIGHTEEN

The morning after her return to Riverford, Christine sat on the front porch shortly after daybreak just as she had done countless times with her beloved Richard. She sipped tea from a dainty cup from their wedding china and looked at the larger cup on the tray, which held his usual steaming robust coffee. This had always been their time together, a quiet hour before the children awoke, the town came to life, and Richard hurried off to the bank. This had always been their hour to plan the day, to determine their priorities.

On this, her first morning home after her weeks in Colorado, she had automatically come to their special place at their usual time. She had come knowing that Richard would not, could not meet her in the flesh. She could not sit next to him, slide under his protective arm, and feel him pull her close to his side. She could not feel his lips press against her forehead, delivering what she had always felt was his morning blessing on her. None of these sensations produced by living arms and lips would greet her this morning. Still … she felt certain Richard would be there, and she wanted to converse with him.

"We are safely home, my darling," she murmured. "The girls are asleep upstairs; the boys are coming. Our little family will be together again, all under the roof of this house you built for us, sharing life just as we always—" She stopped. "No, it will never be the same!" A quiet sob escaped her lips. "How can I go on alone?"

"You will learn." Christine heard her father's voice followed by the thud of the screen door closing behind him.

"How?" Anguish tightened her chest as she extended her arms, desperately grasping for answers. "I am confronted by a gaping hole—empty, empty—where Richard stood. I shall never be able to cross it. Never!"

"We don't cross such holes, my dear. We learn to walk around them." He took her hands in his. "And you have already made that journey."

"I thought I had. Oh, Father, I grew in Colorado. I became someone I never dreamed of being. But now I am devastated again."

"Only for a short time. My dear, the hole is still there. It always will be. You cannot fill it in. There is no substitute for the lost loved one. No experience, not even one as remarkable as your weeks in Colorado, can fill it in. Neither can another person, even a beloved person. The hole is unique, shaped by the person we have lost. In all of history, there has never been another Richard Boyd, and there will not be another in the future. That is the way God works. He creates; He never duplicates."

"Oh, Father! That is hardly a consoling thought!"

"No ... but it is a freeing one."

"Freeing? I feel myself slipping into the chains of despair."

"And so you could and stay there until you draw your last breath, if you choose. Or you could confront the reality that the unique creation we called Richard Boyd may be gone, but the unique creation we call Christine Boyd is still here, and it would be a sin for her to shut her life down by embracing grief as her identity."

Christine dropped her head into her hands. "This is so confusing."

"Then let me simplify it for you." General Gibbes sat down next to her, pulled her hands from her face, forced her chin up, and peered into her eyes. "You have a choice to make. You will go on breathing as long as God wills, but how you spend the days He gives you depends on you. Will you withdraw from life and deny the world the gifts God has given you to deliver to the world? Or will you courageously stay in the world, allow yourself to blossom, and allow God to bless the world through you?"

"I do not know ..."

The general's quick laugh startled her. "Well, I *do* know, my child, because I know *you*. I have led thousands of soldiers and never met a single man with your courage."

"I do not know how you can say such a thing when I feel so weak, so frightened."

"My dear daughter, when I came home from that Yankee prison camp, I found that while I had been away at war and behind bars, my little girl had become a young woman who would confront Satan himself in order to rescue the helpless. You have not changed; look how you defied most of Riverford to take Victoria to Colorado. Oh no! Richard's death will not stop you; it will only double your efforts. Will you not honor him by taking up his causes as well as your own?"

Christine straightened. "Well, of course I will!"

"And you are a mother …" her father added.

"The boys are coming home." Christine sprang to her feet. "They arrive tomorrow evening!"

The general smiled as he rose. "Yes, they do. And Ceci played the piano for me last night. Juli showed me her drawings and laid out her entire life's plan as an artist. And that, my dear, is just the family. While you were gone, Mrs. Bellows formed a committee to persuade the school board to charge country children a fee to attend the town school."

Indignation burned through Christine. "That is ridiculous! The sharecroppers could never pay such a fee for their children. What is the woman thinking?"

The general chuckled as he picked up his straw hat. "I very much fear you will find out before the day is over. She is sure to pay you a visit."

Christine wearily closed her eyes as she nodded her head.

"As for me," the general said as he clapped his hat on his head, "I'm off for my morning constitutional. When I return, I should like to accompany you to Richard's grave, if I may." He paused as Christine dropped her gaze to the wide boards of the porch floor. "That is where you are going this morning, is it not?"

"Yes, of course it is. I want to see the headstone and be sure everything is—" Tear-filled longing rose in Christine. "Oh, Father. I just need to be with him."

"Of course you do, but I must warn you that the headstone is not in place."

Startled, Christine jerked her head up. "Not in place? You mean the grave is …"

"The grave has been well tended, I assure you, and the headstone is ready to be placed. It occurred to me that it would be a help to the boys to participate in marking their father's grave. Perhaps a quiet, private ceremony of some kind."

"Yes. Of course. Oh, Father, once again your wisdom serves us all so well." She raced to his side and hugged him. "I have been so worried about helping the boys accept the loss of their father."

"I think it is time for us to formalize the Boyd and Gibbes plots, perhaps bring them together with a low-lying fence. After all, the plots lie side by side. I have long wanted to plant some flowering shrubs near your blessed mother's grave."

"Azaleas, of course. Mother loved her azaleas and Lady Banks' roses. Remember the enormous, Lady Banks' rose she had in South Carolina?"

"Indeed, I do. It covered the entire roof of the carriage house."

"Such a delicate yellow color, so like Mother." Christine's spirits rose at the memory.

"Yes, she was refinement itself but had the strength of iron. And you have that same strength, my dear. Never doubt it," General Gibbes assured her. "Our job now is to pass it along to your children. The girls are young, but the boys will soon be men. I want them to spend time at the bank while they're here, especially on a Saturday when the farmers and sharecroppers come in. After all, some day they will own all that Richard has built up. They need to start learning, not only about banking but also about compassion."

Christine picked up the tray and looked down at her husband's untouched cup of coffee. "Yes, Richard was the most compassionate man … Strange to think of the boys changing into men so soon. I suppose we shall see great changes in everything. A whole new century is around the corner. Think of it. Only one more year left in this one. Sometimes, I fear …"

"No need to fear, my dear. God resides in every day, in every night. We can name the year 1898 or 1900. He still controls every second of it."

Christine nodded. "I will go dress and be ready when you return from your walk."

He kissed her on the forehead, opened the screen door for her, and set off on his walk. Christine stood in the shadows of the entry, turning her head slowly as she gazed into the beautiful rooms Richard had supplied for their family. The drawing room on her right, the dining room behind it. The ornately carved staircase straight ahead with its bright window, edged in stained-glass flowers, at the landing. The library, Richard's favorite abode, to the left of the stairway. And finally on her direct left, her beloved music room. The morning sun streamed gently through the curved bay window, over the aqua velvet of the window seat, and spotlighted the mahogany grand piano. As she walked to the beloved instrument, she remembered the long walk across the Chautauqua stage, how endless the distance to the piano had seemed. Yet she had managed it, and once she had begun playing, the world, with all its joy and all its pain, had drifted away. Only the music had remained, and she had become one with it, dwelling on a height she had never dreamed of. A thrill shivered through her. She had changed; she knew it. She would seek that height again. She would always mourn Richard, but she *would* seek that height again.

CHAPTER NINETEEN

The minute Ceci finished breakfast, she complained, "Mama, I've missed two whole days of practice!" Nothing would do but that Christine should accompany her to the music room and have the little girl sight-read a short Bach piece. Christine marked the music with a pencil, suggesting fingering for Ceci's small fingers, and set her to learn it.

Juli, of course, responded by insisting that she must "go to work on my art." Hoping to placate the little girl, Christine hastily arranged a crystal vase of brightly colored zinnias and positioned them on a white wicker table on the front porch.

"There!" Christine forced unfelt enthusiasm into her voice. "Those bright colors will certainly make a lovely drawing."

Juli scowled. "I don't want lovely. I want drama."

"Drama?"

"There has to be contrast, Mama! There's no 'story' to those dumb zinnias, and Miss Victoria says there's always got to be 'story' or the painting won't sing."

"Sing?"

Juli sighed loudly as she shook her head in an exaggerated display of patience. "I'll fix it." She snatched a cobalt blue runner off the tea table, and returning to the zinnias, she wrapped one end of the fringed runner around the vase and trailed the other end over the edge of the table.

"That looks quite lovely," Christine encouraged her.

"I'm not through!" Juli roughed up the precise arrangement, bending both orange and yellow zinnias down over the blue cloth and snatching several stalks out of the vase to strew around. "There! Now we have drama."

"We certainly do," Christine agreed diplomatically as she kissed Juli on top of the head and wisely slipped back into the house.

There she discovered that Nancy had taken control of the housekeeping with a vengeance, wrenching authority from the younger Josie by objecting to her plans for today's dinner. "Ain't no tellin' what that girl got planned for the week!" Nancy warned Christine. "We gotta get our heads together, Miz Christine 'fore them boys gets here." So Christine hurried to her desk in the music room and spent half an hour writing out a menu that included the boys' favorite dishes. Nancy scanned the plan, nodding at times, grumbling occasionally, even though Christine knew the servant couldn't read a word. It was a scene Christine was accustomed to playing, pretending Nancy could read to protect the woman's pride, while casually commenting on the dishes she had listed so Nancy could guess at the words.

Once Nancy left her, Christine stared at a blank page she had set before herself, trying to think of pleasant activities to fill the days of the boys' visit home. Her mind refused to fill with anything but pictures of her sons standing next to the slightly raised hump of grass in the town's cemetery. *They will never see their father again!* The cruel thought tore through her so viciously it forced a sob from her lips, and Christine dropped her pen and lowered her head into her hands. How grateful she was that the sounds of Ceci's practice covered her own gasps as she fought for control of herself. How would she ever carry the load that now resided on her shoulders? She snatched up a photograph of her two sons in their Citadel uniforms and clutched it to her breasts. *They need Richard!* A wave of panic rolled over her at the thought that she was now their only parent, the one they would turn to for guidance. How would she ever rise to the task of guiding them into a man's world when she had only lived in a woman's?

Christine's emotional free fall was halted when Ceci slammed her hands down on the keyboard. "Mommy! I can't reach the notes. My hands are too small." Christine heard the coming tears in her daughter's voice and scrambled to avert them.

"Stop struggling with the Bach for a little while. Play something simpler."

"What?" the impatient child demanded.

"Just open the hymnal and play whatever you see."

"But I want to play the Bach!"

"And you will. But for now, go to something you know."

Christine heard Ceci sigh impatiently as she scrambled through the stacks of music for the hymnal and finally flopped open the heavy book on the music stand. After another exaggerated sigh, Ceci let her little fingers fly across the keys, and the randomly chosen tune transformed into familiar words for Christine. "On Christ the solid rock I stand. All other ground is sinking sand ..."

Christine smiled through her tears. Her father's words of encouragement, spoken just hours before, returned to comfort her. "No need to fear, my dear. God resides in every day, in every night."

CHAPTER TWENTY

"I feel guilty," Hayden confessed as he watched Victoria gaze up at the Rocky Mountains from the train station at Raton Pass, New Mexico.

"Guilty?"

"Yes. For dragging you away from a place that obviously fills your soul and gives you joy. On top of that, I'm dragging you back to the heat of Texas."

"It will end soon, just a few more weeks." Victoria linked her arm with Hayden's and leaned her head on his shoulder. "Besides, I couldn't bear to be parted from you again, and your life revolves around Riverford."

Hayden turned and kissed her lightly on the lips. "My life revolves around you, my darling girl. I just want to be with you."

"Ah …" Victoria cocked her head and grinned at him. "So that's why you kept dragging me back into that bed. And all those days I thought you had ulterior motives!"

Hayden feigned shocked innocence. "I was only thinking of your health, your need for rest. Why … what else would I be thinking of?"

"I can't imagine!" Victoria laughed as she turned her gaze back to the towering fir-covered mountains. "Oh, how I'll miss this beauty. If I didn't know I could come back, I simply couldn't leave."

"By next summer, we'll have a cottage of our own to house us."

"Cottage! Hayden Hodges, you drew up plans for a four-bedroom house complete with servants' quarters and—" The shrill train whistle shattered the calm and commanded them back to the stuffy enclosure of a railroad car. "Oh, no!" Victoria wailed. "The time has come. We really are leaving the mountains behind." She took one last long, hungry look at the towering peaks and the rail line that wound its way up the pass to the grandeur of the jagged, rocky peaks behind Raton Pass.

"Once again, I take you away from your heart," he muttered.

"No." She met his eyes. "You are my heart, my dearest. I made that decision three years ago when I chose to marry you and come back to Texas."

"Listen, Victoria." He grabbed both her arms. "I want to make a pledge to you. I'm going to do everything in my power to protect your creative time when we get home. I want you to have that exhibition in New York you're yearning for. Your dream is my dream, my love."

"I can't accomplish it if I continue to give equal time to Riverford's social life and to my painting."

"Put your painting first. Forget Riverford. Just don't forget me."

"Never!" She threw herself into his arms, and together they stood and watched the mountains sink lower and lower on the horizon.

At noon the next day, Victoria paused on the platform of the rail car and surveyed the Riverford train station as Hayden bolted ahead of her to clasp General Gibbes' extended hand. *How small, how insignificant Riverford looks!* she thought. *There's a whole world out there. Experiences, challenges, victories …*

"Victoria!" a beloved voice called over the din.

Victoria's eyes traveled to its source, a lady dressed in black. *No widow's veil!* Delighted, Victoria waved gaily as she descended the steps and hurried toward her friend.

"How I have missed you!" Christine threw her arms around Victoria. "You cannot imagine how dreary Riverford is without you."

"And hot!" Victoria fanned her face. "Whether I'm here or not."

"Believe it or not, it is actually cooler today. Early in the morning, it almost feels like autumn."

Victoria laughed. "You're always the optimist." She glanced around. "But where's Sarah?"

"At school. Classes begin on Monday, and her first faculty meeting is in the morning. She has to have the bulletin boards in her classroom decorated by then. She was absolutely miserable when she realized she could not meet your train."

"Just think of it. Sarah's preparing her own classroom. Oh, I can't wait to hear all about it!"

Hayden rushed up and gave Christine a gentle hug. "You shouldn't be out in this noon-day heat," he chided. "We must get you ladies home to a shady porch."

"Indeed we must," General Gibbes agreed. He raised Victoria's hand to his lips and kissed it. "Welcome home, my dear lady. What a cheering sight to see you well again! Riverford has been a dismal backwater without you."

Victoria planted a kiss on his cheek. "Thank you, General. Happily, I'm quite recovered and full of plans to enliven Riverford."

General Gibbes laughed heartily. "My response is a direct quote from your husband. 'Batten the hatches, Riverford. Hurricane Victoria has made landfall.'"

"And the next thing she gotta do is go home and take a nap," Frances insisted as she hurried forward. "I ain't gonna have her gettin' sick again 'cause of this heat."

Victoria laughed as she looked up at Hayden. "See what a monster I created by taking Frances to Colorado?"

"I'm quivering in my boots," Hayden answered. "Or I would be if it weren't so hot. Off we go now!" He marched her forward.

"But Christine and I have so much to catch up on," Victoria protested.

"I will come by after supper when it is cooler," Christine called after her.

* * * * *

"Sam, why are you sneaking around like that?" Sarah asked the elderly servant as she descended the stairs the next morning. "You look like a kid playing hide-and-seek."

"*Shh!*" Sam's finger crossed his lips. "I ain't playin' no game, Miz Sarah. I's hidin'."

"From whom?"

"From that woman Miz Victoria done brought back from Colorado."

"What woman?"

"The one I's married to. She be tearin' 'round the kitchen jerkin' everything outta the cupboards and just be throwin' a hissy fit 'bout everything in general. Seems me and Delphie done everything wrong the whole time she's gone. This place be a disgrace, and we's just slovenly as all get out."

"Goodness! I hope she doesn't awaken Miss Victoria." Sarah glanced back up the stairs.

"Oh, ain't no need to worry 'bout that. Miss Victoria been in her studio tearin' apart everything in there since dawn. She bound and determined to stretch some of that canvas of hers over a frame she made me build, and ain't hell nor high water gonna stop her neither."

"Well, why aren't you in there helping her?" Sarah asked. "Is Mr. Hayden in there?"

"Oh, no, ma'am. He be gone to the bank to check on things. Course he was up 'fore dawn, stompin' 'round in the back garden and writin' things down on a paper he got with him. I tell you, Miss Sarah, you best be careful. They's all gone crazy."

"Yes, it certainly sounds like it. I'll go calm Frances down, and you go help Miss Victoria stretch the canvas."

"Oh, no, ma'am! I ain't goin' back in there. She done told me to get out 'cause I ain't fit for nothin'."

Sarah's mouth fell open in surprise, but she quickly took command of herself, slammed it shut, and straightened her spine. "Now Sam, I don't believe that Miss Victoria actually said you're worthless."

Sam's hand shot to his head, and he began to scratch it as perplexity covered his face. "Well, it might of been Frances that said that. I can't rightly recall 'cause they's both in such a tizzy."

Sarah patted him on the shoulder. "Just go sit out under the trees for a while, Sam. I'll deal with Frances, and then—"

"Ain't nobody gonna deal with Frances!" Sarah swung around and found a furious Frances standing behind her with a broom in her hand. "And he ain't goin' nowhere except back out to the kitchen to help me clean up the mess he made out there."

Sam held up his hands. "Now, Frances, you gotta just stop this. I's a man, and I ain't supposed to know nothin' 'bout kitchens. Besides, Miss Sarah been back here a couple of weeks, and she ain't complained 'bout—"

"Miz Sarah's a lady now! Why they even had her teachin' the other teachers up at that Chautauqua place." Frances shook her broom at him. "And you knows when the ice box pan ain't been emptied and the water be drippin' on the floor and rottin' the boards 'til they look like swamp mud. You may be a man, but you ain't stupid!"

"What in the name of heaven is going on out here?" Victoria's voice sliced through the air. "Have we abandoned every semblance of civilization in this house?"

Sam was struck dumb, and Frances lowered her broom and lifted her chin. "No, Miz Victoria, we's gonna be civilized if I have to kill somebody."

Victoria turned to Sarah as the fury in her eyes dissolved into suppressed laughter. "Isn't it wonderful, Sarah, how travel always educates and elevates one?"

Sarah bit her lips to stop her own laughter from exploding and gravely nodded.

Having regained control of her mirth, Victoria turned back to Frances. "I'm hopeful that it won't be necessary to kill anyone, Frances, but if it should become necessary, I'm confident you will take care to protect the rugs."

"You can count on me, Miz Victoria!" Frances glared at Sam. "Ain't nobody gonna bleed on my rugs."

Victoria nodded. "Yes, I know I can count on you, and I'm greatly comforted by that knowledge. Perhaps you might mention any need for repair of the kitchen to Mr. Hayden."

"Yes, ma'am. You!" She pointed to Sam. "You come with me."

As soon as Frances had dragged Sam away, Victoria collapsed onto a chair.

"Welcome back to Riverford." Sarah laughed.

"And I thought I was going to just get up early, stretch a canvas, and cover it with a coat of gesso before breakfast." Victoria shrugged her shoulders as she released a dramatic sigh. "Never mind. Look at you!" She jumped up to admire Sarah's new outfit. "Off to your first faculty meeting. But aren't you going to have breakfast before you go?"

"Oh, I couldn't eat a bite. I had some tea, and Delphie stuck some scones and an apple in my satchel. I confess I'm all jitters. Do I look okay?"

"Very professional. And I'm very proud of you."

CHAPTER TWENTY-ONE

"*This* is the magnificent Sarah Novak we have been blessed with." Mr. Morris Hunt's sarcastic tone at the first teachers' meeting obliterated Sarah's eager happiness on the first day of her teaching career. "Stand up, Miss Novak!" She flinched at his shouted command, and her stomach turned with fear as he took a menacing step toward her, paused, and pointed his bony finger at her. "*Do* let everyone get a good look at the prodigy among us mere mortals." Sarah struggled not to show the sickening fear that quivered through her nerves. Mr. Hunt released a derisive laugh into the silent room. "*Do* allow us to view what can be created from a cotton-picking sharecropper's daughter by a meddling outsider."

The principal's veiled but vicious reference to Victoria instantly shifted Sarah's reaction. Her fear fled as cold fury surged through her. *How dare he snipe at Victoria! How dare he try to humiliate me!* She rose with exaggerated dignity. Before her, Sarah saw the entire faculty of Riverford School, the eight primary schoolteachers as well as the six high school teachers. All were female; all were dressed in the near-uniform of dark skirt and plain white blouse. The few who met her eyes did so with disdain.

"Miss Novak has not only risen from sharecropper's daughter to teacher's college graduate," Mr. Hunt sneered, "she has also traveled *all the way to Colorado*—" He paused for dramatic effect, and Sarah heard several snickers. "A mighty feat indeed!"

All too familiar with the abusive, bullying tone of the principal, Sarah ordered herself to demonstrate complete composure. She conjured up and copied the image of Victoria standing erect, her chin slightly raised as she leveled her gaze on the teachers until each one had raised her head and met her eye.

Mr. Hunt stepped close to her. With a leer on his face, he looked her over, his eyes beginning at her boots and traveling upward until they stopped at her bosom and remained. "Sit down!" he commanded.

Sarah flinched at his shout, but she remained standing as she locked eyes with him.

"I said sit down!" He flung his arm downward. "Are you deaf?"

"No, sir." Sarah kept her voice even but strong. "My hearing is good, as are my manners."

Mr. Hunt's face turned near purple with rage, but Sarah turned her back on him, swept her eyes across the room of upturned faces, and addressed the women before her. "I wish to thank each of you for your warm welcome. I'm looking forward to working with you. No doubt I shall gain immeasurable benefit from working with teachers of your experience."

"Are you finished, Miss Novak, with your sentimental remarks?" Mr. Hunt barked. "I'm sure it will surprise a novice like you, but we do have actual work to accomplish this morning."

Turning back to him, she narrowed her eyes. "The only thing that surprises me, Mr. Hunt, is your unprofessional tone." She sat down in a fluid, graceful movement.

"Well—well—really!" Mr. Hunt stammered, then loudly cleared his throat. "See me after this meeting adjourns, Miss Novak!"

When Sarah entered the principal's office an hour later, she found him standing behind his desk, his arms clasped behind his back, his face rutted with a scowl. "I will *not* have my authority questioned, Miss Novak!" he barked without the slightest prelude. "I am the boss here."

"I do not question your authority since the school board has assigned it to you, Mr. Hunt, but I will *not* be bullied. Is there anything further you wish to say? If not, I will return to the primary school meeting." Sarah waited, her feet positioned to turn sharply and leave.

"Now, now, Miss Novak ..." Mr. Hunt's tone softened as he slid around the desk toward her. "What's your hurry? Why don't you take a seat and let us get to know each other on a personal level." He motioned to a chair with one hand while he slipped the other around Sarah's upper arm.

Sarah stiffened at his inappropriate touch. "I prefer to keep our relationship professional, Mr. Hunt." She shrugged her arm away from his hand.

"Oh, I see." He raised both hands as he shrugged his shoulders. "You're angry with me. But of course you are; you don't understand what I'm doing for you." He leaned toward her. "You're such a beautiful young woman, and it was for your own good that I put you in your place in front of the other teachers. They're all so dried up. They would hate you if they thought I favored you." He smiled knowingly into her face. "As, of course, I do."

Sarah's skin began to crawl; her throat tightened. Her response, which she meant to sound firm, came forth as a stutter. "I—I don't seek to be favored."

Mr. Hunt lifted his hand, clutched the locket that lay on her bosom, and fingered it. "But of course you do," he murmured as he lifted his eyes from her bosom to her face. "It's the best way to get ahead."

Horrified, Sarah pushed his hand away, turned on her heel, and ran from the room. She hurried toward the nearest outside door, flung it open, and bounded through. *Stop! You can't run away.* Her reason fought her fear as she gasped in the fresh air. "I have to think," she muttered. "Where can I hide?" Her eyes darted around her surroundings until they lighted on a shadowed corner. She hurried toward it and leaned heavily against the brick wall, her face in her shaking hands. "You're okay," she comforted herself. "You can handle this. You must!" A quiver ran through her whole body as she remembered the weight of Mr. Hunt's hand on her bosom, and for one horrible, panicked moment, she thought she would break down and sob. "You mustn't," she ordered as she wrapped herself in her arms. "He's trying to break you. You can't let him win!"

Confusion washed over her. *But why? What's happening?* Her mind grew fuzzy, and all she could think to do was to breathe, to wait. She slid down the wall, sat on the grass, and forced herself to take deep, calming breaths until finally her mind cleared.

"Okay," she whispered to herself. "What are my options? To tell someone?" Unaccountable shame washed through her. "No! I can't bear for anyone to know!" She wrung her hands, which suddenly felt filthy. "No one must know! I'll just have to handle this myself. But how?"

She heard a bell ring in the building and realized she was missing the next meeting. Scrambling up, she hastily brushed off her linen skirt. "I can't think about this now." Sarah ran back into the building, stopped for a moment to compose herself, and entered the classroom where her supervisor, Miss Agnes Grimm, was addressing the primary teachers.

Without altering her cadence, Miss Grimm nodded at her, and Sarah gratefully slipped into a student desk. She heard little of what was said as she replayed the scene with Mr. Hunt and reshaped it into a memory she could bear. *Perhaps I only thought ... surely he wouldn't. I can't afford to make waves ... I'll just stay away from him.*

By the end of the day, she had convinced herself that she had overreacted, and she told no one.

CHAPTER TWENTY-TWO

Christine's heart was heavy as she accompanied her family on their solemn journey to the cemetery. Across from her sat her father, rigidly upright with his face set in his sternest military expression. Next to him her sixteen-year-old son, Andrew, sat. Struggling to match his grandfather's composure, Andrew held Ceci on his lap. *He is determined to be a father to his sisters now. How will I ever convince him to stay in military school?* She turned her eyes to her fourteen-year-old son, George, who sat beside her holding Juli, who had buried her face under her brother's chin. *They are too young to lose their father!* As for her, she was weary to the bone and struggling to hold herself together. The boys' visit had forced her into reliving her own grief at the same time she tried to support them in theirs. Tomorrow they would be returning to school; she was determined she would appear strong and capable so they could leave with free consciences. She stiffened her spine, sending a sharp pain up to her neck and into her throbbing head.

The carriage rolled to a stop in front of the newly designed family plot, which the boys had spent the last two weeks designing and constructing. From the vantage point of the high carriage, she inspected their work. "It looks splendid," she complimented them on the iron-fence-enclosed area. "You have chosen beautiful evergreen plantings, and the garden bench under the oak is the perfect place to sit and reflect." When her eyes fell on the newly installed gravestone of her husband, she gasped.

"Mother?" Concern dredging lines in his face, Andrew leaned across and took her hand. "Are you sure you're able—"

"Yes," she choked the word out, but could say no more.

George peered at her. "We could just go home if you're too upset—"

"I'm sorry," Christine managed to murmur. "It's just the shock of seeing ..."

General Gibbes sat forward. "Your mother has exhausted herself trying to help you children through the sadness of the last two weeks."

"When we should have been taking care of her!" Andrew's voice was heavy with condemnation as he looked across at his brother. "We have been selfish and—"

General Gibbes held up a hand to stop him. "As you experience more of life, Andrew, you will learn that it is a mother's privilege to sacrifice herself for her children."

"Yes, that's exactly right," Christine agreed. "You are my children. I would give my life for you ..." She swallowed hard, forcing her tears back, and took another tack. "I am so very proud of you boys." She struggled to steady her voice. "And your father would be—no! Your father *is* proud of you. This is the essential fact we must all remember. Your father is here with us right now. I do not understand how this is possible, but I feel his presence. He will never leave us, and one day we will all be reunited." She stopped to take a deep breath. "Now, we have come to pray together in this special place that you boys have created for the family. Let us follow our plan."

George leaned forward. "I see other carriages on the road."

General Gibbes descended the carriage step and held up a hand to help Christine. "Reverend Neville and Lavinia will be joining us, and no doubt some friends are coming too."

"I did not know that they—" Christine's inbred hospitality took over, and she rose quickly. "Come, children, we must prepare to greet our guests."

After all the children were in bed, Christine sought the relative coolness of the night air on the front porch and was glad to find her father there before her.

"Sit down, my dear." He patted the cushion next to him. "I would insist you go to bed, but I am sure your heart is too troubled to sleep."

Christine nodded. "I cannot bear for the boys to leave tomorrow. The thought of their being alone at school … and yet, I cannot bear for them to abandon the plans their father made for their futures. I feel so torn."

"School is the distraction they need, and they will have each other. They will grieve, of course, but they will be well served by the discipline. It is we who are left behind who will suffer the most."

"Yes … the girls."

Christine felt her father's comforting hand enclose hers. "They will take their cue from us, and I know you well enough to know that you will create cheer in this house regardless of how you are feeling. No, I am not worried about the girls; I am worried about you."

"Surely I will have my hands full."

"But not your heart and mind. Victoria has been telling me about Madame Makarova and the joy you received from studying with her and from performing."

"It was a blessed reprieve from grief, but it is over."

"Only if you choose for it to be. I have just reread the reviews of your concerts, my dear. It is clear to me that while you will likely never travel the world as a concert pianist, you could share your music with many."

"Are you suggesting that I perform? Oh, Father! I have already been so thoroughly criticized by the Riverford ladies—"

"Who should be ignored!" General Gibbes' voice was emphatic. "No doubt it will surprise you, my dear, but I find myself thinking like Victoria Hodges these days."

"You?"

He chuckled. "I may be old, but I am not dead, Christine. And since it has been God's will to call Richard home, my duty is clear. My duty and my joy."

"To take care of us, you mean."

"Yes. It is the least I can do for the man who saved my beloved wife and daughter when I could not."

"So long ago … the War and that horribly painful reconstruction period."

"Reconstruction, bah! A season of thievery and cruelty; that's what those nine years were. But it is history now, and we are approaching a new century. The human experience is being quickly and radically changed. Some of the change is good; some is bad. As much as we might prefer to live in the past, we know we cannot. We must all stay engaged in the present moment in order to enhance the good and defeat the bad."

"I agree, of course, but I fail to see what part I can play beyond Riverford."

"The most significant good that can come is the empowerment of women."

"Father, are you feeling well?"

"Better than a man who has reached the three score and ten years of age the scriptures limit us to should expect to feel. Daughter, I am a realist, and I have long understood that the goodness of humanity does not naturally dwell in the male of our species. We men must be taught to be humane, to be civilized, and what little we have learned, we have learned from the female models in our lives. So I say, let the female models take the stage. Give women the power to shape our arts, our science, even our politics. If the nineteenth century has taught us anything, it should have taught us that we need better models for the twentieth."

"You are taking my breath away!" Christine exclaimed. "How many hours have you spent with Victoria?"

The general laughed as he lowered his head to his daughter's. "Enough to know that your talent is sizable and must not be hidden. It will be the world's loss if you do not share your gift. And you will be miserable."

"You know, Father, I had no intention of performing that second time in Colorado, but then I saw that the restriction I was placing on myself was teaching Ceci that she must restrict herself. She is vastly more talented than I shall ever be."

"That is hard to believe."

"It is true. Madame Makarova says that our Ceci is a prodigy, that if she were in New York—"

"But she is not. She is here with us, and the question is, what doors will her mother open for her?"

Christine sprang to her feet, walked to the edge of the porch, and peered up at the stars. "I do not want her to be denied the opportunity that I was—" She quickly covered her mouth with her hand to stop her words. "Oh, Father, I am sorry."

"There is no need to be. Your mother and I did not choose to bring a war into your young world. And perhaps, even without the War, a young girl's musical genius would not have been supported at that time. But Ceci will be a child of the twentieth century; she need not have the restrictions you had."

"I must find the best teacher for her."

"Can you not teach her?"

"I can. I will. But, oh Father! You should have seen her bloom under the tutelage of Madame Makarova."

"Victoria tells me that you will be able to return to Colorado next summer."

"Yes, but we cannot wait that long. Ceci needs the best teacher now."

"New York is a long way off, my dear, but the mail service is quite dependable. Why can't this Madame Makarova be employed to create a weekly program of study for Ceci, which you could oversee?"

A thrill of excitement raced through Christine as she hurried back to his side. "Of course! Ceci has already developed the highest regard for Natalya. She would do anything to please her."

"And she would see herself as a serious student studying under a famous teacher," General Gibbes added.

Christine laughed. "Not just a little girl learning piano from her mother." She hugged her father. "You, sir, are a very wise man. I'll write Natalya today.

CHAPTER TWENTY-THREE

Sarah's shiny new black boots tapped on the battered wooden floors as she walked briskly down the central hall of Riverford School on the first day of class. *I am a teacher! I made it!* She was so excited, she could have twirled in circles outside the door to her very first classroom. Instead, she inspected her image in the door's window and straightened her new red-and-navy-striped silk scarf. She had tied it in a droopy bow under the collar of her crisp white shirtwaist that morning after she had tucked the blouse into her new navy five-gored skirt. She patted her curls one last time and took a deep breath in a last-ditch effort to calm her excitement before she opened the door. When she breezed into her sun-drenched classroom, she jerked to a halt right before colliding with her supervisor, Miss Agnes Grimm.

"Good morning, Miss Grimm," Sarah greeted the gray-haired woman in spite of the woman's frown.

"What is that thing dangling from your neck?" Miss Grimm demanded as she pointed a long, accusing finger at Sarah.

Sarah raised her hand to her crisp, white collar. "Why, it's a scarf, Miss Grimm."

"Entirely too flamboyant for a teacher. Did you not listen when I dictated the teachers' dress code?"

"Yes, ma'am. I did listen. You said we must wear dark skirts and boots with white or ivory shirts and a tie."

"That is not a tie!" Miss Grimm's raised hand began to shake with palsy. A cloud of fear crossed her face as she snatched her hand to her waist and imprisoned it in her other hand. Her tone softened and turned pleading. "You did not see that, Miss Novak."

"No, ma'am." Sarah resisted the urge to pat the woman's shoulder. "Perhaps I could retie my scarf and flatten it."

"Yes, I'm sure that will suffice." Miss Grimm glanced at her shaking hand, then cleared her throat and took on her commanding tone again. "There are other matters I need to discuss with you. Matters about your classroom. I see that you have assigned desks already."

"Yes, ma'am." Sarah looked with pride at the individual signs she had created for each of her students' desks. She had painstakingly scrolled in calligraphy the name of each student, then created an elegant but dignified border—floral for the girls and classical for the boys—on each card.

"This arrangement will simply not do."

"Why not? I separated the boys from the girls, as you instructed."

"So I see, but you have failed to separate the town children from the—" Miss Grimm gave Sarah an apologetic look. "From the other children."

Anger flashed through Sarah, but she forced herself to keep her tone calm. "You mean, from the *immigrant* children?"

"Miss Novak, it is not my intention to offend you or indeed to lessen the status of any student. My personal belief is that every— well, never mind about my personal belief. The rules are the rules. Mr. Hunt insists that immigrant children must sit in the back of the classroom."

"But Miss Grimm—"

Agnes Grimm held up her hand to silence Sarah's protests. "We might as well lay our cards on the table, Miss Novak. Mr. Hunt does not want to encourage immigrant children to come to Riverford School, and he has the backing of the school board. As you probably know, some townspeople have petitioned the school board to impose a tax on all children who don't live in town."

"Yes, I've heard, and it's an outrageous idea! Why can't those people understand that education of the population, all the population, benefits everyone?"

"I'm sure I can't explain the thinking of such people, and it's not my job to do so. My job is to require all the teachers to conform to Mr. Hunt's directives. That being the case, you must seat the immigrant children in the back, and you must not allow them to take textbooks home."

"But how can they do their homework?"

Miss Grimm sighed. "They can't." She looked Sarah full in the face. "If you want to survive as a teacher here, Miss Novak, you will lay aside your personal opinions, the causes you are tempted to fight for."

"I am an immigrant's child, Miss Grimm, and I have fought to be here."

"I know that. Now you must fight to stay." She turned her back on Sarah and walked to the bulletin board where Sarah had pinned a map of the world and letters, which she had painstakingly cut out, that announced "Diversity is strength."

"This must come down, Miss Novak." Miss Grimm pointed to the letters. "Such a statement is offensive to many tax-paying citizens of Riverford."

Sarah lifted her chin and narrowed her eyes. "But not to *all* tax-paying citizens of Riverford, Miss Grimm."

"I have your well-being at heart, Miss Novak. I wish you would believe that."

"Then you will wish me success in my endeavor to change the minds of the bigots of this town, for you see, Miss Grimm, I shall not be content until I do."

Miss Grimm nodded curtly. "I regret that our acquaintance will be short-lived." She walked to the classroom door but turned back to Sarah. "At least retie your scarf, Miss Novak, and in future wear nothing that labels you as fashionable. Your cause is too admirable to fail due to your personal dress code."

"I do not intend to fail, Miss Grimm."

A sad, faraway look crossed Miss Grimm's face. "No," she murmured. "No teacher intends to fail when she begins. But the long, empty years ..." She jerked herself up straighter. "I hear the students coming down the hall."

Sarah's initial excitement was dimmed by angry frustration and a strange wave of grief as she fumbled to untie her bow and straighten the scarf into a facsimile of a man's tie. She turned to the bulletin board and snatched off the letters that spelled out "Diversity is strength" just as the first students flung open the door and entered, their voices raised in excited chatter. When she turned back to help them find their assigned seats, she was startled by the diversity of sizes and ages that Mr. Hunt had assigned to her seventh-grade classroom. Clearly, the town children were all about twelve, but the poorer dressed farm children were in their teens.

When all of her students were seated, Sarah wrote her name on the board and turned to greet the class. Just as she opened her mouth to speak, a young girl's hand shot up, and she blurted out, "I don't want to sit here!"

Sarah glanced at the seating chart she had made. "That is your assigned seat, Stephanie Sharp."

"But my mother won't like it," the girl persisted.

Sarah forced herself to smile and keep her tone light. "Your mother is not in this class. No doubt she graduated long ago."

The class giggled as Stephanie scowled at Sarah, then wiggled around to look at several other well-dressed girls.

Another girl's hand shot up. "We want to sit with our friends," she blurted out.

"Before long we shall all be friends, Leanne Proper," Sarah replied.

"Her name ain't Leanne," a boy shouted. "It's Prissy 'cause that's what she is. Just a prissy girl!"

Most of the boys broke into laughter and chanted, "Prissy Proper, Prissy Proper!"

"Thank you for that information, Julius Octavius Lynch," Sarah replied coolly.

"My name ain't Julius Octavius!" the boy protested amid howls of derision from the class.

Sarah pretended innocence. "But it says right here in my grade book that your name is—"

"No!" The boy jumped up, his fists clenched, his face scarlet. "My name's Buddy!"

Sarah smiled at him. "Sit down, Buddy." She widened her gaze to include the entire class. "I think we should all be allowed to choose what we want to be called, don't you?"

Surprised, the children glanced from side to side, checking out each other's responses. They began to nod.

Sarah glanced at Leanne. "Welcome to my class, Leanne." She turned her eyes on Julius. "Welcome, Buddy."

Admiration grew in the eyes of the children sitting before her, and Sarah took advantage of the moment to change the subject. "Now, class, I have a mystery for you to solve." She turned to the blackboard and printed *E PLURIBUS UNUM*. "Can anyone tell me what this phrase means?"

"It ain't English," a well-dressed boy blurted out.

Sarah glanced at her seating chart again. "That's right, Willis."

"Could you call me Willy, Miss Novak?"

"Certainly. What language is this on the board? Does anyone know?"

Jerome Nelson raised his hand and eagerly announced. "It's Latin. It's like the words over the door of the school."

"Exactly, Jerome. It is Latin. Now, what does it mean?"

The students squirmed in their seats and shot furtive looks at each other.

With obvious hesitation, a handsome but shabbily dressed boy with an earnest expression behind his gold-rimmed spectacles stood, and Sarah called on him. "What does it mean, Piotr?"

"It means 'out of many, one,' Miss Novak."

"That is correct. And how did you know that, Piotr? Have you seen the phrase before?"

"*Tak.* I mean, yes, ma'am. I seen it on the papers they give when we leave ship from Poland in Galveston."

The room filled with giggles as the students whipped their heads around to stare, but Sarah noticed that Stephanie's expression quickly changed from derision to admiration when she saw the tall boy.

Sarah rushed on to make her point as Piotr sat down. "That Latin phrase was on those papers because it is the motto of the United States of America. Can anyone tell me how the United States was formed?"

Stephanie waved her hand in the air, and Sarah nodded at her. "It was made out of thirteen colonies. They all signed the Declaration of Independence."

"Very good, Stephanie!" The girl beamed and cast a furtive glance at Piotr. "And where did the people in the thirteen colonies come from?"

"I know!" A boy in the front row leaned across his desk and waved his hand wildly. "They came from other countries, like England and places."

"That's right, Russell Quince." Sarah watched the boy's face turn red. "Or do you prefer to be called Rusty?"

"Yes, ma'am! I'm Rusty." He pointed to the boy next to him. "And this here's my best friend, Billy Gerhardt."

"Glad to meet you, Billy." Sarah smiled at the boys and quickly returned to the subject. "So what you're telling me is that the United States was formed by people who came from England. Right?"

"Naw," Billy Gerhardt protested. "I ain't English. My great-grandpa came from Germany."

"My great-grandfather was an aristocrat who came from France," Leanne announced as she looked down her nose at Billy.

"Who cares where your great-grandfather came from?" Rusty sneered at her. "We're all Americans now."

"Exactly." Sarah intervened to prevent a fight. "We're all Americans now."

"Where do you come from, Miss Novak?" Leanne asked. "My mother says you're nothing but an ignorant immigrant."

"I am the child of immigrants, Leanne, just like all the rest of you. My parents came here from Bohemia. As for being ignorant, we're all ignorant until we become educated."

"But if you're ignorant, you can't learn anything!" Leanne retorted.

Much of the class broke into laughter, but Sarah turned to the blackboard and wrote *ignorant* and *stupid* on it. "You are using the wrong word, Leanne. There's a big difference in the meaning of these two words. Ignorant simply means a lack of information, a lack of education." She looked down at Jerome. "Can you tell me what stupid means, Jerome?"

"Stupid is when you don't have enough brains to learn anything."

"That's right," Sarah agreed. "Some people are not born with enough brains to learn, but everyone in this classroom has plenty of brains, and we're going to learn about the countries we came from. Just think how much we can learn about the world if we share our knowledge." She moved to the map on the bulletin board. "This is a map of the countries of Europe and the United States. Here is Texas, and here is Riverford. Now, let's put pins in the countries where our families came from. Piotr, would you like to begin by putting a pin in Poland?"

"How come he gets to be the first one?" Buddy demanded.

"'Cause he's the newest one here." Stephanie sneered at him. "Guests always get to go first."

"After he puts his pin in Poland, he'll no longer be a guest." Sarah held up a pin. "He'll be one of us."

Before Piotr could come forward, the tiny girl in a patched homespun dress sitting next to Stephanie stood. "I'm Nadia." She stopped as a quiver ran through her body, and her eyes filled with tears.

"Where are you from, Nadia?" Sarah softly asked.

"Po—Po—land." Another quiver shook her small frame, but she straightened her shoulders and brushed away the tears that were now cascading down her cheeks. "Please, can I put pin in Poland?"

"Naw!" Rusty Quince protested. "Let Piotr do it. He's a boy; she's just a girl. Besides, she's so short, she can't even reach the map."

As the boys laughed, Sarah intentionally focused on Stephanie.

"I'll help her!" Stephanie shot out of her chair. "Girls are just as important as boys." Sarah smiled at her, and Stephanie took Nadia's hand and dragged her to the bulletin board. "Nadia's gonna put in the first pin!" Stephanie lifted the thin girl to the map, then glanced at Sarah for help.

"Poland is here." Sarah pointed to the country as she turned to Piotr. "Come, put your pin in too, Piotr."

"I wanta put one in for Germany!" Willy jumped up.

"And France!" Leanne called out.

"Good," Sarah agreed. "Let's take turns."

"But what if we don't know where our families came from?" Rusty asked.

"Ask your parents tonight," Sarah answered. "In fact, your first homework assignment, class, is to write a paragraph about the country your family came from."

The students groaned, of course, but Sarah ignored them. "If you know where your family's from, come forward quietly and put your pin in. When you return to your desk, turn to page thirty-four. We're going to read 'Rip Van Winkle' by Washington Irving this morning."

The classroom filled with the inevitable clatter of students moving around, but finally grew quiet again as they settled back in their desks and opened their books.

"This is a fascinating story about a man who falls asleep for twenty years," Sarah explained. "When he finally wakes up, his whole world has changed. Can you imagine?" The students shook their heads. "Just think how things will change in your lives in the next twenty years, students. We're about to enter the twentieth century!"

Recess time came an hour later. Sarah was only half finished reading the story, and she was thrilled when the students complained about stopping and forming a line to march outdoors. Once outside in the fresh air, the boys began a game of baseball, and the girls jumped rope. Sarah took deep breaths of fresh air, reveling in her success of the morning. She had not only headed off the hostility toward the few immigrant children in her class, as well as toward herself, she had actually managed to start the students thinking about America as a nation of immigrants.

Grateful for the breeze that was cooling the September sun a bit, she tried to tame her wayward silk scarf that fluttered freely. Just as she finally secured it in the waistband of her skirt, she glanced to her right, and there stood Mr. Hunt watching her from the shadows. Sarah felt a cold sweat break out on her back, and she instinctively moved closer to the children, offering to turn the heavy jump rope for the girls.

CHAPTER TWENTY-FOUR

"May I join you, General?" Hayden hailed his neighbor passing Hodges House on his early morning walk.

"Certainly." The general kept up his quick pace, and Hayden had to scramble to catch up. "Are you going to the store this early?"

"I am. I hope to finish my Christmas orders before the staff arrives and presents me with endless interruptions. By the way, congratulations on winning the school board seat."

The general laughed. "Surely you and Victoria and Lee deserve the credit. You practically rammed me down the voters' throats. As for me, I cannot imagine why I took on another challenge at my age."

"Because you knew you were the only one we could possibly get elected who would press for fair rulings."

"I thought I was doing it for Sarah's sake, but it looks like we are going to have a much bigger fight on our hands."

"Much bigger. Sarah's already been ordered not to let the immigrant children take home textbooks. Heaven only knows what'll happen after the harvest is in and her class suddenly doubles in size."

"We will have a full-scale rebellion. People like Mrs. Sharp and Mrs. Lynch will never accept the mingling of their darlings with children who speak with strange accents and wear shabby clothing."

Hayden bit his lower lip as he shook his head. "I don't understand what motivates such hatred."

"Fear. They are comfortable with what they know."

The men walked on in silence until Hayden, with a wave of his hand, turned to go to the back of the store and the general proceeded down Main Street. The Christmas order immediately took control of Hayden's mind, and as he approached the back door of the store, he was engrossed in calculations.

"Good morning, Mr. Hodges." Hayden was startled by a boy's voice with a distinctively Scottish accent. "I'm Alban MacKenna. I'm new to town, sir, and have come to offer myself as an employee."

"Well, young man, I'm sure you're going to school, so you must be wanting a Saturday job."

"Nay, sir, it's full-time employment I be seeking. Ye'll find I'm a diligent worker, sir. I'll be here early and stay late."

Hayden forced himself not to smile because he sensed a grown, seasoned man in the boy. Forthright, determined, aware of his powers. The spirit of generations of hard-working, hard-fighting, stubborn Scots seemed to be distilled down into a syrup that was the blood that flowed through the boy's veins. Hayden heard phantom bagpipes and imagined tartans. "Where are you living, young man?"

"The Reverend Wright has kindly given me lodging after a mighty fire destroyed part of the Buckner Orphanage in Dallas."

"Well, if you're living with Reverend Wright, I'm sure he wants you to go to school, and you'll have no need to earn a living. Perhaps a little pocket money—"

"Nay, sir. It's my intention to earn a great sum so I can rescue my sister."

"Rescue your sister?"

"Aye, sir. She's being forced to work like a drudge on a cotton farm near Dallas. I'll not rest till I've freed her."

"Freed her? Surely you exaggerate, young man."

"Nay, sir. She was chosen by a farmer when we came in on the orphan train. He promised to let her go to school if she'd keep house for him."

"But this farmer did not choose you?"

"Aye. He chose me and promised me an education if I'd work at chores, but when I objected to the way he treated my sister, he threw me off his farm."

Driven by a force he could not name, Hayden held out his hand. "You're hired, lad. But I insist you go to school, and I mean it. You can work in the evenings and on Saturdays.

"Nay." Alban waved Hayden's hand away. "I'll not be taking charity. Your store closes at five o'clock every day; you don't need evening workers."

Hayden intentionally matched the boy's gruffness. "You'll get no charity from me, sir. The work doesn't stop because the public doors are locked. You'll sweep and mop and carry. Believe me, you'll earn your wages!"

Alban thrust out his hand. "Then we are agreed, sir."

"Agreed." Hayden felt the strain in the boy's hand as he endeavored to strengthen his grip to match a man's.

The boy swiveled smartly toward the door. "Where will ye have me begin, sir?"

Hayden wanted nothing more than to send the boy back to the Wrights' house for a hearty breakfast. Instead, he took him to the janitor's closet and directed him to clean the store's front entrance. When Hayden returned to his office, he telephoned Reverend Wright at the Baptist Church.

"So that's where he is!" Reverend Wright exclaimed. "Well, at least he hasn't run off again."

"Again?"

"Yes, again. You see, Hayden, I just brought the boy to Riverford from the Buckner Orphanage in Dallas. They were having a terrible time keeping him from running off to a cotton farm north of there to rescue his sister."

"Yes, he told me about his sister."

"She's only fourteen or so. There's no room for her at Buckner, even if the farmer would let her go. They still haven't raised the funds to rebuild the houses they lost. That's why I was up there in the first place. Trying to see what the church could do to help. Anyway, I wasn't there five minutes before this strapping Scottish boy ambushed me and insisted I help him 'free' his sister."

"That's the word he used when we talked."

"He's convinced she's in danger at that farm. Seems the owner is a widower, so there's no woman overseeing things. Sounds like it's a big operation with a lot of men working around the place. Anyway, Alban's worried, and believe me, that kid doesn't take no for an answer."

Hayden laughed. "So I discovered this morning."

"Sorry he's been bothering you—"

"He hasn't. Not really. In fact, I suspect he's quite a hard worker. Anyway, I've got him downstairs mopping the entrance. We'll see …"

"The boy has a home here with us if he'll just accept it, but there's not much we can do about his sister. Apparently, she agreed to work on that farm until she's eighteen so the farmer would take Alban and her in."

"Sure sounds like that farmer was quick to rid himself of Alban. Can't help but wonder why."

There was only silence on the other end of the line. Then the reverend exhaled loudly. "Yeah. That bothers me too. Wants to keep a pretty girl, but not a strong, hard-working boy?"

"And Alban says they were promised education."

"I imagine lots of the folks who take in these orphan train kids offer more than they plan to deliver. Not right, of course, but let's face it; most of those kids are just taken as workers."

Both men fell silent.

"I think I'll check into the matter." Hayden finally broke the silence.

"Sure glad you're back home, Hayden. Without Richard Boyd … well, there just aren't too many men I can turn to in this town."

"We all miss Richard. Guess we always will. I'll see what I can do."

"Thanks. Let me know if I can help."

"You can register Alban in school for a start. That was a condition of my hiring him."

"Glad to." Reverend Wright sighed. "Just hope he hangs around long enough to go to school and doesn't head off to rescue his sister."

"Me, too. I'll be in touch." Hayden heard a click on the other end of the line. "Need more information," he muttered as he rose and left his office.

When Hayden reached the front entry, he found that Alban had finished the floor and was outside polishing the brass sign embedded in the bricks next to the double glass doors. An unreasonable pride grew in Hayden as he watched Alban make the raised words *Hodges Department Store* break free of their dark background and gleam in the morning sun. "Hope you're not planning to rub my name off the building," he growled at Alban.

The circular movement of the boy's arm stopped, but before turning around, he gave a definitive down swipe at the word *Hodges*. "Not yet, sir." Alban boldly met Hayden's eyes as he turned. "Not yet."

At that moment, Hayden felt his heart expand and pull the boy into his affections. "Tell me about your sister," he commanded.

Startled, Alban dropped his polishing rag to the sidewalk, and Hayden could see the muscles in the boy's throat contract as he struggled to take control of himself. "She's too bonnie a lass to be left in the company of men."

"You got a plan to rescue her?"

"Aye, sir."

"I'd like to hear it. When you're finished here, come up to my office."

CHAPTER TWENTY-FIVE

Sarah told herself she was just stepping into the bathroom to check her hair before going downstairs to greet Lee, but she knew better. She felt compelled to wash her clean hands one more time. As she soaped and scrubbed them, she caught a glimpse of herself in the mirror. The anguish she was feeling was on clear display for all to see.

Why is he doing this? The question played in her mind like a phonograph record stuck in one groove as she remembered Mr. Hunt's startling visit to her classroom only hours before. She had gaily called out good-byes to her students as they rushed away to enjoy their weekends, then turned to the blackboard to erase it. How pleased she had felt to think she had finished her first week of teaching! But when she turned back to her desk, Mr. Hunt was standing in front of it. The shock of his sudden appearance had caused her to lose her breath. Scrambling feebly for the support of her chair back, she leaned on it as she fought back a wave of fear.

"But he said absolutely nothing!" she told her image in the mirror. "He just stood there, staring at me, that filthy look on his face." Sarah's stomach turned, and she grabbed a washcloth, soaked it under the tap, and held it to her forehead.

"Sarah?" Victoria's voice made her jump. "Are you sick?" Victoria hurried into the bathroom, dampened another washcloth, and wrapped it around Sarah's neck.

"It's just the heat," Sarah mumbled. "I'll be okay once I get out on the verandah."

"Perhaps you should come to my room and lie down under the electric fan. I'll go get some ice—"

"No!" Sarah fought back a sudden rush of tears but not soon enough to escape Victoria's eagle eye.

"You're crying. Something has upset you. Someone ..." She took hold of Sarah's shoulders and turned her away from the mirror. "What's happened? This should be a happy evening for you, the celebration of a successful first week of teaching. Yet ... you're clearly upset."

"Just nerves ... and the heat." She forced herself to stand up straighter, look Victoria in the eye, and laugh lightly. "I guess I've been a little frightened all week but wouldn't let myself feel it." She shrugged. "I guess it's all finally caught up with me."

Victoria looked dubious.

"I'm okay now. Let's go downstairs out of this heat."

"Lee just arrived. And Lavinia and John are already out on the verandah."

Sarah jerked the damp cloth off her neck. "We must go then." She fanned her face with her hand. "So wretchedly hot up here."

"Yes." Victoria took her bare arm. "Let's get you downstairs. There's a breeze on the verandah, and Frances is serving iced tea."

"You won't say anything to Lee ..."

"No, of course not. But perhaps you should talk to him about whatever it is that's bothering you."

"Oh, I couldn't!" Sarah regretted the words the moment they flew out of her mouth.

Victoria took her arm and stopped her from descending the stairs. "Then you better talk to me later. Sarah, clearly you need to talk to someone."

"Yes ... later." She met Victoria's loving eyes. "Not now. I can't."

Victoria nodded.

"Ah, here's our victorious *professoressa* at last!" Hayden called out.

"Why, Hayden! You're beginning to sound like Antonio," Victoria teased.

"Bite your tongue, woman!" Hayden protested. "I won't tolerate such abuse."

Everyone laughed as Lee rushed to Sarah's side and kissed her lightly on the lips. "My conquering heroine."

Sarah managed a smile while the others applauded.

"How was your first week?" John asked. "Tell us all about it."

"Give her a chance to sit down." Lavinia's face took on a worried expression as she spoke. "Here, Sarah." She pulled Sarah toward a wicker settee and sat down next to her. "Let me pour you some cold tea."

"Are you all right, Sarah?" Lee asked as he pulled a chair close.

"Of course!" Sarah made her voice light. "It's just been quite a week."

"I hear you had more immigrant children than you expected this week," John said.

"Yes," Sarah answered between sips of the refreshingly cold drink. "But how did you hear about that?"

"Not now, John," Lavinia murmured.

A new apprehension rose in Sarah. "How *did* you hear about that, John?"

"I had a visit from several parishioners ..." John glanced at the Bellows' house. "Accompanied by your neighbor."

"I don't care what they said!" Lavinia exclaimed. "Sarah, your lesson proving that all Americans are immigrants was a brilliant way to confront their bigotry head-on and defeat it."

Sarah's pulse began to race. "Apparently, I didn't defeat it if some of the parents went to see John."

"What did they want, John?" Victoria's cool tone didn't match the angry flush of her cheeks.

"They were asking for my signature on the petition they're planning to present to the school board." He turned his face toward Sarah. "Naturally, I declined. As for your success, Sarah, there's no doubt you changed some of the town children's minds. That's why these women were so upset."

"Unfortunately, the children have no sway over the school board." Sarah's tight throat forced her words to sound raspy.

"But we do!" Lee grabbed her hand. "You've done a great thing, Sarah. You've exposed the bigotry in Riverford in your first week of teaching, and you've changed some of those young minds."

"And their hearts," Lavinia added.

"We're proud of you, Sarah," Victoria said. "And you have our unqualified support."

"Victoria's right." Hayden's voice was serious. "We knew this school year would bring the question of whether the sharecroppers' children should be allowed to attend the town school to a crisis point. It was inevitable because the number of immigrant sharecroppers has grown, and these families from abroad want education for their children."

"For their sons, at least." Sarah's tone reflected the resistance she had encountered to her own fight for education.

Lavinia took her hand. "I'm convinced, Sarah, that your presence as a female teacher, the daughter of an immigrant, will convince many of the newly arrived immigrant parents that they should indeed educate their daughters."

"Lavinia is right!" Victoria insisted. "We teach best when we teach by example."

"Absolutely!" John agreed. "Just keep your focus on the classroom, Sarah, and the rest of us will do battle with the town."

Sarah sighed as she leaned back against the pillows. How had her first week of teaching descended into a political fight? She had expected the week to be challenging, but she had thought the challenges would be learning to dispense new information and motivating the children to learn.

"Let's give the subject a rest," Victoria suggested. "I'm eager to hear the plans for Lavinia and John's wedding."

"Good idea." Hayden's tone was light. "We men need to prepare ourselves for the romantic fantasies we've got to endure in a few weeks."

Lavinia laughed. "There are no romantic fantasies, Hayden. We're going to have the simplest wedding possible given the fact that we must invite the entire congregation of St. Paul's."

"Saturday afternoon, October fifteenth at four o'clock," John added. "That way, Lavinia and I can catch the six o'clock train to Galveston for a honeymoon." He winked at Lavinia, and she blushed.

"And the reception?" Victoria asked.

"In the church hall. It's the simplest thing to do," Lavinia answered.

"But surely you need at least one elegant event," Victoria protested. "Why don't Hayden and I host a dinner party the evening before?"

Lavinia glanced at John before asking, "How would we ever choose the guest list without offending someone?"

"But every bride needs one special event," Victoria insisted.

"All I need is John."

Lee squeezed Sarah's hand as he asked. "Are you listening to this amazingly reasonable woman, Sarah? She sounds like the perfect role model to me."

"Forget it, Lee!" Victoria verbally pounced on him. "Sarah's having the grandest wedding Riverford has ever seen."

"Here comes Hurricane Victoria!" Hayden exclaimed. "Have you two set a date?"

"We're not sure since it will be Christmastime," Sarah answered. "School is out the twentieth. Should we choose a date before Christmas Day or right after it?"

"Before!" Lee insisted. "More time to honeymoon before school begins again."

"I'm with Lee." Hayden laughed. "The sooner the better."

"Be reasonable, men," John intervened. "Sarah will need a day to rest before a grand wedding. How about the twenty-second or twenty-third?"

"I vote for the twenty-second." Lee raised his voice. "Then we're off on a Christmas honeymoon."

Lavinia held up a hand to stop the merriment. "Perhaps you men should ask Sarah what she wants."

Anxiety rose in Sarah as she felt all their eyes focus on her, waiting for her decree. But how could she set a wedding date when so many challenging weeks of school teaching—and even a fight with the school board—lay ahead? And what about Mr. Hunt? Together, it was too much. Her mind fogged; she could not think.

"Sarah and I will discuss this later," she heard Lee say. Tears of relief, of gratitude swam in her eyes. She heard the creak of wicker as Lavinia stood, and quite miraculously, Lee was at her side, his arm slipping around her shoulders, his free hand stroking her cheek.

"How about some more iced tea?" Victoria's overly cheerful voice sounded distant to Sarah.

When Sarah was able to reconnect to the conversation around her, she realized that Hayden was telling the story of finding Alban at the store earlier in the week.

"And the boy had dreamed up the most fantastic plan for rescuing his sister," Hayden said.

"So what was his plan?" John asked.

"He was going to stow away in one of our delivery wagons, head north, kidnap his sister, bring her back to Riverford in another of our wagons, and hide her at the store."

John Neville frowned. "What is the background of these children, Hayden?"

"Alban told me that his family had owned a small general merchandise store for several generations, but when the farmers around their village suffered several years of bad crops, they began to emigrate to America. Eventually, the village population shrank so much it could no longer support a store. Alban's father made the hard decision to bring his family to this country to start over. Unfortunately, both parents died on the trip, and Alban and his older sister, Alison, were left at the mercy of the authorities in New York."

"How horrible!" Lavinia exclaimed. "How old is this boy?"

Hayden chuckled as he shook his head. "He won't say. I'd guess he's about twelve, and it sounds like Alison would be fourteen or so."

"But why won't he tell you his age?" Lavinia asked.

"He's probably trying to convince Hayden he's older than he is," Lee answered. "I'm surprised he doesn't just lie about it."

"That's what impresses me the most," Hayden mused out loud. "The boy refuses to lie."

"Integrity." Victoria's voice was quiet.

"And unbreakable determination. Hard worker too. You've never seen even a grown man work as energetically as that boy. He's got a dream. He's not sharing it, mind you, but he plans to make it come true. And the first step is reuniting with his sister."

"But how did they come to Texas?" Lavinia asked.

"On one of those orphan trains we've read about in the papers. The train came to Fort Worth, and the people in charge of that program stood them up on a platform like the slaves before the War and let the farmers—"

"Stop it!" Sarah was surprised by the shrillness of her voice but couldn't stop her words from tumbling out. "I can't sit here on this comfortable verandah a minute longer when that boy—so many children are—" She turned to Hayden. "Where is he?"

"Sarah's right." Victoria agreed. "This tale of yours should be shaming us, not entertaining us. Where is he, Hayden?"

Hayden raised both hands to calm them. "The boy's okay. Reverend Wright rescued him. He's well fed and perfectly safe now."

"But where's his sister?" Sarah demanded.

"Working on a cotton farm just north of Dallas. It seems the farmer only wanted her. Ran Alban off. I can't imagine why."

"Can't you?" Victoria glared at him. "Think harder."

Hayden looked confused. "All I know is Reverend Wright met Alban at the Buckner Orphanage and brought him to Riverford."

"And Reverend Wright felt no need to help the girl?" Victoria demanded.

Hayden shrugged. "I don't know, Victoria. I can't speak for the man. He … I'm sure he …"

"Didn't think the girl was worth helping." Sarah's voice was stone cold as she sprang off the settee. "I have an errand to run." She strode across the verandah to the steps.

"Sarah, where are you going?" Lee called after her as he jumped up.

"To see Reverend Wright!" Victoria answered for Sarah as she sprang up. "Wait for me, Sarah. We'll take the buggy."

"Now, Victoria," Hayden grabbed her arm. "Let's stop and think this through. Exactly what do you hope to accomplish—"

"More than you have, Hayden Hodges!" Victoria shook her arm loose and joined Sarah at the base of the steps.

"I'm going too!" Lavinia stood up.

"Well, then, I better go with you," John offered as he started to rise.

"No!" Lavinia's lips quivered as she motioned him back. "No, you men have had your chance."

"At least let me hitch up the buggy, Sarah," Lee called after her.

Sarah's cold fury turned hot as she turned back and glared at him. "Don't bother! I've been hitching up buggies all my life. I can handle one more."

Lee watched the women disappear into the dark, then turned back to Hayden and John. "What just happened here?" He flung his hands upward. "Sarah's furious, and I'm drowning in shame over a situation I didn't even know existed a few minutes ago. How did this happen?"

Hayden shook his head. "It seems, boys, that I've taken far too cavalier an approach to the plight of Alban's sister."

"It *is* a serious problem." John's voice was grave. "Across the state, more and more immigrant girls are being put out to hire, being put at risk."

"But what can Riverford do?" Lee asked.

"Take care of the ones God sends our way," John answered. "Find them permanent homes. Weave them into the life of the town."

"That won't be a popular idea in Riverford," Lee muttered.

"No, it won't," Hayden agreed, "but what does that matter? Right now, I think we better just catch up with the ladies, who are far ahead of us in many ways."

"And I better plan to travel north and find this boy's sister right away," John added. "This sounds like a situation the church needs to get involved in."

CHAPTER TWENTY-SIX

At dawn, a cool breeze waved the ruffled curtains in Christine's bedroom before floating across the room to greet her. Like a lover planting an early morning kiss, the refreshing, chilly air swirled around her face. As Christine grew conscious of the coolness, a smile lifted the corners of her mouth. *The first fall weather.* The thought brought quiet joy to her heart as she opened her eyes and turned them toward the window. "Thank you, Lord," she breathed as she saw the yellow light of early morning and watched the curtains sway in the invigorating dry air. "Summer is over. We have made it to a new season." The thought of a new beginning lured her to leave her comfortable bed, don her lace-embellished wrapper, and slip downstairs through the quiet house to the front porch.

The effects of the ferocious thunderstorms of the previous night, which had shaken the house with deafening cannon shots of thunder and streaked the sky with jagged, blinding light, were quite evident. The front garden was littered with small limbs and ragged leaves, but the plants that had withstood the attack were glimmering with thousands of tiny water crystals. Christine surveyed the plantings until her eyes fell on the Russian sage. Its blue spires glistened as they pointed straight upward to the approaching light of the new day. A thrill of encouragement rose within her. She hastened down the steps and, picking her way carefully through the debris, went to the bush. It towered over her as she lifted her hand to stroke the length of a floweret-covered branch. She reached, determined to hold the highest tip in her hand. She stood on her tiptoes and strained upward, but still she could not quite touch the pinnacle. *A man's reach* should *exceed his grasp* ... The words of Robert Browning, admired and memorized long ago when she first came to Texas with Richard, sounded in her mind. It was Richard's voice. He had said that every time they had encountered difficulty that required more effort on his part. *Yes*, Christine thought as she stared up at the tip of the stem. *A man's reach should exceed his grasp, and so should a woman's.* She smiled and finished the quote, "Or what's a heaven for?"

Tears turned the distinct fine lines of the branch into a blur of blue. "And you have finally reached your heaven, my darling," she murmured to the love of her life. "You reveled in the reaching required to create and care for our family. You thrived on building this town. And now you are able to grasp. Not just reach … actually grasp." She wrapped herself in her own arms. "And now, I shall reach again."

"Mommy, who are you talking to?" The tug on her gown, coupled with the voice of her youngest, doubled the happiness Christine had attained in her moment with Richard. She glanced down and saw that Juli was shivering as she stood, barefoot, on the moss-covered bricks of the walk in her thin white dimity nightgown.

"Where are your slippers and robe, darling? You are shaking with cold."

Juli giggled and shook her body as violently as she could.

Christine opened her lips to insist the child march back into the house, but no sound came forth. Her words had been eclipsed by the first stream of sunlight that beamed straight onto Juli's head and revealed shimmering red highlights in her hair. Christine broke into happy laughter as she shook her head in disbelief.

"Hold me up high, Mommy!" Juli demanded. "I want to see the top of the blue bush. I'm going to paint it today."

"I have no doubt of it," Christine answered as she lifted Juli up.

"Higher! I want to see the top!" Juli pointed at the highest, sun-kissed tip of the bush.

Christine strained to lift the little girl higher. "Of course you do, my darling. You are your father's child."

"Mother, the postman just brought a package from Madame Makarova!" At mid-morning, Ceci raced into the music room, a brown-paper-wrapped flat box in her hands. "Maybe she sent us some new music!"

Christine stopped her efforts to memorize the first page of a Schubert sonata and turned toward her eager daughter. "I suspect she has. Get my scissors out of the writing table, and we'll cut through this twine and soon find out." She watched Ceci hurry to the desk, noting that even though her older daughter was truly excited, she moved with the composure of a debutant. *How different my girls are … I would never dare send Juli for anything sharp.*

"Oh, I hope she's sent my new lessons." Ceci's face was flushed with excitement as she hurried back to her mother as quickly as her idea of composure would allow.

"I hope so too." Christine took the scissors and began to clip the white twine that bound the package. "Your grandfather and I have been talking about your future musical training, and we have decided that you must be given every chance to achieve your dreams."

"Really? Does this mean—will I go study—"

"I am not certain what it means at the moment. Perhaps this package will give us the information we need to make a plan. Before we left Colorado, I asked Madame to guide us."

Ceci's attempt at decorum vanished as she ripped the paper off the package in her mother's lap. "It's music! Oh, look! One of them has my name on it." Ceci snatched the volume out of the pile and opened it. "And there are notes in it. See, Mother?" She held up the book. "This is Madame's handwriting. Just like in Colorado. She's telling me how to play it. Oh, can I get started right now?"

Christine's heart swelled with love and pride as she looked into the eager face. This longing to learn was a feeling she remembered well from her own childhood during the War, when her mother had been forced to move her from one relative's house to another. "Of course you can," she answered her daughter as she glanced at the clock on the mantel. "It's ten o'clock. Let us decide right now that at ten every morning except Sunday I will give you a music lesson." Christine held out her hand, and Ceci shook it.

Christine turned to the new music book and opened the first page. "Let's start right here." She pointed to a short Bach piece. "Now, can you sight read this for me?"

"Of course I can!" Ceci peered up at the music and slowly began to play.

Almost immediately, Juli burst into the room and raced to Christine's side. "Mommy! Look what I painted. It's blue like the bush outside."

"Go away!" Ceci insisted. "I'm having a piano lesson."

Juli pushed her painting on top of the piano keys, but Christine firmly removed it.

"From now on, Juli, I will be teaching Ceci from ten o'clock until eleven o'clock. I will not be able to play with you for that hour."

"But I want you to—"

Christine placed her fingers over Juli's lips. "Not now. From now on, I am not available between ten and eleven. Go paint some more or go outside and play on the swing."

Juli snatched her painting from Christine's hands and stomped out of the room.

CHAPTER TWENTY-SEVEN

As Victoria stepped back and appraised her painting of the teacher driving the tent stake into the ground, her concentration was broken by the sound of the front door knocker. "Who on earth is calling at this hour? Well, someone else will just have to handle it. I have set aside the mornings to paint, and paint is all I'm going to do."

The knocker attacked the door more ferociously. Victoria felt her temper rising, but she forced herself to keep her eyes on the canvas. "Discipline," she murmured. "A professional has discipline. In the mornings I am a painter, not Mrs. Hodges!"

"'Scuse me, Miss Victoria, but they's a delegation come to see you." Sam stood in the doorway, his eyes narrowed with worry.

"A delegation?"

"Yes'm." He took a step closer and whispered. "Mighty fearsome ladies."

"Tell them I'm not at home."

"Don't bother!" Mrs. Bellows' angry voice preceded her as she stormed into the room. "You are dismissed, Sam!" She pointed to the drawing room door behind her.

"I believe I just go out this way." Sam cast a fearful glance at Victoria as he hurried to the outside door of her studio.

Victoria turned a cool eye on Edith Bellows. "I do not receive company in the mornings—"

"Oh, I know that! Everyone in Riverford knows you pretend to be a painter in the mornings." She scowled at the oversized canvas depicting Sarah in the mountains. "Good heavens! What's this monstrosity?"

"Nothing that concerns you." Victoria plunked her brush into a container of turpentine and swished it around.

"For mercy sake! The smells in this room are revolting enough. Must you do that?" Mrs. Bellows sidled past Victoria to get a close-up view of the canvas. "Why, it's Sarah! Why on earth would you paint a picture of a sharecropper's daughter?" She screwed up her nose as she turned away. "Must we stay in this smelly room?"

If it will make you leave sooner! Victoria thought as her temper flared hotter. "What do you want, Edith?"

Edith clasped her hands in a prayerful pose. "I've come on a mission of mercy." She pointed to the drawing room doorway. "Mrs. Sharp and Mrs. Proper are with me. We feel that it's our Christian duty to warn you about Sarah and her disgraceful behavior."

Her pulse quickening at the accusatory tone surrounding Sarah's name, Victoria decided she would be wise to control her tongue and hear the women out. "Very well." She gestured toward the drawing room door. "Let's join the …" Victoria swallowed hard before she could utter the word. "The *ladies*."

"Good morning, Mrs. Hodges." Fanny Sharp's voice sliced the air as Victoria stepped into the shadows of the drawing room. "Mercy! What are you wearing?"

"A painter's smock over a pair of old bloomers." Victoria followed her sharp response with a quick turn toward Louise Proper. "Surely you ladies haven't dressed up so elegantly to examine my clothing. What's on your mind, Mrs. Proper?"

A visible shiver of disgust ran through Louise's body, shaking the silk flowers on her straw hat, as she looked Victoria up and down. "To think that Hayden Hodges married you! His mother is surely turning over in—"

"For mercy's sake, Louise!" Mrs. Bellows waved Mrs. Proper away as she confronted Victoria head on. "Sarah is endangering our children. There's the long and short of it."

"I wasn't aware that you had any children, Edith."

"You know what I mean! She's endangering the children of Riverford, and we're not going to stand for it. We're going to get her fired if you don't control her. There! It's out in the open now. What are you going to do about it?"

"Exactly how is Sarah endangering your children?"

"She forces them to sit next to filthy sharecropper children!" Mrs. Proper's voice trembled with indignation. "Heaven only knows what diseases our innocent children will contract from those unwashed, ragged—"

"Ragged, perhaps." Victoria raised her voice to interrupt. "But not unwashed. They may bathe in a creek, but they come to school as clean as your children."

"They carry hideous diseases from those foreign countries they came from," Fanny Sharp declared.

"What diseases?" Victoria demanded.

"You know what I'm talking about. Slum diseases, conditions a lady doesn't speak of."

"And the scandalous ideas they're being taught by that sharecropper!" Mrs. Bellows' face turned purple with rage. "That's the worst of it. Never in the history of Riverford has—"

"What ideas?" Victoria cut her words off.

Mrs. Bellows' nostrils flared as she pulled herself up to her tallest height. "She is teaching our innocent Riverford children that we are all immigrants. Think of it! Calling pure-blooded Americans immigrants."

"Absolutely outrageous!" Mrs. Proper pumped her head up and down. "Why, my family has been in Texas since—since—"

"Since it immigrated here from France and changed the spelling of its name from *Propre* to *Proper*." Victoria paused to calm herself before going on. "Ladies, Sarah isn't your enemy. She is trying to promote respect for one's fellow man. She is teaching that diversity is not to be feared, but to be embraced. There is strength in unified diversity. Surely we can agree that Riverford's children will benefit from unifying our community and working together for a better future."

"I won't have my children unified with foreign children!" Fanny Sharp snapped.

"Fanny is absolutely right," Louise agreed. "Respecting something foreign is just one step away from embracing it. We must act now to protect our children, and if you won't stop Sarah, then we will."

"The very idea of forcing my little Stephanie to sit next to a Bohemian girl!" Fanny Sharp's voice was shrill. "If my darling doesn't die of some hideous disease, she'll start thinking like a foreigner."

"What's a Bohemian?" a high-pitched child's voice demanded from the drawing room door and startled the women into silence.

"Good heavens!" Louise Proper exclaimed. "It's Mrs. Boyd's little girl. Juli, what on earth are you doing here?"

Juli held up her child-sized suitcase. "I ran away from home. I'm going to live with Miss Victoria now."

"Horrors! You most certainly are not!" She marched across the room, her arms outstretched, ready to snatch Juli away. "It is my Christian duty to rescue you from this den of iniquity."

Victoria exhaled her disgust as she gathered Juli to her side. "It is your Christian duty to expand your concern to all the children of this county, Edith. Don't you realize that we're one year away from a new century? Riverford is going to change. It has to in order to survive. And you are blessed to have such a caring teacher leading the change for your children."

Fanny Sharp snorted. "We'll just see what the school board has to say about that! Come, ladies, our duty is obvious. We must save the youth of Riverford."

"Hadn't we better save Juli Boyd this very minute?" Louise Proper asked. "Her mother must be frantic with worry."

"Oh, she's okay," Juli breezily announced. "She's teaching Ceci piano. She doesn't even know I'm gone."

Mrs. Bellows clucked as she gravely shook her head. "Poor Christine's judgment flew away when Richard died. Then she spent all those weeks in the company of … of …"

"Women who think for themselves and are not afraid of new ideas," Victoria finished her sentence.

"This is pointless." Fanny Sharp's voice was ice cold. "Let's just get on to our next step."

"Our next step?" Louise Proper asked.

Fanny glared at Victoria, an undeniable challenge in her eyes. "We're going to exclude the immigrant children entirely from the school. After all, it's Riverford's school, and those foreign children all live outside the city limits. Their families don't even pay taxes. Why should they be allowed in our school at all?"

Outrage flamed through Victoria. "Shame on you! How do you dare to lift your prayers to God with a vicious plan like that in your mind?"

"This is our town!"

"Children are gifts from God, and He loves them. Every last one of them!" She shook her finger at the women. "You are not the Almighty, ladies. And if I were you, I wouldn't be in such a hurry to cross Him."

Fanny Sharp tossed her head. "I'm not afraid. Come, ladies, we've done our best to reason with Mrs. Hodges. Now, let's go pay a much-needed visit to several members of the school board."

"I don't like you!" Juli shouted at the women as they bustled out of the room. "You're mean!"

Victoria knew she should correct the child, but she agreed with her too much to try. Instead, she shepherded her out to the studio, collapsed onto the settee, and pulled Juli into her lap.

"I like that painting." Juli pointed at the large canvas. "But what's the lady doing?"

"She's driving a metal stake into the ground with that big hammer."

"Why?"

"Because the tent will fall down if she doesn't."

"It looks hard. That lady must be really strong."

"Most things worth doing are really hard, Juli."

"Things like stopping Mrs. Bellows from hurting children?"

Victoria was stunned by the child's question. "Yes," she finally managed to answer. "Things like that."

"I want to be strong. That's why I ran away from home. It's time for me to get ready to be a real artist." Her brow furrowed with earnestness. "I'm going to be five soon!" Her hand, with its fingers splayed wide, flew up toward Victoria's face.

"Five!" Victoria exclaimed. "Goodness, you're getting old."

Juli's head bobbed up and down in an exaggerated nod. "I can't wait any longer. I have to commit."

"Commit?"

"That means get really serious about something. I heard Mommy tell Ceci all about it. She's got to commit to the piano, or she'll never play on big stages like Madame does." Juli jumped down and ran to Victoria's easel. "I'm going to commit to painting like this." She pointed up at the large canvas. "Then maybe …" Her feisty voice dwindled. "Maybe Mommy won't …"

"Won't what?"

"Forget about me." Juli whirled around and revealed her distressed face. "Mommy doesn't have time for me anymore. But if I become an important painter—" Tears began to stream down her face.

"Oh, darling, come here." Victoria held out her arms, and Juli raced into them. "Your mother will never, ever, ever forget you." She pressed the sobbing child against her breast and stroked her head. "Now, let's stop this crying and talk because I want to know what happened to make you feel this way." She reached into her pocket and produced a handkerchief. "Sit up and blow your nose and talk to me."

Juli blew vigorously into the handkerchief and, true to her nature, spouted the whole story of the arrival of Madame's package and Christine's plans to teach Ceci. "So Mommy won't have any time for me ever again." Juli tossed her head. "But I don't care!"

"Yes, you do. You feel abandoned."

"What's 'abandoned'?"

"Left all by yourself by the people who should love you."

Juli fell silent and stared at Victoria. "Like you?"

Victoria gasped as the tiny girl's words unwittingly slashed open her heart, revealing old wounds that never seemed to heal.

"No, not like me," Victoria managed to say before she had to pause to press her quivering lips together. "I know you want to be an artist like I am, darling, but you do not have a family like mine. Your mother adores you, and she always will. Now, come here. I want to show you something."

Victoria reached for a sketch pad and pencil and drew a straight line on it. "Do you see this line?" Juli nodded. "And here's another line right next to it but not touching. That's the way my family has been all my life … two lines that run close to each other, but never touch." Victoria swallowed hard and drew two spirals that wrapped around each other. "This is your family. See how the lines wrap around each other? Sometimes they move apart, but they always swirl back together."

Juli traced one spiral with her finger. "This is me."

"That's right. And this is your mother." Victoria ran her pencil along the curves of the other spiral; then she added a third. "And this is Ceci."

"And make one for Andrew and George too," Juli demanded. "And what about Daddy? Is he still part of our family?"

"Absolutely." Victoria added the necessary swirls. "See, you're all separate but twined together in love."

Juli nodded so hard her curls bounced as she eagerly grabbed the pencil from Victoria's hand and drew a new spiral. "This is you." She added another spiral on top of it. "And this is me because I'll always love you." Victoria's eyes filled with tears as the child continued to add spiral on top of spiral and to name each one. "This is Mr. Hayden; this is Sarah."

CHAPTER TWENTY-EIGHT

Sarah was teaching Texas history to her class when an older student tapped on the door, entered immediately, and thrust a note into her hand. When she glanced at its contents, she temporarily lost her breath and began to fan herself with her hand. *See me after school regarding a complaint from a parent. Morris Hunt, Principal.* The note was terse, but its double threat struck Sarah hard. Not only would she have to spend awkward, maybe even frightening, time with Mr. Hunt, but she also would have to deal with a complaint from a parent.

"Are you okay, Miss Novak?" Stephanie Sharp asked.

"Yeah," Buddy blurted out. "You don't look so good."

Sarah stashed the note in her desk drawer as she struggled to regain her composure. "Just a notice of a meeting," she murmured. "My, but it is getting warm in here, students. Buddy, would you open the windows, please, so we can have more breeze."

"Sure!" Buddy shrugged his shoulders before sauntering over and jerking windows up.

"I'm sure we'll be more comfortable now." Sarah forced control back into her voice. "Now, let's go on with the story of the Battle of San Jacinto, so we can finish it before lunchtime."

When the dismissal bell rang at three thirty, Sarah wanted nothing more than to prolong her teaching day, but the students raced out the door, eager to embrace their more carefree hours. Dread rose in Sarah like a malignant fog that had waited for its moment to darken her mind. She sank into her desk chair and pulled out the note from the principal. *I must keep this meeting professional ... I must behave with perfect propriety.* She jerked her head up and glanced out at the students' desks as if she were confronting a jury. "But I behaved appropriately last time!" she defended herself. "I did!" Her defiant, certain words could not cover the niggling accusation in her mind. *You must have done something ... something that encouraged him.* "But I didn't!" Sarah's angry voice was choked with tears.

She wiped her perspiring face as she rose. Thinking about it was making it worse. Better to get it over with. She left the safety of her room, walked down the no-man's-land of the hall, and stopped to straighten her clothes before entering the battle zone of the main office. Her worst fears were realized. The secretary was absent from her desk, and Mr. Hunt's door was cracked open. She forced her shaky legs to cross the room and knocked lightly on the door.

"Come in, Miss Novak." Mr. Hunt made it obvious he was waiting for her.

When she pushed open the door, she found the principal propped against the front of his desk, his arms crossed, a satisfied look of empowerment on his face. It was obvious that he intended to keep her standing in front of him like a penitent student.

"I received your note." Sarah forced her voice to be steady as she entered the room.

"Close the door."

Sarah flinched. "I'd rather leave it open."

"Would you really?" Mr. Hunt approached her, his eyes malicious. "And allow everyone to hear about the complaint that has been made against you? I think not." He passed her, and she heard the door knob click.

Sarah decided to take the initiative. "Kindly inform me what the complaint is."

Mr. Hunt stood close behind her, his breathing becoming more labored. "Oh, we needn't waste time on that. As I told you before, Miss Novak, I am extending my special favor to you, and that favor includes my protection."

Sarah quivered in spite of herself.

"I'm sure that now you've had time to think it over, you've decided you want my special favor, don't you, Miss Novak?" Mr.

Hunt's hand caressed her shoulder and slithered down her back to her waist.

Turn around! Confront him! she ordered herself, but her legs had turned to jelly. "No." She heard the weakness in her voice, and it infuriated her, but she couldn't form another word.

"You don't really mean that." His oily voice carried some indefinable filth she didn't understand. He squeezed her waist as he walked around to face her. "Do you?" He leaned forward, his face close to hers. "My, my, it looks like your tie is crooked."

Sarah watched in horror as he raised his hand and began to fumble with the silk tie that lay on her bosom. The smell of the man revolted her. Her stomach threatened to heave, and the thought of embarrassing herself by throwing up shoved her into action. She slapped his hand away, turned, and ran for the nearest girls' bathroom. Once inside, she raced to the sink and frantically scrubbed her hands with the gritty lye soap. *I'm so ashamed!* The irrational words howled through her mind. *I just want to crawl into this sink and scrub my whole body!*

"Did he touch you?"

Sarah's heart stopped, then raced into a gallop at the sound of the sudden voice behind her. She grasped the cast-iron sink as she fell forward in a near faint.

"He ... he ... touches me ... here."

Sarah struggled to raise her face, to look into the mirror over the sink, to see who stood behind her. She found another teacher's distraught face and her quivering hand pointing below her waist. "I have to let him," the woman cried as she ran toward Sarah and jerked her around. "I have to! Don't you see? I have to have this job. I'm not like you. I don't have powerful, wealthy friends. I have to let him—" Her words were cut off by an escaping sob.

Sarah's nausea doubled, but she fought it down. Filled with compassion for the pathetic woman in front of her, she struggled to think what to say.

"I am a bad woman," the other woman wailed. "I used to cry every time he did it, but I don't even cry anymore. That's how bad I am." Her head bowed as her shoulders slouched. "Please don't tell anyone. I'm so ashamed."

Shame! Sarah winced as her own sense of degradation returned. She turned back to the mirror and peered at her own face. *I have done nothing! Why should I be ashamed?* Once again, she felt the principal's fingers moving on her bosom, but this time her temper flared. "How dare he touch me?" she shouted. She saw the woman behind her shrink back, so she turned and addressed her in a quieter tone. "How dare he touch you?" Sarah's furious words were curtailed by a new, more shocking image that flew into her mind. "Did he ... did he force himself on you?"

"No." The woman's whole body quivered with revulsion. "He just touches."

Sarah reached up and swept her hair away from her face as she struggled to clear her clouded, confused mind. "I don't understand. How dare he do such things?"

"Because ..." The woman sighed and lowered her head. "Because he can."

"No, he can't!"

"You're wrong, Miss Novak. He can."

"But why? Why can he?"

The teacher shrugged. "Because he's the boss."

"We must stop him."

"It's too late, Miss Novak. If anyone finds out, my life will be ruined. They will do nothing to him, but they will fire me. And there are others ..."

"Others?" The single word conjured up a history of suffering, a sudden understanding in Sarah's mind. "Yes, of course. There would be others. Such a man would ... would approach other teachers ... inappropriately."

"And students too."

Horror swept through Sarah. "Students?"

The teacher nodded. "But only the poor ones, and they just drop out of school and find someone—anyone—to marry them."

Sarah was stung by the revelation. *Another reason sharecroppers' daughters are stuck in lives of misery. Another reason they have no choices in their lives.*

"I don't know what to do," Sarah muttered. "I don't understand why he's doing this."

"Because he can! I told you already. He's the boss, and he can do whatever he likes. He's got his eye on you now, so just stay as clear of him as you can. That's all you can do."

A wave of intense anxiety washed over Sarah, and she reached for the locket she always wore, the locket that held the miniature portrait Victoria had painted of Sarah's mother. *Mama! She's fought all my life to raise me to this teaching position. I can't fail now.*

"You look pretty sick, Miss Novak. Maybe you better wash your face with cold water. It won't do for Miss Grimm to see you like this. She'll take it for weakness."

CHAPTER TWENTY-NINE

"I'm so glad you ladies could come," Victoria exclaimed as she opened the front door for Christine, Ceci, and Juli. "And don't you look pretty!" She turned her attention to the girls' dresses.

"This is for you." Ceci shyly held out a tussie mussie.

"We picked the flowers all by ourselves, and I got stuck by a thorn." Juli grimaced as she held up her finger for Victoria to inspect.

"Oh, I'm terribly sorry."

"It's okay." Juli's breezy voice replaced her tragic one. "It's not my painting finger. See." She held up her other hand. "It's still good."

"Thank heavens!" Victoria exclaimed, and Juli nodded solemnly. "Well, why don't we abandon this steamy house for the side verandah? Frances has laid out a very special tea for us."

"Come on! I know the way." Juli grabbed Ceci's hand and dragged her out of the hall.

Christine sighed. "Sometimes I wonder if I will survive Juli's childhood."

"You will," Victoria assured as she guided Christine through the drawing room and out onto the porch where they found Juli swinging her legs so she could kick out the flounce on her skirt.

"Can we have some cookies now?" the child demanded.

Ceci swatted her sister. "Stop kicking your skirt, and don't ask for cookies."

"Why not? I'm hungry."

Ceci shook her head in disgust. "Because you're supposed to practice proper eti … eti …"

"Etiquette," Christine finished the word as she sat down.

"Ah, here comes Frances with our tea tray." Victoria changed the subject. "And I see several kinds of cookies on it."

Juli rushed to her mother's side. "Can I have *real* tea like a grown-up lady?"

"You may have a little bit of tea in your milk if you sit down and comport yourself appropriately."

"What's comport?"

"Behave," Christine answered as she pointed at the seat Juli had abandoned.

"Yes, ma'am." Juli sighed as she dragged herself back to the wicker settee.

"Will you take milk and sugar in your tea, Miss Boyd?" Victoria addressed Ceci in her most formal tone.

"Yes, ma'am, please." Ceci sat up primly and folded her hands in her lap.

"Frances, please offer the ladies some cookies."

Juli's face lit up.

"I understand that Hayden has a new employee, a very young one," Christine said as Victoria gave Ceci her cup of tea.

"He certainly does. A very energetic immigrant from Scotland."

"Who has a sister, I hear." Christine gave Victoria a knowing look. "Lavinia came to see me."

"Ah, then you know the dilemma. Hayden and John are investigating and trying to arrange for her to join her brother and—" Victoria spotted Sarah standing in the door. "Why, Sarah! What on earth is wrong?"

"I didn't know you had company," Sarah murmured as she backed away.

"We're having cookies," Juli called out.

"Yes, so I see."

Victoria's worry heightened as she watched Sarah force her downturned lips into a crooked smile before adding, "How nice!"

"Will you ... can you join us?" Christine rose, her face covered with concern, and extended her hand.

"No ... that is, I need to rest." Sarah started to turn away.

Victoria sprang to her feet. "Frances, didn't I hear Sam say that the cat in the barn had some new kittens?"

"Kittens!" Juli squealed. "Mommy, can we go see the kittens?"

"Of course. Go with Frances."

Juli slid off the settee and raced to Frances' side, but Ceci gave her mother a worried look. "You go too, Ceci," Christine insisted. "We'll give Sarah some tea and help her rest."

Ceci reluctantly left with Frances as Victoria pulled Sarah onto the verandah and pressed her down into a cushioned chair.

"What's happened?" Victoria demanded in a low voice. When Sarah didn't answer immediately, Victoria's pulse began to race. "Has someone been hurt?"

"No," Sarah blurted out. "I'm just having some trouble at school."

"With the students?" Christine asked.

Sarah shook her head. "With Mr. Hunt, the principal. He's … he's said horrible things about me in front of the other teachers."

"But why?" Christine asked.

Victoria's experience of the world made her jump to a conclusion. "To put her in her place. What he considers her place." Before Sarah could answer, Victoria plopped down on the ottoman in front of Sarah and grabbed her shaking hands. "What else has happened? You wouldn't get this upset over a few unkind words. What's he done?"

Sarah took a deep breath, snatched her hands away, and wrapped them around her shoulders. "He called me into his office. He said he was only pretending to dislike me in front of the other teachers. He said—he said he really likes me." Sarah began to ramble. "He will make it easy for me, be on my side—"

"If you do what?" Victoria demanded.

"I—I don't know. I ran. Like a child, I just ran." She began to sob. "I'm so ashamed!"

"I don't see why!" Christine exclaimed, but when she started to say more, Victoria held up a hand to silence her.

"Did he touch you, Sarah?" Victoria waited, struggling to control her growing fury.

Sarah nodded.

"Where?"

"He grabbed my arm. He was standing so close behind me I could hear him breathe. Then he grabbed my arm."

"We must tell Lee," Christine insisted. "This man's advances are unacceptable."

"No! You can't tell Lee. I'll lose my job. After all my mother's struggles and my own work, I can't lose my very first teaching experience."

"But Lee would want to protect you," Christine argued.

"I know he would, but don't you see? I have to prove that I can protect myself. I'll probably have to face worse things than this in my teaching career. I've got to toughen up. Please don't tell anyone!"

Christine exchanged a questioning look with Victoria.

"We'll let you try to solve this," Victoria said. "But if it gets worse in any way ..."

"I'll ask for help. I promise I will." Sarah dropped her head into her hands. "I'm so tired. All I want to do is sleep."

Victoria pulled her to her feet. "Go upstairs to bed. Rest until suppertime."

Sarah nodded and drifted back into the house.

"What are we going to do?" Christine asked the moment Sarah was gone.

Victoria paced the room, her fists clenched. Finally, she stopped and exhaled a sigh of frustration. "Nothing until Sarah's ready for us to intervene."

"I do *not* agree. At the very least, we need to tell Lee or Hayden."

"Can you imagine how Lee will react? What he will do?" Victoria demanded. "I know what *I* want to do, and Lee's reaction will be considerably more violent than mine."

"Nevertheless, Sarah needs help." Christine paused. "Victoria, do you get the impression she has not told us everything?"

Victoria clenched her jaw and narrowed her eyes as she nodded. "We must do something!"

"Let's give Sarah a little more time to work her own solution out. She's smart, and she's right that she needs to toughen up and learn to confront whatever is thrown at her in the professional world."

"Just a little more time. I will not stand by and see her hurt."

Victoria's temper blazed into a bonfire. "Do you think I will?"

"No." Christine took Victoria's clenched fist in her own hand. "But promise me you'll let the men handle this."

"I can't."

CHAPTER THIRTY

"This is a pleasant surprise!" Victoria exclaimed as she looked from her easel to her studio's outdoor entrance and saw Christine entering. "What brings you over?"

"A visit from Edith Bellows and comrades. I confess I'm quite concerned about the fight ahead. They're furious."

"They'd be even angrier if they knew John Neville and Alban went to Dallas last night to bring Alban's sister back to Riverford."

"So he did go?" Christine asked. "I knew he was talking about it, but his wedding to Lavinia is tomorrow. I thought, perhaps, he might—"

"Postpone?" Victoria laughed. "Not a chance. Not with both Lavinia and Sarah pushing him."

"You are right, of course," Christine agreed as she moved closer and examined the large canvas. "It's magnificent, Victoria. You have captured so much more than that teacher driving the stake. You've captured the determination, the spirit of the new woman facing the new century. All the hopes and plans and new visions for women, everything we discussed in Colorado."

"Oh, to be back there!" Victoria exclaimed. "With no Edith Bellows and Fanny Sharp to worry about."

"Yes, but we're not." Christine relaxed in a pillow-stuffed chair. "I wish I could think about music only, but we must figure out how we can help the immigrant children."

"I have some ideas about that," Victoria's voice sounded menacing, "but I could never return to church if I uttered them!"

"I know how you feel, but we will serve the children better if we tackle the actual complaints against them and nullify them. The immigrant children must not be refused access to the town school!"

"I'm listening."

"As you know, Mrs. Bellows insists that the sharecroppers' children are unclean and unhealthy. That complaint worries me the most because the school board will listen to it."

Frustrated, Victoria waved her hand in the air. "That's absurd. Sarah says the poor children come to school perfectly clean. Their clothes are in tatters and they have no shoes, but they are clean."

"I think we should have Dr. Shockley examine the children and certify that they are in good health. And then, perhaps we can find a way to supply new clothing for the children."

"And school books." Victoria added.

"School books?"

"Mr. Hunt, the principal, has decreed that the immigrant children may not take school books home."

"But how are they to study?" Christine demanded.

"Exactly. This ruling is nothing more than an attempt to discourage the children until they drop out and go back to the fields."

Christine sprang from her seat. "Absolutely unacceptable! Well, he will not get away with that." She whirled back to Victoria. "It is time for Riverford to have a library!"

"Of course!" Victoria felt a new spark of inspiration ignite in her spirit. "But it can't be a Riverford library; it must be a county library, and the first books we'll buy will be multiple copies of the textbooks!"

"I thought we could mobilize the Women's Literary Society to raise funds. All we need is a building."

"We could even offer classes!"

"Classes?"

"Yes, like the Chautauqua. On the weekends, the sharecropper families come to town. We could offer English classes, history classes—"

"But the immigrant children are already studying those subjects in school."

"The few who are coming to school. Sarah says that most immigrant children are still working in the fields and will continue until the harvest is in."

Christine's face lit up. "The library could provide a place to educate the children who are not coming to school, even the girls. I mean, if they're already coming to town on Saturday ..."

"Exactly!" Victoria exclaimed. "And if the school board passes the tax they're debating, we'll be able to circumvent them entirely. We'll no longer be dependent on them for education for the sharecroppers' children."

"I hope it never comes to that. We must work within the system if we can. After all, our ultimate goal is to shatter this ignorant prejudice against newcomers, to open Riverford to the growth that comes from new ideas."

"Why, Christine Boyd, underneath that sedate exterior you're a revolutionary!"

"I do not intend to leave this world before I see more justice enter it."

"Justice for everyone, even the poor."

"Especially the poor!" Christine exclaimed.

Victoria laughed. "Riverford worries about 'Hurricane Victoria' when they should be worried about 'Earthquake Christine.' If they had the slightest idea what you have in mind, they—"

"Victoria!" Hayden's voice rang out as the front door slammed. "Where are you?"

Startled, Victoria jumped up, gave Christine a worried look, and hurried into the drawing room. "Here," she called out as Christine followed. "I'm here, Hayden."

Hayden bounded into the room. "Thank heavens you're home. Now listen carefully; I haven't a second to spare. John Neville's in jail in Dallas."

"What?" Victoria exclaimed.

"He and Alban got into some kind of fight trying to deal with the farmer who has Alison. I don't know any details. I just received a telegram from him. Anyway, they're holding him until Monday."

"But he's getting married tomorrow!" Christine exclaimed.

"Not if I don't get him out of jail he's not." Hayden pulled out his pocket watch and glared at it. "I've got five minutes to get to the station to catch the noon train. You two go talk to Lavinia— No, wait until you hear from me. No point in upsetting her now." Hayden turned back toward the main hall, talking as he moved. "I'll telegraph you as soon as I know more. And no matter what, keep this quiet!" The front door slammed, and just as suddenly as he had appeared, he was gone.

"Poor Lavinia!" Christine exclaimed. "What if—"

"Don't even say it," Victoria insisted. "We have to believe that Hayden can—"

"Does this mean I can't be a flower girl tomorrow?" Juli wailed from the studio doorway.

"Good heavens!" Victoria jumped at the sound. "When did you get here?"

"You are supposed to be taking a nap, young lady!" Christine exclaimed.

"Isn't Miss Lavinia going to get married?"

Christine hurried to Juli and, grabbing her hand, pulled her to a settee. "I think we better have a talk, darling."

"I don't want to have one of those talks!" Juli wrenched free of her mother and ran to Victoria. "Why is Reverend Neville in jail?"

Her mind racing, Victoria fell to her knees in front of the child. "I don't know. Not yet." She grabbed Juli's hands. "But isn't this exciting? You and your mommy and I know the biggest secret ever!" She leaned closer to the child's face. "Do you think we can keep anyone else from finding out?"

Juli's face lit up. "Not even Ceci?"

"Not even Ceci. No one but Miss Lavinia must know. Can we do it? Can we keep the secret?"

"I can!" Juli whispered as her head bobbed up and down. "I'm good at keeping secrets."

As Victoria gathered the child into her arms, she looked up at Christine who was rolling her eyes and clasping her hands in a prayerful pose.

"Of course you are," Christine agreed. "Let's go home now and practice keeping our secret."

Juli twirled out of Victoria's arms. "I know a secret! I know a secret Ceci doesn't know!"

Christine grabbed her hand and hurried her toward the door. "Let me know when you hear from Hayden, and I'll meet you over at the Logan house," she called back.

"But I want to go tell Miss Lavinia the secret!" Juli protested.

"Oh, you can't do that," Christine insisted. "Ceci would be sure to guess that something is happening she knows nothing about."

CHAPTER THIRTY-ONE

"He's what?" Lavinia demanded three hours later.

"I think you better sit down, dear." Mrs. Logan pressed Lavinia onto a sofa. "And you too, Victoria. Shall I send for some tea?"

"Tea?" Lavinia's voice was shrill. "How can you even think about tea?"

"Because tea enables crisis resolution," Victoria answered for Mrs. Logan. "And we are going to resolve this crisis."

"How? It's twenty-four hours until the wedding, and my husband-to-be is in jail in another city. If the congregation finds out John's in jail, they'll toss him out entirely."

"I better tell Nonnie to use our largest teapot." Mrs. Logan's agitated hands fluttered as she hurried out the door.

"Hayden will bring John home in time. I'm sure of it."

Lavinia's eyes filled with tears. "But how can you be sure?"

"Because I know Hayden. He's smart, and whatever John has done—"

"John has done nothing wrong!" Lavinia bristled as she sat up straight and angrily whisked the tears from her cheeks. "John is a man of integrity. He has set out on a mission of mercy, and I will not have him defamed!"

"No one doubts John's integrity, Lavinia," Mrs. Logan insisted as she returned. "At least, no one who knows him."

Lavinia glared at the polished tea table her mother moved in front of the sofa. "There are people in Riverford who would gladly gossip him out of town for trying to save an immigrant child."

"Yes, there are," Victoria agreed. "And that's why we're going to take every precaution—" Her words were interrupted by a knock on the front door.

"Heaven help us!" Mrs. Logan declared as she hurried out of the room. "Not another well-wisher with a gift. Not now!"

"It's most likely Christine." Victoria comforted Lavinia. "I sent her a message to join me here."

"Christine knows?" Lavinia asked. "But how?"

"She was visiting me when Hayden rushed in on his way to the train."

"My dear Lavinia." Christine hurried to Lavinia and hugged her.

"Does you want me to serve the tea now, Miz Logan?" Nonnie asked from the doorway.

"Yes, now."

Silence fell on the room until the servant left.

"I have a telegram from Hayden." Victoria broke that silence as she pulled a paper from her pocket. "He's seen John, learned the circumstances of his arrest, and seen the judge."

"Father has also had a telegram," Christine added. "He is taking the next train to Dallas."

"The General knows about—" Lavinia fell silent as Nonnie carried in a heavy silver tray and placed it on the tea table.

"How delightful!" Christine exclaimed. "I am so glad we were able to gather for a quiet tea before all the bustle of the wedding begins."

"Just think, Lavinia." Victoria picked up Christine's social tone. "The next time we ladies gather for tea, you'll be a married lady."

"And a very happy one, I'm sure." Mrs. Logan smiled bravely. "Thank you, Nonnie. I'll call you if we need anything."

"The girls are so excited," Christine said as the servant left. "They keep trying on their dresses and practicing their march down the aisle. I declare they are going to—"

"Why did Hayden telegraph General Gibbes?" Lavinia broke in.

"It seems that the judge who is holding John fought under the General. Hayden thinks that Father can convince him to free John."

Mrs. Logan fanned herself with her hand. "Oh dear! If Hayden can't convince the judge, if it takes the intervention of General Gibbes …" She turned to her daughter. "What on earth are you going to do?"

Lavinia sat up straighter, reached for the teapot, and began to pour the golden liquid into a delicate cup. "I'm going to pour the tea, of course. I'm going to pour this pot and all the hundreds of pots ahead of me as I live as Reverend John Neville's wife."

"Well said!" Victoria applauded. "Now, let's make a plan."

"A plan that includes a wedding tomorrow afternoon at four o'clock," Christine added.

"Absolutely," Victoria agreed. "The General and Hayden will do what must be done in Dallas. They'll probably all come back to Riverford late tonight or early in the morning."

"Early in the morning?" Fear flashed in Mrs. Logan's eyes. "On Lavinia's wedding day?"

"Yes." Victoria cleared her throat. "Hopefully before the bishop arrives at ten."

"The bishop!" Lavinia sprang from the sofa. "Coming here?"

Victoria pulled a second telegram from her pocket. "That's the good news that arrived today. The bishop sent Hayden a telegram announcing that he's coming to surprise you and John. He's going to marry you."

"This is a disaster!" Mrs. Logan exclaimed as she abandoned decorum and sank back against the sofa pillows.

"We must protect John!" Lavinia declared. "At all costs." She turned to her mother. "Do you hear me, Mother? We will do whatever it takes, but we *will* protect John."

Tears filled Mrs. Logan's eyes as she smiled at her daughter. "My, how you've changed, my darling girl! Where is that little mouse of a woman who hid herself among her books?"

"She is in love." Christine smiled up at Lavinia. "Love creates courage."

Victoria met Sarah in the main hall when she returned from school that afternoon and told her of the dramatic events of the day.

"Poor Lavinia!" Sarah exclaimed. "How is she holding up?"

"You wouldn't recognize her," Victoria answered. "She's determined to protect John's reputation at all costs."

"I just hope that doesn't mean trying to keep the bishop from finding out John's in jail."

In spite of her doubts, Victoria chose to project confidence. "Oh, I'm not too worried. Hayden will bring John home late tonight. Now, shall I send for a pot of tea?"

"Yes, please. Sounds like we could both use a bit of relaxation. My students were so eager for the weekend, I could hardly—" A knock on the front door stopped her.

Victoria groaned. "I'm afraid to answer it," she called back as she hastened to the main hall.

By the time Sarah caught up with her, Victoria was dismissing the boy from the telegraph office.

"Maybe it's good news," Sarah suggested as Victoria ripped open the envelope.

"'Missed judge in town. Stop. Going to his farm. Stop. Be home tomorrow. Stop. Hayden.'"

"Tomorrow!" Sarah exclaimed. "What is Lavinia going to do?"

"Wait, I'm afraid."

"You don't think she should postpone the wedding?"

"No, I don't. I believe in Hayden. He will have John home in time for the wedding."

"What about the bishop?"

"Christine, you, and I will meet his train," Victoria answered. "We'll tell him what John is doing, and he'll understand."

"We'll tell him John is in jail?" Sarah demanded.

Victoria flicked her hand in the air in a dismissive gesture. "There's no need to mention that part." She grinned as the thrill of a new challenge coursed through her blood. "By the time I get through with him—I mean, *we* get through with him, he'll be ready to nominate John for sainthood."

"Victoria ..." Sarah cocked her head, apprehension spreading across her face. "What are you going to do?"

"Just tell him a woeful tale about the plight of a helpless immigrant girl in a desperate situation. And after I have him close to weeping, I'll tell him about John's heroic efforts to save her."

"Heaven help Lavinia!"

The minute Sarah woke the next morning, she climbed out of bed and sank to her knees to pray for Lavinia and John. "We need a miracle, Lord. Victoria's charm will only go so far. And surely John shouldn't be penalized for trying to help a young girl." It all seemed quite logical to Sarah, and she certainly had faith in God's ability to do anything. So why was she so nervous? She glanced at the rose-colored silk dress she would wear as maid of honor at four o'clock. *If there's a wedding!* Sarah's chest clenched at the thought, and thinking of Lavinia's plight, she added on to her prayer. "Oh, dear God, please comfort Lavinia. What a panic she must be in!" Sarah rose and hurriedly dressed. Not surprisingly, she found Victoria downstairs ahead of her, already at work on her plan.

"Here are the critical facts to remember about the bishop, Sarah." Victoria whisked around the dining room table, placing her finest china. "He's essentially a political creature. Keeping the peace in the church is what he values most, and he'll look the other way to avoid scandal. What we must do is give him a way to do just that."

"I don't understand."

"If we give him a believable story that supports the status quo, which specifically keeps him from having to take action that causes waves in the church, he'll latch onto it. Even if he has questions, he won't ask them."

"So we keep him focused on John's heroic rescue of a girl named Alison."

"An *orphan* girl. A girl in danger from an unscrupulous man. Remember, John is a hero. He has risked everything to save this girl, even the possibility of being late to his own wedding."

"What else do we do?"

"We *feed* him. The bishop likes nothing better than a fine meal."

Sarah's anxiety reared its head. "Victoria … It doesn't sound like enough. Isn't there more we could do?"

"Yes, there is."

Sarah wheeled around at the sound of a voice behind her. Lavinia stood in the dining room doorway. "Forgive me, Victoria, for just walking in. No one heard my knock."

"You look beautiful, Lavinia!" Sarah exclaimed as she scanned Lavinia's new suit. "But isn't that your going away suit?"

"It is, but I need it now more than I do later in the day. You see, I've been praying all night, and it has come to me that the most persuasive thing I can do to convince the bishop to support John is to show him how fervently I support John."

"You're going to the train station with us," Victoria guessed.

"I am, and I'm also inviting myself to the dinner you're preparing for the bishop. I hope you'll forgive me, Victoria."

Victoria raced to Lavinia and hugged her. "Completely forgiven and completely right. Your example of faith in John is the strongest card we can play."

"But it won't be playing because I do believe in John. I know he'll be here if he can, but I also know that he has his priorities properly set. The most important thing is to rescue this young girl, this Alison."

Sarah was surprised when Lavinia walked toward her and took her hand. "Sarah, John must have seen something truly dangerous for the girl. Otherwise, he would never have taken an action that would get him thrown in jail."

Anger began to boil in Sarah. "I hadn't thought of that," she muttered.

"I believe John will bring Alison home with him, and she will undoubtedly need a lot of support. I won't be here next week. One way or the other, I'll be married and off on my honeymoon. You must take care of the girl."

"You can count on it!" Sarah's voice shook with emotion.

"I knew I could." Lavinia hugged her, then turned to Victoria. "This is going to be quite an interesting day, isn't it?"

"That's quite an understatement," Victoria responded. "And so is this: you are amazing."

Sarah had never seen a more shocked man than the bishop when he descended the steps of the train and found the bride awaiting him. Much to her relief, the jovial man immediately donned his "shepherd of the flock" persona and became engrossed in comforting Lavinia in her "time of trouble."

Throughout the early luncheon, Sarah noticed that the light-hearted chatter of the ladies was interspersed with many glances at the doorway in hopes of finding John standing there. She, herself, kept one ear strained to hear the slightest movement at the front door, while she also tried to participate in the conversation at the table. By twelve thirty, it was apparent that John had not arrived in Riverford on the noon train, and the faces around the table became more strained. At one o'clock, when Victoria suggested they adjourn to the drawing room, the bishop cleared his throat and took Lavinia's hand in his.

"My dear Miss Logan." The bishop adopted his most pastoral tone. "While I haven't a doubt in the world that John will arrive in time for the wedding, perhaps we would be wise to make an alternate plan."

Lavinia rose from the table. "John will be here," she said quite simply. "Thank you for the lovely luncheon, Victoria. Now I must go home, rest a bit, and dress."

"But my dear ..." The bishop also rose. "Perhaps it would be prudent ..."

Lavinia shook her head. "I prefer faith to prudence, Bishop. John will be here."

"I'll have Sam drive you home," Victoria said.

"There's no need, Victoria. It's such a short walk, and a few minutes in the bright sunshine and cool air will do me good."

"I'll walk with you," Sarah suggested.

"I'd like that."

Sarah's nerves grew more frazzled as she listened to the clock ticking away in the main hall as Lavinia thanked Victoria again and said her good-byes to Christine and the bishop. The last thing Sarah did before exiting the front door was to cast a furtive glance back at the clock. It was one twenty. What was she to do? Should she try to prepare Lavinia for John's failure to arrive, or should she support Lavinia in her faith?

As they descended the steps, Lavinia settled the question for Sarah. "Send word the minute he arrives."

"Of course." Sarah tried to match Lavinia's confidence.

Lavinia abruptly stopped walking and peered toward the gate. Sarah's eyes followed her gaze and discovered the station master hurrying up the brick-paved walk, waving a paper in his hand.

Sarah's heart sank, but as she turned to comfort her friend, she discovered that Lavinia's face was jubilant. "He's on the three o'clock train. Oh, thank you, Lord!" she exclaimed as she rushed forward.

The minute the station master saw her, he called out, "He's coming, Miss Lavinia! He'll be here at three o'clock."

Sarah burst into tears, but Lavinia raced forward, grabbed the telegram, and clutched it to her heart. "Tell the others," she called back to Sarah as she waved and hurried off.

The others! Victoria, Christine, and— "Oh dear! What do I say to the bishop?"

"Sarah!" Victoria called from the verandah, and Sarah turned to find all three of them waiting for her.

"He's on the three o'clock train!" Sarah shouted as she ran up the walk.

"Thanks be to God!" the bishop intoned from the verandah steps as Christine and Victoria hugged. "Now, let's get organized," he added. "Mrs. Hodges, if you'll have your driver take me to the rectory, I'll clean up and go to the church to greet early arrivals. You ladies couldn't look lovelier, but I suspect you have new dresses you want to slip into."

Christine pulled Sarah aside and asked, "Is Alison with him?"

"Of course she is!" the bishop answered before Sarah could speak. "John Neville would go to the gates of hell—" His eyes twinkled. "Or anywhere else to rescue a damsel in distress." He gave Victoria a knowing look, followed by an exaggerated wink.

Victoria donned her most innocent look. "Why, Bishop, are you asking me a question?"

"No, ma'am! I never ask questions I don't want answers to." He chuckled as he shepherded them back into the house.

When Sarah started her walk down the aisle promptly at four o'clock, John Neville had been back in Riverford for less than an hour. Nevertheless, there he stood, awaiting his bride at the front of the church with Hayden standing next to him as best man. From the second pew, Victoria beamed back at her. Next to her stood a beautiful, auburn-haired young woman dressed in an outfit that had been hastily contrived by Victoria from both her own and Sarah's clothing. It was hard to believe that Alison MacKenna was only fourteen years old. She was tall, stately, and composed. Alban, his face badly bruised, stood next to her.

As Sarah approached the altar, she veered to the left and turned back to look up the aisle to watch Ceci and Juli sprinkle flower petals from their baskets as they made their way down the aisle. Finally, the organist played the fanfare announcing the coming of the bride, and with Lee escorting her, Lavinia began her walk to her destiny as John Neville's wife, as the wife of a clergyman. Sarah forced back her tears of joy for her friend and wondered if she would ever be able to equal Lavinia's faith.

"What an exhausting day!" Sarah exclaimed as she collapsed on a settee in the drawing room at Hodges House.

"But what a beautiful ending," Christine added as she also sat down. "Have you ever seen a sweeter wedding?"

"I'll never forget the look on Lavinia's face when she said her vows to John." Sarah sighed. "My, how she loves that man!"

"I think she's certainly proved that in the last two days." Lee took Sarah's hand in his as he joined her on the settee.

Sarah watched Victoria pace the room. "Come sit down, Victoria. All that pacing won't make Hayden return any sooner."

"Where is the man?" Victoria demanded. "How long can it possibly take to deliver the bishop to the train station?"

"He can't just drop him off, Victoria," Lee said. "He's got to wait till the bishop's settled on the train and it pulls out of Riverford."

"How can all of you be so calm?" Victoria asked. "Aren't you dying to know what happened in Dallas?"

"I've hardly had time to think about it," Christine admitted. "The way we all rushed off to the church, my concerns that the girls would perform well as flower girls, and then the reception and saying our farewells to Lavinia and John."

Sarah heard the front door close.

"He's back!" Victoria exclaimed. "Hayden, we're all in here," she called out.

"Well, good evening, everyone," Hayden was obviously fighting to suppress a grin as he entered the room and hugged Victoria. "Glad to see all of you, but I'm afraid I'm worn out, so I'll just be off to bed—"

"You will not!" Victoria swatted at him. "Tell us what happened in Dallas!"

"They're having beautiful weather up there …"

"Hayden! Stop teasing us." Victoria grabbed his arm and dragged him to a settee. "Now sit and tell us everything that happened. How did John end up in jail?"

"Okay, okay." He pulled Victoria down beside him. "As ya'll know, John and Alban went up to the Bronson farm early yesterday to check on Alison's well-being. Well, it seems that Alison ran out the front door to hug Alban just about the time Mr. Bronson came around the corner of the house. He ordered Alban and John off the property in words I can't repeat in the presence of ladies."

"How do you know what kind of language he used?" Victoria demanded. "You weren't there yet."

"This all came out in the hearing we finally had about noon today." He looked across the room at Lee. "Can this still be the same day? Seems like a week's passed."

"Oh, go on!" Victoria exclaimed.

"Well, John tried to talk to Bronson, tried to discuss the possibility of gaining Alison's freedom, but Bronson flew into a rage and ordered Alison back in the house. When she didn't go immediately, he grabbed her by the hair and started dragging her—"

"He what?" Sarah sprang up, her fury sending her heart into a wild gallop.

"Bronson started dragging her toward the front door. Alban tackled him. Bronson shoved Alison through the door and hit Alban. Once Alban was on the porch floor, he started kicking the boy."

"Heavens!" Christine exclaimed.

"That's when John went into action and slugged Bronson." Hayden looked at Lee and grinned. "Don't ever make John Neville mad, friend. From the looks of Bronson at the hearing, I'd say that John's got quite a powerful right hook."

"This is not funny!" Sarah exclaimed as she plopped back down.

"No, I guess it's not." Hayden exhaled loudly. "Well, a couple of farmhands pulled the two men apart, and they hauled John and Alban into the sheriff's office. The sheriff locked up John but refused to lock up Alban because of his age. Alban had the good sense to telegraph me, and from that point on, I guess you know the story."

"The judge refused to free John so you sent for the General," Lee said.

"Right. I found out the judge had served under General Gibbes. Seemed like he was our best chance. The General talked him into holding a hearing at noon even though it's Saturday, and once he heard the whole story, especially the part about Bronson's treatment of Alison, he turned John loose."

"And what about Alison?" Sarah asked.

"The judge ruled that since Bronson had not kept his part of the original agreement with the officials who organized the orphan train, Alison is free of any obligation to him. The judge asked her what she wanted to do, and she said she wanted to come to Riverford with us."

Sarah's heart leapt with excitement. "She's going to live here?"

"With Reverend Wright, so she and Alban can be together."

"They'll both be able to go to school!" Sarah clapped her hands together. "They'll be considered town children."

Victoria laughed. "No special tax for them!"

"And Lavinia and John are married and on their honeymoon," Christine added. "What a lot we have to be thankful for."

CHAPTER THIRTY-TWO

Sarah's gait was jaunty, just short of a skip, as she walked to school on Monday morning. Her mind was full of images of Lavinia's wedding and dreams about her own. The cool, dry air of late October invigorated her as it blew down the street, swirling raked piles of leaves into disarray. She looked forward to welcoming new students to her class today, for the harvest was finally in, and the sharecroppers' children were free to attend school at last.

Once the school building was in sight, she set aside her wedding dreams and turned her focus to plans for catching up the new students. It was going to be quite a challenge! The new students would have different native tongues and different levels of previous education. She fervently hoped the immigrant families would allow the girls to come. Repeatedly, she cautioned herself to temper her expectations, to be grateful for every new student and every bit of learning she could instill in all of her students.

The wind was particularly playful when she reached the school building and tried to open the door. After three tries, she finally managed to keep the door open long enough to scoot through. Laughing, she paused inside the hall, dropped her book satchel, and removed her badly skewed shawl. She was shaking it out when she became aware of someone standing in the shadows. "Good morning," she offered to the unknown figure, and Miss Grimm stepped forward.

"You may not think so for long," she whispered as she motioned Sarah to step back into the dusky corner.

Sarah's chest tightened as her light-hearted mood shifted to anxiety. "What's wrong?"

Miss Grimm's fingers instantly went to her lips to silence her. "Just listen carefully. Mr. Hunt is in your room waiting for you."

Sarah sucked in her breath as her heart galloped into full speed.

"He has assigned many of the immigrant students to your class— too many for one teacher to handle."

"Doesn't he want me to be able to teach them?"

"No. He's trying to cause trouble in your classroom. He's trying to upset the town parents so they'll demand that the school board deny the immigrant children access to the school. Be careful, Miss Novak!" With that sharp warning, Miss Grimm hurried away.

Light-headed, Sarah leaned against the wall and took slow, deep breaths to steady her pulse. *Self-control*, she counseled herself but immediately recognized her inadequacy. "Dear God, help me help these children," she whispered a fervent prayer. She took one last deep breath, picked up her book satchel, and resolutely walked to her classroom.

When she entered, she saw Mr. Hunt placing name cards on the desks that he had arranged at the front of the room. Behind the desks, benches were lined along the back wall. There was a definite aisle between the desks and the benches.

"Ah, good morning, Miss Novak!" He scanned her figure, settling his eyes on her hips. "I've rearranged your classroom."

"So I see."

"The town children are to sit in the desks at the front." He held up a name card. "I am assigning their seats."

Sarah nodded.

"I shall add a large group of sharecropper children to your class today. They are to sit on the benches at the back, and under no circumstances are they to be allowed to cross the aisle I've created. Do I make myself clear?"

"Completely." Sarah walked to the coat stand in the corner and draped her shawl over it.

"There will be an outcry from the town folk, of course." Mr. Hunt walked up behind her and changed his voice to a raspy whisper. "I could have saved you from the approaching trouble had you made the slightest effort to be friends with me, but alas! You have not chosen to do so. Perhaps after today you will." He placed his hand on her shoulder for a few seconds before striding to the door. "Ah, here come your town students, and I see that Miss Grimm is holding back your country students, as I ordered." He raised his voice. "Come in, children, and find the desk with your name on it. That's it. Hurry up now. We have new students to add to your class today."

Sarah watched her regular students' faces as they filed in, searched the name cards, and settled in their desks. Most looked confused, but Leanne Proper looked smug, and Stephanie Sharp looked disturbed.

"Bring in the additional immigrant children, Miss Grimm," Mr. Hunt called out into the hall. "Line up in front of the desk," Mr. Hunt ordered the new children as he picked up a wooden rod he had brought with him. "In front of the desk!" he repeated in a louder voice as he waved the menacing rod.

Sarah watched as ten shabbily dressed children of varied ages and sizes filed in. Most of the boys looked at her hopefully. All of the girls kept their eyes on the floor—all but one. Sarah was startled to see that Alison MacKenna was included in the group. Her brief talk with the girl at Lavinia's wedding had convinced her that Alison was fairly well educated and surely capable of more than grade-school work. Besides, she was a resident of the town.

"Now, children, listen carefully!" Mr. Hunt rapped the rod on Jerome's desk and made the boy jump. "These desks are for the town children." He pointed to the benches with the rod. "You will sit in the back on those benches, and under no circumstances are you to associate with the town children. Furthermore, you are not to interrupt the education of the town children in any way whatsoever. You will remain quiet at all times. No questions! No comments!"

Sarah scanned the children's faces, trying to gauge how much they understood. Clearly, they understood their rejection. The boys' faces were angry; the girls' faces were frightened. All but one. Alison MacKenna stared coolly at Mr. Hunt, and he noticed.

"You!" He pointed the rod at her. "You are the girl from Scotland, I believe."

"Aye, sir, I am." Alison stood ramrod straight, her ice-blue eyes piercing him.

The room fell totally silent as Mr. Hunt looked her up and down. "Most attractive," he murmured.

Sudden fury blazed through Sarah. Fury at the man and fear for the girl. She stepped between them. "Alison, kindly lead the children to the back benches."

"Oh no!" Mr. Hunt moved closer and leered at Alison. "This young lady must have a desk."

"Nay, sir!" Alison's retort was sharp. "I'll not be needing a desk."

"Oh, but you'll grow tired sitting on a backless bench, and there's a free desk right over by the window."

"You may throw your desk in the river, sir, for all I care. And yourself along with it!" Alison took the hand of a small shaking girl and marched to the back. The younger children scurried after her, but Piotr and a much larger boy held their ground.

"Move!" Mr. Hunt shouted at the boys as he pointed the rod toward the back wall.

Piotr began a slow retreat to the back, but the larger boy jerked the rod out of Mr. Hunt's hand and glared at him.

Determined to protect the boy's future in the classroom, Sarah forced herself to step forward and hold out her hand. "I'll take that."

"*Dobrý. To patří vám*," the boy muttered in Czech as he handed it to her. He glared at Mr. Hunt over his shoulder as he lumbered to the back of the room.

"Yes!" Sarah adopted her teacher tone. "It does belong to me." She turned to Mr. Hunt and Miss Grimm. "Thank you for delivering the new students." She turned back to class. "Please stand, students." She raised her hands to suggest rising and pointed to the American flag in the corner. "As always, we will begin our school day with the pledge of allegiance to the flag."

All the children stood, and the town students chanted the pledge as Mr. Hunt and Miss Grimm left. Next, Sarah led them in reciting the twenty-third psalm as she slipped over to the door to be certain no one was in the hall. When she turned back to the class, she was startled to see Stephanie Sharp walking to the back of the room.

"Where are you going, Stephanie?"

"I want to sit next to Alison." Stephanie plopped down on the bench.

"Well, if she can sit where she wants to, so can I," Billy Gerhardt announced as he abandoned his desk. "I'm sitting next to Piotr. He's smart."

"But you can't!" Leanne Proper exclaimed. "Mr. Hunt said—"

"Ah, I don't care what he said," Billy retorted.

"Me neither." Rusty jumped up. "And I'm sitting next to that big guy."

"Your mother is gonna have a fit, Rusty Quince!" Leanne warned.

Rusty shrugged. "Who cares? I want that big guy on my football team."

Leanne turned to Sarah. "Do something, Miss Novak!"

"Of course." Sarah smiled as she walked to the window, opened it, and threw the rod outside. "Open your English books, class, to page seventy. And if you'd like to share your book with someone who doesn't have one, please do."

Normally quiet Betsy Benson stood, walked to the back of the room, and grabbed Nadia Burzynski's hand. "I'm sorry, Miss Novak, but Nadia always shares a book with me." She dragged the reluctant Nadia to the empty desk next to hers as Sarah fought back tears of joy.

Sarah wasn't surprised when Mr. Hunt stalked into her room after the final bell had rung and the children had departed. What did surprise her was that he showed no anger that his orders had been defied. Instead, he sidled up to Sarah and grabbed her upper arm. "This is your last chance, Miss Novak, your last chance to be my friend."

"All I want is a professional relationship with you, Mr. Hunt." Sarah made her voice as firm as she could. "Turn loose of my arm."

"Come, come, Miss Novak. I know what you foreign women are like. None of you can resist a man."

"What do you mean by that?" Sarah wrenched her arm free.

Mr. Hunt's gaze fell below Sarah's waist. "Well, you foreign women do breed like rabbits, don't you? And you made your interest in me quite evident at the first faculty meeting. A man of the world knows when a woman is interested in him."

"Are you saying that I—" Fury exploded in Sarah. "How dare you? I've done nothing wrong."

"Haven't you? Why, the way you smiled at me …"

Sarah's mind reeled.

Mr. Hunt laughed. "But it's too late now, Miss Novak. You had your chance, but I've no more time for you." He glanced at the bench at the back of the room. "After all, you're no longer the prettiest immigrant girl in my school. Her name is Alison, I believe." He grinned and sauntered out of the room.

Horror washed over Sarah. Images of the beautiful young Scottish girl floated through her mind. Her long, flowing, auburn hair … her ice blue eyes … her young womanly body. Sarah gasped. "No! He won't! I won't let him." She turned, and without picking up her books or her shawl, flew out of the room.

CHAPTER THIRTY-THREE

Victoria clasped the letter from Antonio she had received that day as she impatiently paced the verandah, waiting for Sarah. She was eager to share the good news that he would indeed play for the benefit. When she finally saw Sarah in the distance, she bolted down the steps and hurried down the walk to meet her, but she stopped when she realized that Sarah was turning into the driveway. *Why on earth is she ...* Victoria's heart constricted with alarm as she realized that Sarah was wiping tears off her cheeks. She turned and raced across the front garden to intercept her.

"Sarah!" Victoria called out as she dashed around an azalea bed to the driveway. "Sarah!" Victoria stopped and watched in shock as Sarah burst into tears and raced toward her. "It's going to be all right." The words automatically sprang from Victoria's lips as she threw her arms around Sarah. "Whatever it is, we can handle it." She pushed Sarah away and peered into her face. "You believe me, don't you, Sarah? There's nothing we can't handle."

Sarah nodded as she sobbed.

"Come with me." Victoria put her arm around Sarah's waist and half supported her as she led her up the remaining drive to the side verandah.

"I don't want anyone to see me like this," Sarah whispered. "Please ..."

"Hayden is down at the store, and the servants are in the house. No one knows you're here." She led Sarah to a wicker couch and pressed her down onto the cushioned seat. "Now tell me what has happened."

"It's awful. Oh, Victoria! I don't understand why he's acting this way."

"Who?"

"Mr. Hunt."

"What's he doing?"

A shiver ran through Sarah as she wrapped her arms across her chest and started crying again.

"Sarah!" Victoria knelt in front of her and looked up into her face. "You're frightened!"

Sarah could do no more than nod.

Victoria sprang to her feet, her face hot with anger, her fists clenched. "What has this Mr. Hunt done? Just tell me straight out, Sarah. I won't have anyone frightening you!"

"That's just it, Victoria. I don't know why I'm frightened of him. I should be angry, not scared. I should be furious with him because of what he did to me and what he's done to others—"

"What did he do to you?" Victoria interrupted her. "Tell me!" she demanded, then, realizing her anger was not helping, she forced herself to lower her voice as she sat down next to Sarah and took her hand. "Just tell me from the beginning what's happened. We'll sort it out."

"You already know how he acted at the first teachers' meeting and that he ordered me to come to his office after the meeting. When I went, he told me he was just pretending to dislike me so the other teachers wouldn't be jealous of me because I'm younger and pretty. Then he …"

"He what? What, Sarah?"

"He picked my locket up off …" Sarah pointed to her bosom with a shaking hand. "He didn't pick it up all the way. He left his hand …" Sarah turned her face away.

Victoria clamped down on the fury that was exploding in her and fought to keep her voice calm. "Are you saying Mr. Hunt fondled you?"

"Not exactly. He just moved his fingers—I was so afraid, Victoria! The way he leered at me, and the feel of his hand …"

"That day you came home so upset. That had just happened?"

Sarah nodded.

"But you didn't tell Christine and me."

"I was afraid I'd lose my job, and I—I was so confused and ashamed. I don't know why."

"You have no reason to be ashamed. He's the criminal."

"I think I began to understand that when it happened the second time, but I—I couldn't ..."

"The second time?"

"He sent me a note, ordered me to come to his office after class. When I got there, he ... Oh, Victoria! I was so nauseated I bolted from the room and ran to the girls' washroom. I clung to the sink trying not to faint." Sarah paused, obviously working to slow her breath and to focus.

"Go on," Victoria encouraged.

"I was startled by a woman's voice. When I turned around, another teacher, a sad, broken-looking creature named Minnie, was standing there." Sarah met Victoria's eyes. "She knew what had happened to me because Mr. Hunt has done the same thing to her ... only worse."

Victoria's fury turned cold. "Why didn't you tell me?"

"I didn't know what to do. I thought I could just stay away from him. Minnie said I'd lose my job if I told. After all that Mama and you have done to help me, I couldn't bear to lose my job—"

"But something else has happened, hasn't it?"

"Just before five o'clock when I was alone in my classroom, he came in and closed the door behind him."

Victoria jumped to her feet. "And?"

"He told me it was my fault. That I had encouraged him. But I didn't!"

"Of course not."

"He said he was through with me—Oh, Victoria! He's got his eye on Alison now. I have to do something; I have to protect her. But how? I don't know what to do!"

"Such a man must be stopped!"

"He can have me fired, Victoria. He can accuse me of something ... of incompetence, of misbehavior ... I don't know what. Anything.

The school board will believe him. They will take his word over mine any day. He's had years of experience, and he's well respected. I'm a nobody."

"You are not a nobody! And Mr. Hunt is going to find that out, but we have to proceed cautiously. Somehow we have to entrap him, so it won't have to come down to your word against his."

"But what will we accomplish if we just force him to leave Riverford? He'll still be a principal somewhere. He'll still be able to force himself on—"

"Who are you talking about?" Hayden demanded from the doorway. "What's going on here?"

"Hayden!" Victoria exclaimed, then quickly tried to normalize her tone. "Why, when did you get home, dear?"

"I've been here long enough to know that some man has abused Sarah in some way. Who are you talking about?"

Victoria glanced at Sarah, who turned crimson as she lowered her eyes to the floor. "Sarah's principal, Mr. Hunt, has ridiculed her in meetings and made unprofessional advances in private."

"Unprofessional?"

Victoria drew a deep breath. "Improper. And she's not the only woman he has approached. He makes a habit of preying on the females in his power."

"Where is he now?" Hayden's voice was cold.

"Hayden, you can't just—"

"Where is he, Victoria?"

"I—I don't know. But Hayden, we must think this through."

"Think? I'm in no mood to think! I'm going to boot that man out of Riverford!" Hayden shouted.

Victoria grabbed his arm. "And let him go to another town and ruin other women's lives? He also goes after students, Hayden. We can't just move him along, somewhere out of our sight. We have to remove him from the field of education. We have to ensure that he never works around young people again."

"Please, Hayden." Sarah raised her tear-stained face. "Think of all the young girls he could hurt over the coming years. Please ... for the students."

Hayden turned on his heel and headed for the door. "I'll take care of it."

"Where are you going?" Victoria raced after him, and Sarah followed her.

"To see General Gibbes."

"The General? Why the General, Hayden?"

"This Mr. Hunt must be stripped of his credentials before I run him out of town. Only the school board can do that, and only General Gibbes can make the school board do their duty."

Victoria grabbed his arm. "And if they won't?"

He turned and looked down at her. "They will! If I have to take a whip to every man on that board, they'll do the right thing."

"Surely the law could be applied."

"What law, Victoria? There are no laws to deal with things like this. Maybe someday there will be—but not now. The only solution is for good men to counter bad men. And that's what I'm going to do." He turned to Sarah. "I promise you that Riverford will be permanently free of Mr. Hunt when school opens on Monday morning. You won't ever have to see him again, Sarah."

"But he'll go to another school."

"No, he won't! He'll be too afraid to ever go near a school again."

"So it comes down to threatened violence?" Victoria demanded.

"Until laws are passed, it does. There's no other way. Good men *must* control bad men. In situations like this, that's the only law there is, Victoria."

"And what about Lee?" Victoria demanded. "What's he going to say when he hears that you've taken this into your own hands and left him out?"

Hayden paused and exhaled loudly as he looked at Sarah. "Victoria's right. I'm going to have to tell Lee. You understand that, don't you, Sarah? He has to know."

Sarah nodded sadly. "It's just a matter of time before the whole town knows."

"No." Hayden disagreed. "At all costs, we must keep this quiet. I hate to say it, but your reputation is at stake."

"Sarah's done nothing wrong!" Victoria exclaimed. "Sarah is the victim!"

"I know that. But there are vicious people here who already want to hurt her, and in situations like this …"

"Women are automatically blamed!" Victoria exclaimed.

"I'm afraid so."

"Despicable!" Victoria's voice was laced with fury. "He ought to be put on trial!"

"I agree, Victoria, but we're stuck with the world we have. Morris Hunt is leaving this town tonight with the fear of God in him, and the school board is going to meet tomorrow to officially fire him for incompetence. Sarah's name won't be mentioned. I promise." He strode from the room.

Sarah sighed as she dropped her head into her hands. "If only I had—had—"

"Sarah! This is not your fault."

A sob escaped Sarah's mouth. "Why does it feel like it is?"

Victoria sat next to her and took her hand. "Because that's what we've been taught to feel."

"Another battle to take on," Sarah murmured. "I don't think I can take on any more, Victoria. When Mr. Hunt added ten new immigrant children to my class today, he made it clear they won't be there long."

"I know. It's just a matter of time. Mrs. Bellows and her gang are going to be able to stop the immigrant children from attending the town school."

"That breaks my heart. Oh, Victoria! I'm so tired …"

"Of course you are. You've been carrying a heavier load than any of us guessed. You need to go lie down. Lee is sure to come by later."

"I don't want to see him."

"Yes, you do." Victoria stood and pulled Sarah to her feet. "He is going to be your husband, and you love and need him."

Sarah nodded.

"One happy thing to think on, Sarah." She pulled the letter from Antonio out of her pocket. "Antonio is coming for Christmas."

"And you think he'll help us?"

"He says he will, and we're going to build that library, and it's going to have classrooms in it. We are going to provide education for every child in this county, Sarah. You can take that thought to the bank and deposit it!"

CHAPTER THIRTY-FOUR

Sarah bent forward against the north wind that threatened to throw her to the ground as she hurried to Christine's house. With the coming of November, the wide Texas sky had disappeared behind a thick bank of gray clouds. Slivers of sleet sliced the air and stung Sarah's face as she turned into the wrought-iron gate and hurried up the front walk. She had been summoned to an emergency meeting of the Riverford Ladies Literary Society. Happily, Nancy threw the front door open as soon as Sarah knocked and pulled her into the cold hall.

"We got a fire going in most every room, but this ole north wind 'bout to blow the house down," Nancy complained as she took Sarah's coat. "The ladies be waiting for you in the drawing room, and they's good and fussed up." Nancy led the way and slid one side of the tall pocket doors open.

"Sarah!" Victoria called out. "Come warm yourself." Still shivering, Sarah waved at Christine and Lavinia who were chatting with Mamie MacDonald and gladly hurried toward the glowing coals in the elegant marble-encased fireplace.

"This is all very mysterious, Victoria," Theodora Benton said as she nodded at Sarah. "Why on earth has Christine dragged us out on such a day for a meeting of the Literary Society?"

"Just the officers are coming, Theo."

"But I'm not an officer," Theo protested. "I'm just a pushy old woman who doesn't care about public opinion."

"Exactly why I suggested she include you."

"I knew you had something up your sleeve." Theo grinned as she gleefully rubbed her wrinkled hands together, turned, and called out to Mamie MacDonald. "Good news, Mamie! Victoria's shaking up the town again, and we get to help her."

"It's about the school board's decision, isn't it?" Mamie asked.

"How did you find out about that?" Christine asked. "They only made the ruling last night."

"It's in the morning paper. Front page!" Mamie's face went red with indignation. "That rascal, Bellows, didn't waste a minute spreading the bad news."

"Never could stand that man!" Josephine Schmidt declared as she strode into the room. "Or his wife."

Christine hurried forward to greet her, then turned back to the others. "Ladies, now that we are all present, let us get right to work." She went to stand behind the writing table and picked up the club's gavel. "Let us call the meeting to order and formalize our proceedings."

"Are you sure you want to do that, Christine?" Theo winked at Victoria. "Wouldn't it be wiser to just have a cup of tea, decide what we're going to do, and tell the other members later?"

Josephine gently slid the gavel from Christine's hand. "What a pity we're the only ones able to brave the coming storm and share this lovely morning tea with you, Christine."

Christine cocked her head as she glanced at Victoria.

"We don't have a quorum present …" Victoria answered Christine's unspoken question. "We couldn't possibly have an official meeting."

"Such a pity!" crowed Mamie. "Sit down, Christine, and let me pour you a cup of tea." Mamie plopped down on the velvet settee in front of the tea table and picked up the elegant violet-decorated teapot and held it up for all to see. "Such a pretty teapot! Is it Royal Worcester, Christine?"

"Don't be a fool, Mamie," Theo chided as she picked up a cup and saucer and held it out to Mamie. "It's older than that. Was it your mother's, Christine?"

Confused by the turn of topic, Christine struggled to answer. "No, I am afraid nothing of Mother's china could be saved when the Union forces invaded Charleston. But why are we talking about—"

"No doubt dear Richard bought it for her," Mamie suggested.

"A wedding present perhaps?" Josephine chimed in as she pulled up a chair and accepted a steaming cup from Mamie.

"Okay. That's enough teatime talk," Theo decreed. "Let's get down to business. Exactly what are we going to do about the school board's decision to charge the immigrant children tuition?"

"Tuition—ha! That's just a fancy word for tax," Josephine declared.

"Makes my blood boil!" Theo raised her voice above Josephine's.

"We're going to bring other educational opportunities to Riverford." Victoria raised her voice even louder to intervene.

"Good! We're going to circumvent the bigots!" Mamie crowed.

"Mamie! What a word to use!" Lavinia protested.

"Just speaking the truth. Do you prefer 'biased bigots' or perhaps 'prejudiced people'?"

"Let us just say that their opinions are unfortunate and miscalculated," Christine suggested.

"Downright mean and stupid in my opinion," Josephine chimed in. "But let that go. Exactly what are we going to do?"

Victoria rapped her knuckles on the table in an effort to take control of the conversation. "For three years now, the Literary Society has wanted to establish a library."

"You mean *you* have, Victoria," Theo jeered. "Most of the Literary Society is content to dress up in their new finery and sit in your fancy parlor and drink tea."

"Hush, Theo!" Josephine ordered. "For mercy's sake, give Victoria time to talk."

"Oh, all right," Theo agreed. "Give us the short version, Victoria."

"We're going to start a public library, a *county* library, where all residents of the county will be welcome."

"By that she means all *white* residents," Theo growled.

"One problem at a time!" Victoria retorted. "There are actual state laws restricting what we can do for the colored folks, but there are no laws against educating the immigrants."

"I just hope I live long enough to see—"

Josephine swatted Theo with her napkin. "You will! You're going to outlive us all and stir up trouble another hundred years."

"As I was saying …" Victoria raised her voice and tried again. "We're going to start a county library that will include classrooms where English and other essential subjects can be taught."

"Where are we going to get the money?" Josephine demanded.

"What we need is a fundraiser," Mamie declared. "Something the wealthy residents of Riverford can't resist attending."

"And we're going to have one," Victoria answered. "If you'll allow me to read a few sentences from a letter I just received." She pulled a piece of stationery from her pocket and began to read. "'Of course I will help you and your friends raise money for your new library. You pick the venue, my dear Victoria, and I will pick the music. But I insist on *bellissima* Mrs. Boyd accompanying me.'"

"Antonio Santoro!" Josephine exclaimed. "Is he returning to Riverford?"

"Of course he's returning, Jo." Theo's voice was impatient. "Don't you listen to the gossips? Mrs. Bellows has been complaining that 'that foreign fiddle player,' as she calls him, will be spending Christmas at Hodges House again."

Josephine flicked her hand in the air. "Oh, I just let everything Edith Bellows says go in one ear and out the other."

"I wish I could," Theo muttered.

"I simply *adored* hearing him play at your musicale three years ago, Victoria," Mamie gushed. "Oh, anyone would pay to hear him!"

"In fact, the ladies of Riverford would pay just to have that Italian kiss their hands!" Josephine declared. "I know I would!"

Sarah, who had been respectfully listening to these energetic older women, burst out laughing, and the group suddenly remembered her presence.

"Good grief!" Josephine declared. "We completely forgot Sarah. Surely we ought to ask her what she thinks."

"Even if we don't pay any attention to what she says," Theo added.

"Oh, I'd rather ask her something else," Mamie protested as she turned to Sarah. "Come sit down, Sarah, and tell us everything you know about the disappearance of Mr. Hunt."

Sarah gasped as the heat of panic flashed through her and her pulse charged into high gear.

"Why should Sarah know anything about that?" Victoria demanded. "She's just a beginning teacher at the school."

"The school board would hardly communicate with Sarah regarding the dismissal of Mr. Hunt," Christine added.

"It just seems odd—" Mamie began.

"But not worth our time," Josephine interrupted. "Never liked the man. Slithered around like a snake."

"Okay, okay!" Theo clapped her hands to gain attention. "We're all agreed that we need a public library in Riverford, and certainly we can start raising money through this fancy concert Victoria has in mind, but the biggest problem still remains. We don't have a building!"

Sarah's pulse began to normalize as the topic of Mr. Hunt was abandoned and a general hubbub of private comments about obtaining a building erupted in the room. Finally, Christine rose and held up a hand to gain their attention. "Lately, I have been contemplating the creation of a memorial to my late husband, something that would contribute to our community. He loved this town and the surrounding lands so—" Her voice broke as she visibly struggled to control herself.

"And we loved Richard, dear Christine," Lavinia assured her as she pulled a handkerchief from her sleeve and dabbed her own eyes. "He was one of the finest men I've ever known. A true philanthropist."

"Yes, he was a true philanthropist," Christine agreed. "And I know without a doubt that, were he here, he would support a library for this county with his time and his assets. That is why I want to offer the original Boyd family home to house our new library."

"The old Boyd house?" Theo asked.

"Oh my goodness!" Mamie exclaimed. "How wonderful!"

"But it's not in town," Josephine pointed out.

"Even better!" Theo exclaimed. "We're organizing a library for everyone, not just the townspeople. We don't want the city council or anyone else dictating to us. Besides, it's just barely outside town. Within easy walking distance."

"It's plenty big enough to have meeting rooms too," Mamie suggested.

"Classrooms," Christine corrected. "Richard would be so distressed to know that immigrant children are being denied access to the town school."

"The Richard Boyd Memorial Library," Victoria intoned. "What a perfect memorial to Richard! A living, growing institution that can serve the needs of the whole county."

Theo jumped to her feet. "Well, let's quit talking about it and get started! What do we do first?"

"Go look it over," Victoria answered. "Clean it up. Probably needs some repairs too."

"What about bookshelves, tables, and chairs?" Josephine asked.

"More important, what about books? We need a plan," Mamie declared.

"This is all going to cost a pretty penny," Josephine warned. "How are we going to fund this dream?"

"This is not a dream!" Mamie protested. "It's a necessity. We need some wealthy donors."

"No," Sarah objected as she stood. "I mean, we do need wealthy donors, but we also need to involve *everyone* in the community, even those with the least money."

"Especially those with the least money," Christine said. "I want everyone to feel welcome, and if they've participated in the project, they will be more likely to use it."

"Even the immigrants?" Theo demanded. "If they can't afford to pay the school tax, how can they donate to the library?"

"There's more than one way to donate," Sarah said. "They can give their time. You just said the building needs cleaning and repairing. We need bookshelves, tables, and benches built."

"Sarah's right," Lavinia agreed. "We must give everyone a way to feel pride in our project."

"I don't know ..." Josephine shook her head. "Half the immigrants won't even let their children come to school. They just keep them in the fields and—"

"We have to stop this generalizing about the immigrants," Victoria insisted. "There's wide variety in that community. For heaven's sake, you make it sound like they all came from the same small town in Bohemia. Well, they didn't! They're from Poland and Germany and—"

"Okay, we get the point," Theo cut her off. "But do they all want their children educated?"

"Of course they do!" Sarah blurted out as her temper flashed. "How can you ask such a ridiculous question? The immigrant families risked their very lives to get here. They left behind everything they owned and everything familiar to give their families a better life. All of them want their sons educated. Some also want their daughters educated. I'm sure they'll want to help create a library with classrooms."

"Sarah is right," Christine quietly insisted. "Those of us who are comfortably situated in Riverford cannot even imagine what these newcomers have endured to get here. They have laid their very lives on the line to provide their children with better futures. We should be ashamed that we have dallied so long instead of helping them."

The ladies fell silent, and Sarah watched as each face turned introspective, as each woman seemed to be examining her conscience.

"It's time to get to work!" Theo suddenly proclaimed. "We do no one any good regretting the past."

"Theo is right," Mamie agreed. "Perhaps we needed the school board's outrageous decision to jerk us out of our complacency and boot us into action."

"Let's get on with it!" Josephine insisted as she stood and looked around at the ladies. "Now, who's going to be in charge of what? We need some committees."

"Obviously Sarah will head the committee recruiting labor from the immigrants," Theo dictated. "Victoria will head the committee for the benefit concert."

"Father and I will inspect the house and ascertain what repairs and cleaning need to be made," Christine offered.

"But where are we going to hold the benefit concert?" Mamie asked. "We need the biggest possible venue, and Riverford has no hall."

"I'm sure Hayden would let us use the tearoom at the store," Victoria offered.

"No." Sarah raised her voice, and they all turned in surprise to stare at her. "Let's use the Richard Boyd Memorial Library building. Let's make the concert the first of many public cultural events to be held there."

"What a wonderful idea!" Christine exclaimed. "We will set a precedent from the very beginning. The library will be dedicated to the cultural and educational enhancement of our entire county!"

"But is the house large enough for such an event, Christine?" Mamie asked.

"Of course it is!" Theo declared. "Why, I remember attending dances there. The Boyds simply slid back all the pocket doors and turned the whole first floor into a ballroom."

"Well, that settles that." Josephine clapped her hands together. "Now, when are we going to have this event, Victoria?"

"The sooner the better." Victoria pulled Antonio's letter from her pocket and raised it in the air. "Antonio arrives December fourteenth. How about Saturday, December seventeenth?"

"A week before Christmas. Oh, I like that idea!" Mamie exclaimed.

"You would." Theo's voice was sarcastic. "You always were a romantic."

"So were you … once," Mamie retorted.

Theo's face colored. "Best leave that bit of history forgotten." She turned to Victoria. "I say yes to the seventeenth. All in favor?"

Every hand sailed up.

"Settled!" Theo declared. "Now where do we start?"

"By examining the house, I think," Christine suggested. "We need an inventory of what needs to be done."

"Then I can ask for help from the immigrant men and women," Sarah said.

"And I'll commandeer the supportive townsfolk into action," Josephine added.

"That won't take long!" Theo's tone was sarcastic.

"Everyone who is willing to help must be given a part to play," Christine insisted. "Our goal is to bring the whole community together—at least all those who will join us."

"Someone needs to apply pressure on Mr. Bellows to gain his support in the paper," Lavinia said.

Every lady present turned her eyes on Theo.

"Oh, all right!" she responded. "I love a good fight, and I've got a baseball bat in the attic I can use on him."

The ladies began to laugh at Theo, but the sound was drowned out by a violent gust of wind that threw sleet against the roof of the front porch.

"We're in for it now," Josephine exclaimed. "We better get home while we can."

"I'll have Davy bring the carriage around to the front gate." Christine hurried to the drawing room door and slid it open. "You ladies start bundling up."

"Tell Reverend Neville he's not likely to see us in church in the morning, Lavinia," Mamie said.

"Speak for yourself!" Theo insisted. "I'm not afraid of a little Texas norther."

Sarah glanced at Victoria, who grinned back at her as the ladies rushed out of the room, bickering with good nature.

CHAPTER THIRTY-FIVE

When Nancy entered the drawing room with a fresh pot of hot tea, Christine invited the remaining ladies to take a seat around the fire while she poured. Unable to sit still, Sarah wandered to the front window of Christine's parlor and watched the ladies navigate the icy walk on their way to the waiting carriage. Theo, her head held high in a defiant pose, trooped toward the front gate, occasionally turning around, scowling at Josephine and Mamie and imperiously beckoning them forward. Sarah sympathized with Theo's obvious frustration. Now that the Literary Society had made a plan, she didn't want to drink tea. She wanted to take action.

"We have less time than I thought if we're going to hold the benefit in the old Boyd house," Sarah heard Victoria comment.

"We should go inspect the house this afternoon," Christine agreed. "But Father has a cold and this weather—" She stopped, cleared her throat, and changed to a lighter, teasing tone. "What a pity Lee is not available to help us."

"Oh, but he is!" Sarah whirled around as she spoke. "He's coming over this afternoon."

"Is he?" Christine feigned surprise as she glanced at Lavinia and winked. "What a happy coincidence. Of course, this weather will certainly discourage him from—"

"Oh no! He wouldn't mind the weather." Sarah's excitement grew. "We could go inspect the house this very afternoon. After all, there's no time to waste."

Victoria laughed. "And houses should always be inspected in sleet storms."

"Why, of course they should, Victoria." Christine's face was covered with a mock grave expression. "What better time to discover if the roof leaks."

Sarah tapped her foot with impatience as her sharp tone cut the air. "This is no laughing matter! I know you're just trying to give us time to be alone, but—" She plopped her fists on her waist. "Don't you understand? The immigrant children are only going to be allowed *one more week* of education. After that, they'll be turned away at the school door unless they can hand five dollars to Miss Grimm!"

"It's regrettable, of course," Victoria conceded. "But how can we make things happen any faster? The children will just have to make up the lost work—"

"When?" Sarah demanded. "In the spring? When they're forced back onto the land from dawn to dusk? These winter months are their only chance for education."

"But, Sarah," Christine intervened. "Even if we had the library classrooms ready in a week, we wouldn't have teachers."

"That's not true." Lavinia's voice was quiet but firm. "I may not be as trained as Sarah is, but I can certainly teach English and arithmetic."

The room grew so quiet Sarah could hear the coal hissing in the fireplace as the sleet hit it. Her heartbeat increased, her lips quivered; something told her they were on the verge of a huge leap forward.

"So can I." Christine's voice was thoughtful. "And so can Theo."

"And Mamie and Josephine," Lavinia added.

Once again, the human voices ceased, but an undeniable excitement, mirrored by the steadily strengthening wind outside, was growing in the room.

Sarah glanced from face to face, certain they were all thinking the same thing. "But where can we hold classes?" She barely breathed the question into the silence of intense thought.

"At St. Paul's!" Sarah's nerves jerked when Lavinia sprang from her chair. "I'm going home to speak to John right this minute."

"But what will the bishop say?" Victoria asked.

"I ... I don't know," Lavinia conceded. "But somehow John will handle him. I know he will!"

"He could at least buy us some time." Christine eagerly rose to her feet.

Sarah blinked back unaccountable tears. "Every day counts when we have so little time with the children before they have to return to the fields."

"We're going to make this work!" Victoria declared. "It may initially be pieced together from scraps like a quilt, but—"

"A quilt is just as warm as an elegantly knitted blanket." Christine stood as she joined them. "After all, we only need a month or two."

"And then we'll have a permanent library with classrooms," Sarah concluded. "I'm going to find Lee right this minute!" She hurried toward the door.

"Wait a minute, Sarah!" Christine called after her. "You'll need a key." She hurried to her writing table. "Here!" She held up a large iron key. "This opens the front door to Boyd House."

Sarah took the key and held it in the air. "To free classes for anyone, for everyone!" she exclaimed.

"To the Richard Boyd Memorial Library," Victoria added.

CHAPTER THIRTY-SIX

"What a fine old house," Sarah declared as Lee encouraged the horse up the pocked driveway toward the porch of the old Boyd homestead.

"I'm stopping here at the end of the porch for the moment," Lee said as he pulled back on the reins. "Wait a second, and I'll come help you down."

"Oh, I can just jump down." Sarah stuck her head out from under the buggy roof and felt the sleet hit her cheeks. "You'll get wet enough getting back to the house after you find a place for the horse." Before he could protest, her feet hit the ground, and holding her basket tight, she dashed under the porch roof.

"I'll be right back," Lee called out as he slapped the reins. "Go on inside."

As the freezing wind blew up her skirt and iced her legs, she raced down the porch and stuck the heavy iron key into the old-fashioned keyhole, but she couldn't make herself turn it. She was being silly, she told herself, but still … This was going to be a memorable moment, and she wanted to share it with the love of her life. She huddled in the doorway to avoid the wind and waited.

"You should be inside!" Lee's words were all but carried away by a northerly gust as he jumped up onto the porch, carrying a coal bucket in one hand, a bundle of kindling under his arm, and a kerosene lamp in the other hand.

"Coal? You thought of coal?" Sarah nearly squealed with delight.

"Can you manage the door?"

"I think so." Sarah struggled to turn the key with her clumsy mittened fingers. Finally, the lock clicked, and she pushed the creaking door open. "Oh, I've always wondered about this old place." She hurried into the main hall. "Have you ever seen the inside?"

"Not until this minute." Lee leaned against the door to shut it behind him. "Wow!" He walked to the center of the extra-wide central hall and turned in a circle under the high ceiling. "This hall is huge. I've never seen one this big."

"Christine said the Boyd family used this hall to entertain guests; they even held balls in this room."

"I can see why. With doors at both ends, it would certainly be the coolest place in the summer."

"And she said these big doors into the parlor slide back." Sarah turned to her left and pushed against a door twice as tall as she. When she gained entrance to the front parlor, a thrill of excitement coursed through her, and she clapped her hands. "Oh, look at these large windows, Lee! On a sunny day, this will be the most welcoming room. Can't you just see the walls lined with bookcases and some writing tables and chairs scattered around?" She grinned up at him as she pointed to the fireplace. "And comfortable couches on each side of a warm fire in the winter months. What a wonderful place to fall in love with books!"

"What a wonderful place to build a fire." Lee lugged the heavy coal bucket to the fireplace and knelt down. "I just hope the chimney isn't full of birds' nests." He lit a match, held it to a piece of paper, and threw both on the grate.

Sarah shivered as she watched the paper blaze and the smoke curl upwards. "This visit will be considerably shortened if we can't start a fire."

"Seems to be drawing all right. Let's risk it." Lee stacked crumpled paper and kindling, then topped it with coal and lit it. "Now we just need some time." He pulled her into his arms. "You're shaking like a leaf in a wind. I better warm you up." He leaned down and kissed her gently, his lips lingering on hers.

"Well, that certainly works!" Sarah giggled as she pulled away.

"If you feel the slightest chill again, I'd be happy to oblige."

"Oh, I wouldn't want to put you to too much trouble, Mr. Logan. Besides, I brought a filled kettle, some tea, and some cups."

He grimaced. "No coffee?"

"A little refinement won't hurt you a bit, Mr. Logan. After all, we're standing in the Richard Boyd Memorial Library."

Lee glanced around. "Which we're sharing with some mice, I'd say, and plenty of spiders." He grinned at her as he shrugged. "No doubt they're tea-drinking mice, though."

"Well, they aren't staying in the new library, no matter what they drink! Mice eat books!"

Lee took her mittened hand. "May I stay in your library, Miss Novak? I never eat books. My taste tends more to the earlobes of female educators." He pulled her to his chest and nibbled on her ear.

"I must warn Miss Grimm at once!"

Lee released her with a groan. "I'm not that hungry!"

"Let's explore this place while this water heats up." She put the kettle on, then tugged him forward. "How many rooms do you think it has?"

"Most likely four on each floor. That's the way they built houses in the early part of the century."

"When do you think this was built?" Sarah asked as she moved back into the hall and crossed to the other side.

"Early 1840s most likely. I think Richard Boyd grew up here."

"It's perfectly grand!" Sarah exclaimed as she entered the square room across the hall. "Look. Another fireplace."

"This was most likely a second parlor, a less formal one for the family."

"I thought it would be the dining room."

"That's one of the back rooms, I'm sure. Remember, the kitchen would be entirely detached behind the house. The other back room was most likely used as an office. Richard's father probably ran his estates from there."

"I want to see all the rooms as quickly as possible. That storm is making it dark in here."

"You do realize there's no electricity, don't you? Not even gas lighting."

A bit of worry flickered through Sarah's mind. "That will be expensive, but we must have electric lights."

"Right." He walked around, checking the windows. "Everything looks sound, though. Needs cleaning and a coat of paint." He looked back at her. "You warm enough?"

"Sure!" Her brave word was negated by her chattering teeth.

Lee didn't smile. "Let's go see if that water is boiling. I've got something I want to talk to you about."

Sarah studied his serious eyes and guessed that their intensity revealed a worry he was carrying. "Sure." She hurried back to the coal-warmed fireplace, knelt, and added tea to the kettle. When she sat back on her heels, she looked up at him. "Something's wrong, isn't it?"

Lee nodded as he joined her on the floor.

"What?" she asked but did not wait for his answer. "You think we're heading into a storm worse than the one outside, a storm of protest from the town, don't you?"

"Yes, I do. I hope I'm wrong, but the malice of Mrs. Bellows and her cohorts seems unlimited. People with such deeply planted bigotry don't change. The road ahead will be rocky, but I want you to know I'll be by your side through every inch of it."

Sarah glanced around the bare room, a haven for a couple who had once fought the dangers of early Texas and had produced not only a family but also a town. Her eyes fell on the glowing fire, the kerosene lantern—all the care Lee had taken for her sake. What a gift God had brought to her! A radiant smile surfaced from deep in her heart as she touched Lee's chest and looked deeply into his eyes. "Actually, you are walking ahead of me, aren't you?"

"That's my plan. I won't be able to predict every obstacle in your path, but I plan to clear a way for your dreams because they are *our* dreams."

"We are a new generation of pioneers ..."

"Yes. This land has been cleared, planted, and harvested on the backs of countless poor people. The land and the people have been made to serve the owners. Now it's time for the owners to clear upward paths for those seeking a better life."

Sarah turned toward the warmth of the fire that Lee had provided and gazed at the transformation of hard black coal into life-sustaining heat. "Do you remember when we met, Lee?"

"Indeed I do! I couldn't decide whether I was more impressed by your beauty or your strength, but you drew me to you like the proverbial moth to the candle flame."

Sarah laughed softly. "I remember the morning you showed up at Hodges House and caught me waltzing around the hall with Victoria. I was so embarrassed!"

"If the historians had been properly on alert that day, they would have recorded the fact that you and Victoria Hodges were dancing together. It was a symbolic moment. No … more than a symbol. It was the beginning of a movement."

"I think that movement began the minute she first stepped off the train in Riverford. She would have changed Riverford whether I existed or not."

"But you did exist, and because you did, more than the arts are being brought to this old town. Opportunity, fresh starts for downtrodden people, elevation of women … And who knows what else the twentieth century will bring."

When he fell silent, Sarah realized that the clatter of ice on the tin roof had stopped. "It isn't sleeting," she said as she rose, hurried to the front window, and peered down into the front garden. "Oh, Lee! How beautiful."

He came to her and wrapped his arms around her shoulders as he looked over the top of her head at the snow gently drifting down. "Well, this day will go down in history for sure. It never snows in Riverford. Plenty of ice storms, but never snow like this."

"It's absolutely magical! Look how it's transforming all the rough edges of the dead grass." She sighed. "Standing here watching this silent transformation is such a happy reprieve from the ugliness of the past weeks. I wonder how many times Richard's mother and father stood here."

"Quite a few, I'm sure. In good times and bad."

"With smiles and tears until their era was over, their work was done. I feel their presence, and it's such a comfort, such an encouragement." She turned to face Lee and pulled his head down until their lips met.

When he finally released her, he stepped back and inhaled deeply. "This is the last thing I want to say to you, Sarah ..."

"What?" Sarah's heart began to pound with alarm. "What's wrong?"

"I'm going to insist we postpone the wedding."

"No! I promised you—"

"I know." He held up his hand to stop her words. "But you can't do all that lies ahead and also get married. I won't let you kill yourself, Sarah. I love you too much."

"But marriage to you is just as important to me as creating this library and setting up classes for the immigrants and continuing—"

He gently placed his fingers over her lips to silence her. "Just listen to what you're saying. That's a lot to accomplish, and I don't think it's going to be an easy road, by any means. I won't let you break your health. Besides, I'm selfish. When we do get married, I want more of you than you can give during the school year."

"But we're going to do all those things together."

"We certainly are, and then we're going to get married the minute the school year ends in June."

"But, Lee ..."

He pulled her to him and stopped her objections with a prolonged kiss.

CHAPTER THIRTY-SEVEN

Sarah fought back stinging tears as the immigrant children gathered around her on their last day of classes at the Riverford School. The girls threw their arms around her and sobbed as the boys stood a few feet back, biting their lips, their faces hardened. Only one thing kept Sarah from collapsing under the weight of the children's sorrow—the small cluster of town girls who had stayed behind when the other town students had gaily run out the door. Those few well-dressed girls, who wept openly with their immigrant classmates, gave Sarah hope. The majority of Riverford adults had denied the poor children an education without a second thought, but these girls were genuinely grieved. *They are the future!* Sarah forced herself to repeat the words silently as she hugged each child.

Through the classroom windows, Sarah saw the dark, low-hanging clouds that had gathered all afternoon, and she worried about the children's long treks home to their sharecropper shacks. "You must start home now," she murmured, but no one moved. Instead, the girls encircled her waist with their thin arms, and the boys rigidly folded their arms as they clenched their jaws.

Alison MacKenna took tiny Michalina's hand. "Come, Michalina, I'll walk with you a way."

"I wish I could stay with you, Alison." The little girl's plaintive tone saddened Sarah further. "You get to live in town. No one can take school away from you."

"Reverend Wright is a good man to take Alban and me into his home," Alison agreed.

"Why don't the town people want us?" Little Nadia Burzynski cried.

Sarah's throat tightened; she could not force a single sound out of it.

"They are stupid!" Sarah whipped her head around at the sound of the familiar voice. Miss Mamie and Miss Theodora bustled in. Between the two of them, they were lugging a large wooden crate filled with canvas bags.

"Come give us a hand, boys!" Theodora ordered. "No time to waste; those clouds outside are about to drop sleet."

"What's in the bags?" Ludvik Svoboda demanded as the children deserted Sarah and gathered around the older ladies.

"Hold your horses, young man! You'll find out soon enough." Miss Mamie thrust her side of the crate into his hand. "But if you help me with this thing, maybe … just maybe you'll get one of these bags."

The children giggled and made way for Ludvik and Piotr to carry the crate to Sarah's desk.

"Are they presents, Miss Novak?" Nadia's face shone with delight.

"I don't know. I'm just as surprised by this visit as you are," Sarah insisted as she shot questioning looks at the ladies.

"You're not the only one in this town who can take action to solve a crisis," Theodora retorted as she pulled a canvas bag from the crate. "Here!" She shoved it into Piotr's hands. "Open it, and let's put all this questioning to rest and get you kids on your way home."

His eyes glistening with anticipation, Piotr eagerly untied the drawstring, opened the bag, and withdrew a stack of books bound by a leather book strap. "*Fantatycnzy!*"

"What's that mean?" Billy Gerhard demanded.

"Fantastic!"

"Do we all get one?" Betsy Benson tried to reach into the box.

"Only the library school students are privileged to have these books," Theo insisted as she blocked the girl's hand.

"But those are *new* books!" Betsy protested.

"Of course they are." Theo snorted. "What do you expect? Library students are *special* students. They get to attend classes in the new library."

"But we only get to go to school one day a week." Piotr's voice was sad.

"I wish I only had to go one day a week," Stephanie quipped in an attempt to make a joke, but the immigrant children didn't laugh.

"We won't have Miss Novak as our teacher." Nadia's eyes saddened.

"That's not true," Sarah answered. "I'll be teaching at the library school every Saturday."

The children broke into excited applause.

"Enough of that!" Miss Mamie insisted. "Let's get these bags dispensed and get you children on the way home before the weather worsens. Mr. Hodges sent a delivery wagon from his store to carry you children out to the farms, and it's waiting outside."

"You mean we don't have to walk?" Ludvig demanded.

"Not today."

"We don't have to walk!" The children cheered as they jumped up and down.

"And remember, I'll see you next Saturday, November ninth at St. Paul's Church at eight o'clock." Sarah raised her voice to be heard over the children's noise. "Don't be late!"

Shy, tiny Michalina raised her hand.

"What is it, darling?" Sarah asked as she clasped the little girl's hand and squeezed it.

"No library?" Tears welled up in her dark eyes. "The town peoples, they say we can no use library?"

Sarah pulled the child to her side and held her close as she spoke in her most confident voice. "Now, I want every one of you to listen carefully. We are meeting at St. Paul's Church for our Saturday classes because your fathers will be working on the library on Saturdays. I promise you that we'll have a full day of classes, and I'll do everything possible to teach you as much as the town children learned the week before."

"In one day?" Piotr asked. "How is this possible? Surely we will fall behind."

Sarah surveyed the children. "Can you keep a secret?"

"*Ano! Tak!* Yes!" In three different languages, the children agreed as they gathered around Sarah. "What's the secret?"

"We're going to have classes for you at St. Paul's Church three days a week."

The children exchanged puzzled glances. "But you will be here teaching the town kids," Ludvig said.

"On Tuesdays and Thursdays, Miss Theo and Miss Mamie are going to teach you. They'll teach you the same lessons I'm teaching here at the school."

"And you better behave yourselves!" Theo's wide grin discounted her threatening voice.

The children broke into laughter and clapped their hands.

"You're all very smart, and most important, you're very determined to learn. You'll keep up with the town children just fine," Sarah assured them.

"Aye, you will." Alison moved forward. "And I'll come and help you learn on Saturdays. May I, Miss Novak?" Alison asked. "I want so much to help. Please let me. After all, I know English, and my father taught me to read."

"You'll be a wonderful help, Alison. Of course you can come."

Alison turned to the other children. "And I will help anybody who wants help on other days too."

"See!" Sarah adopted her most confident tone. "Not a single one of you will fall behind. There are plenty of people just waiting to help you learn."

"But the town people don't want us to learn." Ludvig's voice was angry.

"Aye, some are naysayers for sure," Alison answered before Sarah could open her lips. "But some extend a helping hand. We must *choose* to ignore the naysayers!"

"Alison is right," Sarah insisted. "All your lives, you'll have to make this very choice. There'll always be people who support you and people who don't. Focus on the positive people; they are God's gift to you."

"Hurry, children!" Theo called. "Each one of you take one of these bags of books and run for the wagons. The sleet is starting to fall."

The children swirled around, claiming book bags and shabby coats and shawls from the coatroom hooks before rushing out the door. "*Šťastný víkend!*" the Czech children called. "*Szczęśliwy weekend!*" the Polish children answered.

"What are they saying?" Mamie demanded.

"Happy weekend!" Billy Gerhardt answered as he grinned at the ladies. "If you stay around here, you'll learn all kinds of things."

"All kinds of good things," Alison added.

"Let's go home!" Betsy shouted to the remaining students, and minutes later Sarah found herself alone.

She hurried to the window to watch the immigrant children clamor aboard the wagon. Her heart melted at the sight of them hugging their precious books, carefully covering them with their meager outer clothing, and she remembered the day that Victoria sent her home with a copy of *Little Women*. How precious those bound pages had been to her! How thrilling the possibility of education! Sarah swallowed the lump in her throat, took a deep breath to steady herself, and quietly called out, "See you next Saturday, children!"

"They won't let you get away with this, Miss Novak." Sarah jumped at the sound of Agnes Grimm's voice behind her. "I wish they would. Truly, I do wish you could help those children, but you can't. Not if you want to keep your job."

Sarah turned and looked into the exhausted face of the temporary principal. "My job is to teach, especially to teach the poorest children."

"That is not what the school board employed you to do."

"The school board has no say over what I do on Saturdays."

"You'll find they can—and will—control every aspect of your life. They will fire you if you continue down this path. I don't want to lose you, Miss Novak. I implore you, leave the education of the immigrant children to the do-gooders of Riverford—to those bored women who want to use these shabby children to give meaning to their lives."

"No child is shabby to God, Miss Grimm. No child is less than another child or more than another child in His eyes."

Agnes Grimm laughed quietly. "How naive you are, Miss Novak!" She took a step closer and leaned toward Sarah's face. "Do you actually believe that it's God who employs you here? Don't be a fool. This is a *school*. Men control this school; they always will."

"But they don't control me."

Miss Grimm's exasperated sigh echoed in the empty classroom. "In the end, I suppose it matters little to me. They'll bring in a man to take my principal's position before next fall. You'll see …" She squinted as she peered into Sarah's eyes. "No, you won't. I see that stubbornness in your eyes. It will end your teaching career. Pity!" She turned and walked away, her feet shuffling.

Sarah clenched her fists as she turned back to the window and watched the wagon carrying the immigrant children disappear around a corner. *Always … always some bitter person comes to steal my hope.* She absentmindedly moved among the students' desks, aligning them as she went, until her eyes alighted on Alison's desk. *Choose to ignore the naysayers.* Angry with herself, Sarah wiped hot tears off her cheeks. "Fine thing, Sarah Novak, when your newest student has to instruct you! When are you going to learn?"

"That you cannot live without me?" Lee asked from the doorway. "Soon, I hope. But while I impatiently wait for you to come to your senses, I plan to take you home so you won't be soaked to the skin."

Sarah rushed to his side and hugged him briefly before she pulled herself back into her proper teacher pose.

"The students are all gone," Lee explained in a loud stage whisper. "We're safe. We could even do something really radical like kiss."

"Not with Miss Grimm wandering the halls." Sarah turned away, hurried to the front blackboard, and began to erase it.

Lee followed her, stopped the eraser from swiping the board, and whispered in her ear. "There'll be no escaping me once I get you in my buggy."

Sarah grinned. "I certainly hope not. Now kindly unhand me, Mr. Logan. I must clean up this classroom before I leave."

CHAPTER THIRTY-EIGHT

Christine stood in the sunshine, which illuminated the bay window of the music room, and looked out at the front garden, where the last of the purple asters and canary-yellow marigolds ran riot in the flowerbeds and spilled over onto the lawn. She marveled that they had survived the recent ice storm. "That's Texas weather," she murmured as she noticed that the browning grass was scattered with large red leaves, the final gift of the old oaks before they slept for the winter. "How beautiful the colors are together!"

She watched her servant, Davy, walk into the garden, rake in hand. Rather than setting to work as he had been instructed, he peered up at the oaks, which still sent an occasional leaf drifting down in a spiral, and shook his head. He planted the rake in the grass, propped himself against it, and glared at the leaf-spattered grass as if he thought he could scold the leaves into piles.

"Good morning, Davy!" Christine's attention was drawn to the front gate where Victoria and Sarah were entering the garden. Love for those two extraordinary women warmed her heart and lifted her lips into a smile. How different they were, and yet, how alike. Victoria strode up the brick walk, her unruly red hair flashing, her tiny brown-booted feet gleefully kicking at the leaves. She sent them swirling as her ankle-length camel-colored coat flapped like low-flying wings. Sarah, on the other hand, had combed her chestnut brown hair into a neat high-perched bun and buttoned and belted her black coat into submission. With each step she avoided the leaves, pulling the hem of her coat aside, protecting the precious garment she had worked so hard to attain.

"Looks like the General has put you to work, Davy," Christine heard Victoria call out.

Davy whipped his battered felt hat off his head and bobbed his upper body in the semblance of a clumsy bow. "Yes'm, that he has. I ain't never gonna corral these here leaves."

Victoria laughed as she kicked a pile toward him. "Oh, but think of the joy of having an excuse to be outside on such a glorious day."

"Mighty cold, Miz Hodges. I's just thinkin' of the joy of settin' by the kitchen stove with a cup of coffee."

"When your work is done," Sarah counseled.

Victoria gestured toward Sarah. "Always the schoolteacher. You better behave, Davy, or you'll have to stay after school and clean the blackboards."

"I guess that be easier than rakin' these leaves. Course I don't know 'cause I ain't never been to no school."

"No." Victoria's face lost its jovial glow as her eyes narrowed and her voice turned dull. "You never had that chance."

Christine watched Sarah pinch her lips together and stare angrily at the ground. Her own lighthearted mood descended as she clenched her teeth. "Today we start changing that injustice." Her words were whispered but fierce.

"What injustice?" Nancy asked from the door. "Is that Davy doin' what the General told him? If he ain't, I's goin' out there and give him a piece of my mind," she threatened as she entered the room. "This gonna be an important day, and he ain't gonna—"

"That will do, Nancy." Christine chose to cut off Nancy's critical comment. "Davy is just getting started." She turned to the servant. "Mrs. Hodges and Miss Novak are coming up the walk. Please see them in, and then bring in the tea tray."

"I's used the Royal Wor ... wor."

"Worcester," Christine finished the word.

"Yes'm. That be the china I's used. I figure this be an important day."

"Indeed it is. Now, please go welcome our guests." Christine watched her leave, then glanced around the room as she waited. The sunlight played across the aqua and rose of the Persian rug before climbing the mahogany legs of the grand piano and dancing on the ivory keyboard. She smoothed the skirt of her new dove-gray wool dress and straightened its white lace jabot. Once again, she wondered if she had given up the starkness of black widow's weeds too soon.

"You look wonderful!" Victoria answered Christine's worrisome question the minute she entered the room. "Sarah, look how beautiful Christine's new dress is." Her face lighted by a bright smile, she crossed the room and kissed Christine's cheek. "Dear, dear friend. You have turned a significant corner indeed."

"Let us hope I have not done so too soon for the sensibilities of Riverford. After all, it has only been six months."

"You'll undoubtedly get a mixed review from Riverford," Sarah assured.

Christine nodded. "What will be, will be, but come—both of you—and see the view of the garden from the window."

"Oh my!" Victoria exclaimed as she approached the window. "Such colors! They make me want to abandon our work and race home to my paints." She turned to Christine. "You shouldn't have shown me this view if you expect me to think of electrical lights and bookcases."

"It occurred to me that these colors are emblematic of our community." Christine leaned across the window seat as she pointed. "They're each unique; they each have power, but together they inspire an explosion of imagination." She turned back to her guests, her heart filled with enthusiasm. "Just think what we could accomplish if we could harness all that diversity to build with."

"Mercy, Christine!" Victoria laughed. "You're beginning to see the world through a painter's eyes. Has Juli been teaching you?"

Christine laughed, but she noticed that Sarah's expression was quite serious.

"Those are the bright colors of the native costumes of the new immigrants," Sarah remarked.

"And like the immigrants, those flowers have survived quite a storm," Victoria said as she turned back and walked toward a round table. "Let's get to work. We can't waste what those new cultures have brought to Riverford. We're here to create a way to include them. Sarah, spread your lists out here."

As the three of them settled in chairs, Sarah began to explain, "I've created a specific list of improvements for each room. I'm only dealing with the downstairs, of course. As you know, we've got four big, square rooms plus the main entrance hall that runs from the front door to the back wall."

"What's the most pressing need?" Victoria asked.

"If we're agreed that we must prepare the classrooms first ..."

"We are," Christine answered. "The sharecroppers' children must have a place to learn. That is the first priority."

Sarah nodded. "You should have seen the immigrant children's sadness yesterday as they finished their last day of classes at the Riverford School. Thank heaven I could promise them the Saturday classes at St. Paul's. John Neville says we may use the church as long as necessary."

"At great risk to himself," Victoria added. "Hayden says the bishop won't support the idea if many of the parishioners object, and we can be sure that some will."

"So we have to work harder to ready the library classrooms," Christine said. "What exactly do we need—"

"Excuse me, Miz Christine, but they's two ladies here to see you." Nancy stood just inside the door wringing her hands, her eyes wide with apprehension. "I told them you's in a meeting, but they—"

"Kindly move out of the way!" Edith Bellows' unmistakable voice sliced through the air and made Sarah spring from her chair. "I declare, you'd think I was a stranger in this house."

"Such a stupid girl!" Another voice joined in. "Why does Christine keep such stupid help?"

"Oh, they're all stupid!" Mrs. Bellows pushed Nancy aside. "Christine, you really must speak to—" Mrs. Bellows fell silent at the sight of Victoria and Sarah.

"Please come in." Christine corralled her anger at the women's remarks and hastened forward to greet the intruders. "What a delightful surprise!"

"Delightful is not the word I'd use," Mrs. Sharp muttered as she locked eyes with Victoria, who remained seated. "I'm not inclined to share the room with this ... with this—"

"Do bring in the tea tray, Nancy." Christine cut her remark off. "Right now!"

"You mean they's stayin'?" Nancy drew her head back in doubt.

"Well, of course they are!" Christine took Edith by the arm. "You two simply could not have come at a better time, Edith. We desperately need your input."

"On what?" Fanny Sharp demanded. "We only came by to thank you for donating the old Boyd house for a town library."

"How very thoughtful of you." Christine smiled sweetly at Mrs. Sharp. "And now we shall have the benefit of your wisdom as we plan how to make the library a reality."

Fanny Sharp looked over Christine's shoulder at Sarah. "You seem to have already chosen your counselors, and rather unwisely I'd say."

Christine forced herself to ignore the slight to Sarah. "Sarah has done the onsite inspection for us and has brought us some very useful lists."

Mrs. Bellows shrugged her shoulders. "I suppose she could at least do that sort of thing satisfactorily."

"Indeed she could." Christine felt that her face would crack from smiling so brightly. "After all, we must certainly remember that it was you, dear Edith, who first recognized Sarah's abilities."

"I did?"

"Why yes! You gave Sarah her first job."

Mrs. Bellows lifted her chin. "I know a great deal more than *some* people give me credit for."

"Won't you take my chair, Mrs. Bellows?" Sarah pulled the chair away from the table so the corpulent woman could sit in it.

Victoria rose slowly. "And do, please, take my chair, Fanny. I believe it's the most comfortable one."

Without directly acknowledging Victoria, Mrs. Sharp strode across the room, sat on the edge of the chair, and folded her hands primly. "We won't be here long," she announced. "Just long enough to thank Christine." She pulled her lorgnette from its brooch, balanced it on her nose, and examined Christine from head to foot. "Is that dress *gray*?"

"Such a beautiful shade on Christine, don't you think?" Victoria asked as she moved another chair close to the table and sat down. "It certainly emphasizes the blue of her eyes."

"What it emphasizes I dare not say!" Mrs. Sharp tossed her head. "Certainly not propriety."

"Ah, here comes our tea," Christine hastened to announce as Nancy and Josie carried trays into the room. "Just put the trays down here, Nancy, and I shall pour. How fortunate we can all be together to begin this enterprise." She looked up at Sarah. "Perhaps you would like to pull a chair up, Sarah?"

Fanny Sharp stiffened, and Edith Bellows cleared her throat.

"I believe I'll stand for the moment." Sarah rattled the lists and seemed to be rearranging the pages. "Shall I begin by reading the needs in the front parlor?"

Christine leaned solicitously toward Mrs. Bellows as she handed her a cup of tea. "What do you recommend, Edith? The front parlor or the main hall?"

"The main hall, of course!" Mrs. Bellows snatched a plate and helped herself to several pastries. "After all, you have to go through the main hall first. Don't you agree, Fanny?"

Fanny glared up at Sarah as she accepted a cup of tea. "Any *thinking* person would certainly begin with the main hall."

"Of course," Sarah agreed more meekly than her blazing eyes suggested she felt. "In addition to cleaning the wainscoting and papering the walls, there are loose boards in the floor—"

"I's sorry to interrupt again, Miz Christine." Nancy's worried voice preceded her sudden appearance at the door. "But they's a whole family done come to see you."

"Who is it, Nancy?"

The servant took a further step into the room. "Some name I can't pronounce, Miz Christine." She added in a loud whisper, "They's strange lookin' foreigners."

"Nancy!" The teapot rattled the spoons on the silver tray as Christine indignantly lowered it. "What a thing to say!" She sprang up. "Show our guests in at once."

"Well … I will if you say so, but …" Nancy glanced at Edith Bellows and rolled her eyes. "They's gonna be trouble for sure."

CHAPTER THIRTY-NINE

"Mercy!" Edith Bellows declared as she clattered her teacup into its saucer. "Stop and think, Christine. You can't have such people in your house. Send Sarah out there to get rid of them. She's one of them; she knows how to deal with the likes of them."

"Give those people an inch, and they'll steal a mile." Fanny Sharp sneered. "The very idea of them invading—"

"Silence!" For the first time in anyone's memory, Christine raised her voice.

"Why, Christine! You are quite overwrought." As Edith reached across the table to pat Christine's arm, she rocked the tiered cake plate and sent pastries flying. "Oh! Just look what those people have made me do."

Hot indignation at Edith's accusation surged through Christine, and unable to trust her words, she pressed her hand across her lips.

"Christine hasn't been herself since Richard died," Fanny Sharp sniped. "Running off to Colorado on a whim, playing the piano in public—"

"That will do!" Victoria sprang up as she glared at Fanny and Edith. "If you two are not capable of conjuring up some semblance of good manners, at least try to remember you're supposed to be Christians."

"Well, really!" Edith settled back into her chair. "I've never been so insulted. Christine, are you going to allow that outlandish artist to speak to your lifelong friends in such a way?"

Sarah stepped forward. "Perhaps it's best if I go speak to the family waiting in the hall, Christine."

"No!" Christine was startled by her vehement tone. She took a deep audible breath and lowered her voice. "Thank you, Sarah, but that is not necessary." With obvious effort, she planted a smile on her face as she straightened her spine, raised her left upturned palm to her waist, and lowered her right hand into the cradle she had created. The southern lady from Charleston had returned. "It is my custom and my honor to receive all my callers—even uninvited callers—courteously." She pierced Edith and Fanny with a sharp look before turning to Nancy. "Escort our callers in."

"Piotr!" Sarah exclaimed the instant she saw the family. "Why, this is my student, Piotr Dobrowski." She rushed forward to greet the adults with him. "And you must be his parents."

The boy's face lit up with excitement as he turned to his father. "How good this is, Papa! This is my teacher, Miss Novak." He turned back to Sarah. "Please, may I present my father, Frederyk Dobrowski? And this is my mother, Antonina Dobrowski."

Christine was delighted to see that Mr. Dobrowski bowed quite formally to Sarah as Mrs. Dobrowski spread the full skirt of her embroidery-edged dress, tilted her scarf-covered head, and curtsied.

"Welcome!" Christine exclaimed as she hurried forward with her hand extended to Mr. Dobrowski.

Confusion clouded his face as he looked at her hand; he hesitated, then gently took it and bowed low over it. Once again, Mrs. Dobrowski curtsied as her husband apologized, "I am sorry. We do not know American customs yet."

"Courtesy is always appropriate no matter how it is expressed," Christine assured him. "You are most welcome in my home."

"And who is this pretty young girl in such a charmingly embroidered vest?" Victoria asked as she hurried to Christine's side.

"May I present my sister, Izabela, madame." Piotr bowed to Victoria.

"How I would love to paint such a beauty!" Victoria smiled at the whole family. "I am Victoria Hodges."

"Mrs. Victoria Hodges." With a slight stumble over the sounds, Mr. Dobrowski repeated the name as he bowed to her, and both the Dobrowski females curtsied.

"We apologize for intrusion"—Piotr dipped his head in a salute to Christine—"but my father wishes to say important words."

"Please come and sit down," Christine encouraged as she turned to point toward the tea table.

"Oh no!" Mr. Dobrowski exclaimed, then softened his voice. "You have the guests. We wish not to disturb. Only to say thank you for giving building for classes for Piotr and Izabela."

"Thank you." Mrs. Dobrowski curtsied again. "We so happy for education for children. No classes in Poland."

Tears stung Christine's eyes as she shot a quick glance at Sarah and discovered the young teacher was beaming with happiness.

Struggling to talk in spite of the lump in her throat, Christine finally managed to say, "It gives me great joy to honor the memory of my husband."

"*Niech spoczywa w pokoju*," Mrs. Dobrowski murmured as she grabbed Christine's hand and kissed it.

"Momma says, 'May he rest in peace,'" Piotr explained. "It is a Polish blessing."

"I'm sure we don't need any Polish blessings on our dead!" Fanny Sharp announced as she stood.

"Please, Fanny." Christine motioned her to be silent. "All good wishes are welcome."

"We go now, but first we say we offer our help to make library and classrooms ready," Mr. Dobrowski said.

"Yah. We Polish women clean the building."

"And we Polish men build bookcases and tables and benches. We are good *cieśle*."

"Carpenters," Piotr interpreted.

"Tak. We fix floors or walls. We build what you need to make building ready for classes."

"What's this about classes in the new library?" Edith Bellows leaned on the table, giving the tea service a good shake, as she struggled to her feet. "I thought we'd settled this issue. The school board has ruled. Only town children may come to classes in Riverford. Everybody else has to pay a tax, and I assure you that tax has been set high enough that people like these can't afford it."

"That's exactly why several rooms of the library will be dedicated to teaching classes to all members of our community," Victoria said.

"But the school board—"

"Has no jurisdiction over a library."

"We have been deceived, Edith!" Fanny Sharp exclaimed as she sprang up from her chair. "I've never seen such perfidy! And to think that you, Christine Boyd, would stoop to such tactics."

"Christine is confused," Edith insisted. "I don't know how they've managed to do it, but it's these two"—Edith jabbed her finger at Victoria and Sarah—"who've led her astray. They're revolutionaries! They care nothing for the sanctity of Riverford's traditions and would cast us into any depth of depravity."

"*Co oznacza to słowo?*" Mr. Dobrowski's face was covered with concern.

"Please, what is this word 'depravity'?" Piotr asked.

"It's the wrong word for the circumstances," Victoria answered before Sarah could. "The proper word is enlightenment." She turned to Edith. "Our goal is simple, Edith. We recognize that our community is becoming more diversified and that our newcomers bring us great gifts of knowledge and experience. We look forward to learning from them as we teach them the English language, American history, and other subjects that will enable them to integrate into our society."

"But we don't want them here!" Fanny Sharp raised her voice. "We want Riverford to stay the way it's always been!"

"Riverford will not, cannot stay the same." Christine tried to bring the voice of reason to the conversation. "The whole nation is changing; Texas is changing. We are entering a new century."

Sarah stepped forward eagerly. "Life can be made better, easier for all by the many inventions of our age. In the near future, we will be able to erase starvation, bring better health to all, elevate through education— The possibilities are endless. Don't you want Riverford to be a part of the future?"

"Not if it means dirtying our town with foreigners!" Fanny's face turned purple with fury as she shouted. "What's next? Will you decided to educate the coloreds?"

"Yes!" Victoria's single word silenced the room.

"Not as long as I have breath left in my body!" Fanny Sharp spewed at her. She pulled her skirts close to her body and, head held at a disdainful angle, strode past the Dobrowski family and out the door.

Edith Bellows followed, pausing only long enough to say to Christine, "It pains me to say it, Christine, but since you've chosen to associate with this riffraff, you and I can no longer be friends." She shook her head gravely. "What would your sainted mother say if she could see you now?"

When Christine heard the front door slam, she turned to the Dobrowski family, who had stepped back into the shadows. "I apologize for the unspeakably discourteous behavior of Mrs. Bellows and Mrs. Sharp. Please accept my assurance that they do not represent all of Riverford."

"*Przepraszam za zhańbienie cię,*" Mr. Dobrowski murmured as he bowed.

"Father apologizes for disgracing you before your friends," Piotr exclaimed. "We will go now."

"But I am not disgraced in the least by your presence," Christine insisted. "I am delighted you are here."

Victoria rushed forward and took Mrs. Dobrowski's hand. "We welcome you." She turned to Piotr. "How do I say this in Polish?"

"Mama understands English."

"I just not speak it good." Mrs. Dobrowski gazed at the floor as she apologized.

"But you will learn," Sarah insisted. "That's why we're planning to have classrooms in the new library."

"My dear Mrs. Dobrowski, we are eager to learn from you," Victoria continued to hold the woman's hand, "to share in your rich culture."

"Indeed we are," Christine agreed. "Why, when I consider the music that the Polish people have given us, I find it includes my favorite composer, Frederick Chopin."

A smile flooded Izabela's face. "You know Chopin? Please, will you teach me?"

"Do you play the piano?" Christine asked.

The girl lowered her head and shook it.

"We had a piano in the church before the pogrom," Piotr explained. "Izabela was taking lessons."

Tears filled Christine's eyes as she turned to Sarah. "I am afraid to ask, Sarah, but what is a pogrom?"

"An attack on a group of people, often because of their religious beliefs. Government troops destroy their villages, burn their crops, and generally make it impossible for them to stay."

"So they come to America looking for freedom," Victoria added. "And we're going to see to it that they have the best opportunity to succeed here."

Unwilling to allow the Dobrowskis to see—and possibly mistake the reason for—the tears flowing down her cheeks, Christine turned toward her piano. "Victoria, please seat our guests. Sarah, ask Nancy to clear the table and bring in fresh tea and the cake she made for Sunday dinner."

She walked to the piano, seated herself, and launched into the dramatic opening chords of Chopin's "Revolutionary Prelude."

CHAPTER FORTY

"Come back inside." Sarah felt Lee pull on her heavily coated arm as he spoke. "They're coming, and standing out here in the cold staring into the dawn won't make them come any sooner. Besides, we need you to tell us if we've got the room arranged correctly."

Sarah reluctantly turned back into the large hall that served as St. Paul's reception room.

"How many students do you expect?" Reverend John Neville's simple question sent a wave of anxiety through her.

Sarah shook her head. "I don't know what to expect. I don't know how many. I don't know what ages they are or how much education they've had or even if they can understand English!"

Lavinia pulled Sarah's hands down and leaned close to her face. "You know the only thing that counts: we're supposed to be doing this. It's the fair thing to do, and we have plenty of volunteers coming."

"God will bless this endeavor." Sarah heard John's encouraging voice. "It may well be chaotic this morning as we sort things out, but we will *not* be solving this puzzle alone."

"'When you did it for the least of these ...'" Sarah's voice broke.

"'You have done it for me.'" John finished the scripture verse.

She felt Lee's strong arms surround her shoulders and his warm breath on her forehead. "We don't need perfection this morning, darling. We just need a beginning."

When a blast of cold air whirled around Sarah and she heard the door bang against the wall, she turned, expecting to see a volunteer. Instead, she saw her mother, Jana, leading in a wagonload of children of all ages, and every face was new to her. "And here is our beginning!" She clapped her hands together. "They came! In spite of the weather, they came."

"And it's barely daybreak," Lee said.

Sarah turned her eager face up to his. "This is going to work! I've never seen a single one of them before. Oh, Lee, they really do want to learn!"

Another blast of cold air made her turn back to the door. Alison MacKenna and Stephanie Sharp laughed and waved as they rushed in.

"Isn't that Fanny Sharp's daughter?" Lavinia whispered.

"Yes!" Sarah's eyes filled with tears so quickly, she turned away. "Oh, thank you, God! We really are making a difference."

"A difference that will change the future," John added.

By eight o'clock, Sarah's carefully considered plan to set up three groups of children according to age had disappeared entirely; instead, out of necessity, she had divided the children according to their level of English usage. Each class was a hodgepodge of ages, but all were eager to learn, and Sarah had decreed that teaching English was the first priority for the two lower classes. The first classes of the day began. With Christine's assistance, Miss Mamie was teaching basic spoken vocabulary to the lowest level in one corner. Theo was teaching reading English in another corner. Lavinia was teaching composition to the most advanced students, some of whom had been Sarah's students before the town had applied the school tax.

"You need another class," Jana whispered in Sarah's ear.

Sarah exhaled loudly, puffing out her cheeks. "I know! I need many more classes. This afternoon I must subdivide these classes and start more individual tutoring. Oh, how will we ever give such a variety of students what they need?"

"You probably won't, but look over there." Jana pointed to Miss Mamie's vocabulary class. "See all the women sitting close by that group? They're trying to learn a few words of English."

"The mothers!" Sarah exclaimed. "I forgot all about them. What a perfect opportunity! If we can teach the mothers English, they can help their children."

Jana laughed softly. "Usually it works the other way around. The children end up teaching their parents."

"Well, I have one other corner left in this room. If only I had a teacher who could speak—" She stopped. "You, Mama! You can teach the mothers."

"I'm not a teacher!"

"You taught me, and while you teach them, you can fill them with enthusiasm for promoting their children's educations. You're the role model they need, and you know English."

"I can teach the Czech mothers, but I don't know Polish."

Sarah scanned the room until she saw Mr. Dobrowski standing in the shadows, a happy smile on his face. "Come with me." She took her mother's arm. "I know just the person to assist you."

As the morning progressed, Sarah listened in to each class, her excitement growing as she watched both children and adults begin to learn English. She made lists of students to group together for afternoon tutoring and thanked God for the volunteers she was expecting from the Literary Society.

"Don't you think we should give everyone a lunch break?" Lee asked about eleven thirty.

Frustrated, Sarah slapped her upper forehead with her hand. "Oh, no! Food! I didn't even think—"

"Hush." She felt his large, capable hands squeeze her shoulders. "Someone else has." He nodded toward the door. When she darted her eyes that way, she laughed with relief. Frances was shepherding Samuel and Delphie in, and each one carried a large pot. The minute she saw Sarah, Frances came bustling across the room.

"Where you want us to set up the soup, Miss Sarah?" she asked in a loud theatrical whisper as she drew herself up to full height. "Miss Victoria done put me in charge of the food 'cause she over at the library telling the mens what to do."

"I—I don't know." Sarah turned slowly in a circle, looking for an empty space.

"You'll have to use the foyer of the sanctuary," John suggested as he joined them. "I'm sure they've all brought food of their own, but they'll be glad to have something hot."

Sarah hesitated. "The foyer, John? I don't want you to get into trouble with—"

John waved his hand. "Jesus fed thousands. Surely we can feed a hundred. We'll set up a serving line in the foyer, and the students can grab a bowl of soup and head outside to the courtyard to eat."

Sarah ignored her own hunger as the students ate and took a short recess in the brisk air outside. Instead of eating, she turned her attention to rearranging the reception room into smaller units of chairs.

"You better let me help you," John offered. "Lee's busy out in the foyer managing the food line."

Sarah laughed. "Are you sure he's the one managing it?"

"Nope. But he's patiently taking orders from General Frances."

"Here's my scheme." Sarah spread her lists on a table. "The problem is I just don't have room to keep a promise to my former students. I told them I'd teach them, keep them up with the town kids. But where am I going to put them?"

"In the sanctuary."

Sarah whipped her head around and stared at him. "Are you sure you want to—"

"I'm sure." He cut her question off as he pointed at the list. "So you'll teach your former students in the back of the sanctuary, and I'll teach the older students who were thrown out of the town school in the front. What do you want me to teach them?"

"Mathematics. That's the one subject they can't study at home by themselves."

"Well, this will be the first time I ever set up a blackboard in a sanctuary. Thank goodness the church owns one." He pointed to the only free-standing blackboard in the room.

"This is a day of firsts."

John nodded as he grinned. "This is a good day!"

"I had to see this with my own eyes!" Fanny Sharp's loud exclamation as she burst through the double doors between the foyer and the sanctuary startled Sarah into silence. "I refused to believe my callers when they came to complain that our church is being stained by such an undertaking as this." Mrs. Sharp turned her furious accusing eyes on John. "Fool that I am, I insisted that our dignified Reverend Neville would *never* allow such a thing." She turned back to the ladies who stood behind her. "I owe you an apology, ladies. Clearly Reverend Neville has taken leave of his senses!"

Louise Proper stepped forward. "John Neville, you get these— these creatures out of our church at once!"

"Don't you realize we ladies will have to clean the church all over again?" Mrs. Matilda Quince demanded. "The parishioners won't dare enter for services tomorrow if we don't."

Sarah hurried to the center aisle where the ladies stood. "I assure you that everything will be left in perfect order and completely spotless. The mothers of these children plan to clean the church as soon as classes are finished."

"Filthy people cannot make a filthy building clean!" Lucille Ferrell shouted.

"That will do!" John exploded, then visibly struggled to take control of himself and lower his voice. "There are no filthy people here. Their clothes may be patched, but they are clean—body *and* soul. I suggest you ladies return to your homes and reflect on your hurtful words. I don't believe our Lord would approve of your behavior."

Fanny Sharp glared at him. "We don't need to reflect. We need to contact the bishop!"

Lucille Ferrell pulled on Fanny's arm. "Come, Fanny! We're wasting our time here. It's obvious he's under the influence of—" She sniffed with disdain as she looked down her nose at Sarah. "One of *them*."

"Come, ladies." Louise Proper covered her nose with a lacy handkerchief. "Let's remove ourselves from this foulness. We have an important letter to write."

Fury overwhelmed Sarah, and she charged up the aisle ready to do battle. *How dare they insult my students!* Only John's restraining hand kept her from reaching Louise Proper and giving her an angry shake.

"Consider the source, Sarah!" John insisted. "Don't lower yourself by responding to them."

"But I can't let such a remark stand! My students heard it," Sarah muttered. "I won't let those women demean these children—"

"They won't *feel* demeaned unless you teach them to by your actions."

Recognizing the wisdom of his words, Sarah drew in the deepest breath possible in order to take control of her temper. "Something must be said to the children," she hissed.

"I agree." John patted her on the shoulder, then turned to the staring children. "Students, I regret that you have heard the words of these women, but I ask you to focus on the loving actions of the townspeople who have volunteered their time today to make your education possible. We all knew when we started this school that there would be opposition. We knew that some people would try to stop us."

"But we will *not* be stopped!" Sarah recognized that her voice was too shrill. "We will not be stopped," she repeated more calmly as she forced herself to relax. "Your parents have traveled across an ocean to bring you to a better life. Education is the fuel you will need to create that life. We plan to overcome every obstacle to your education because, quite simply, you are worth it."

Nadia Burzynski's hand shook as she raised it and stepped out into the aisle. "Please, Miss Novak, can I read next?"

Sarah stared at the child's thin face and found herself so mesmerized by her large, fervent brown eyes she couldn't speak.

Michalina, usually too frightened to speak at all, pushed past her sister and, tattered hand-me-down skirt flying, ran up the aisle to Sarah and grabbed her hand. "Come! We learn now," the child encouraged. "We are strong."

CHAPTER FORTY-ONE

Another wave of indigestion rolled through Bishop Randall's ample midsection as the train to Riverford made the last turn and the station came into sight. This was not a trip he relished taking; both his health and his peace of mind had been robbed from him by the scathing letter he had received from Mrs. Fanny Sharp over a week ago. After all, what did it matter if St. Paul's Church was temporarily used to teach a few immigrant children their ABCs? And the bishop definitely did not relish a fight with Hayden Hodges. He poked his finger between his clerical collar and the folds of skin that overlapped it and struggled to stretch the thing a bit. *Why do these blasted things have to be so tight anyway?* He looked up to the roof of the car that swayed more aggressively as the engineer applied the brakes and immediately repented. Bishop Randall had long ago made a deal with God: he would allow himself a harsh word every now and then—not to mention an occasional glass of sherry when he was certain, absolutely certain, that no one was around—and then he would repent posthaste. *It really is the only way to survive these upheavals in churches.*

The last time he had been in Riverford, he had come to marry Reverend Neville to that scholarly woman, Lavinia Logan. *Now I ask you, would a clergyman who made such a sensible choice for his wife be likely to attempt to overthrow the church?*

"Certainly not!" The bishop answered his own question aloud, drawing the annoyed attention of the lady across the aisle. "I beg your pardon." He bowed his head as he apologized.

Still, Mrs. Sharp's letter, a letter that accused John Neville of everything short of actual blasphemy, had been signed by several other members of the parish. "Better remember those names," he murmured as he withdrew several letters from his coat pocket. He was, after all, likely to be met by an outraged self-appointed committee of women set on defrocking Reverend Neville if they could.

The train lurched to a stop as the bishop scrutinized the signature on the top letter. His indigestion rumbled. *Lord have mercy!* He glanced at the ceiling of the car again. The letter was from General Gibbes. A no-nonsense, crisply worded warning that he was ready to do battle in support of John Neville. *Oh me! What if he's also waiting for me?*

"Riverford!" the porter called as he walked down the car.

Bishop Randall sighed wearily as he heaved himself off the train seat and jerked his tight vest down. *Spent my whole life trying to rise to the top and this is what ...* He stopped the thought, glanced at the ceiling, and started his walk down the aisle. *Lord, have mercy. What am I about to get into?*

"Bishop Randall!" a male voice called from the platform the moment the bishop emerged from the car. "Over here, sir!"

The bishop's spirits rose as he scanned the platform. No group of angry ladies. No General Gibbes. Just Reverend Neville with a man he had never met. He descended the steps, careful not to lean his hefty body too far forward and fall on his face.

"John!" The bishop held out his hand when he was still some distance away. After all, best to show support for the clergy as long as possible. Especially in public. "Good to see you! Good to be in Riverford again." He glanced around at the swarm of passengers. Yes, that bow to Riverford seemed to have produced positive reactions.

"Allow me to introduce Reverend Wright," John said as he shook the bishop's hand. "He's the minister of the First Baptist Church of Riverford."

What? Had the bishop heard that correctly? The Baptists were in on the fight? "Pleasure to meet you," he boomed a little louder than necessary. "Always a pleasure to meet a colleague in the fight against ... against ..."

"Sin." Reverend Wright finished the bishop's sentence as his mighty grip crushed the bishop's hand.

"Mrs. Neville has prepared lunch for us at the rectory," John announced. "Come this way, Bishop."

"Wonderful lady, Mrs. Neville." The bishop improvised until he could figure out why he was lunching with a Baptist minister. "Quite the scholar. Most unusual for a lady."

"Yes," Reverend Wright agreed. "I've known her since she was a child." He leapt into the carriage ahead of the others and took up the reins.

"Kind of you to meet me," the bishop offered between pants as he struggled up the single step. The springs of the seat complained as he lowered his body. "Much better than the committee of women I was expecting ... if you know what I mean." He winked at John.

Reverend Wright burst out laughing as the horses leapt forward. "We can't protect you forever, Bishop."

"No, indeed." Bishop Randall sighed. "No escape for the wicked. But tell me, Reverend Wright, are you here in support of John or to condemn him?"

"I'm here in support of the immigrant children, and I'm mighty proud of your Episcopal priest here for bearing the blows from his congregation over this matter. I hope to convince you to support him."

Reluctant to take sides until he had to, the bishop nodded and changed the subject. "How is married life suiting you, John?"

By bedtime, the bishop was thoroughly exhausted and would have gladly checked himself into a monastery for the foreseeable future. Who would have thought a group of church ladies could have been in such violent disagreement? "And voiced their sentiments so forcefully!" The bishop looked at the ceiling of the guest room in the parsonage as he spoke. "What am I to do? Clearly, Lord, the majority of them don't want the immigrant children within a mile of the church." He thought of the children he had seen today in the Saturday classes. Their faces were so eager, their eyes so bright. What harm were they doing, really? The bedsprings protested even louder than his stomach rumbled as he sank onto the edge of the mattress. He rubbed his miserable midsection and rested his crossed arms on his belly.

The bishop hated discord, would gladly have walked a country mile to avoid the slightest disagreement. "Ten country miles," he declared. "Blasted, confounded prejudices! Why can't people just get along?" He glanced at the ceiling, his customary act of contrition for angry words.

"Well, there's no getting around it." He jerked off his clerical collar and spoke directly to it. "If I'm going to wear you, I'll have to make a ruling. Enough to make me resign!" He stretched himself out and, still fully clothed, gratefully sank into the welcoming feather mattress. "You don't have a choice, Randall." His voice was firm as he counseled himself. "You'll just have to do it. But let John deliver his homily before you break his heart." He shook his head. "Too bad really. After all, they just need the church until early February. Then the children start going to that library ... No, wait, John said they need the church for adult classes." The bishop pounded on his chest to relieve his indigestion. "Blast! Hope he doesn't quit the priesthood. Hope he sees that it's just a matter of numbers. Got to keep the church solvent."

The next morning at the ten thirty worship service, Bishop Randall sat in the Bishop's Chair facing the congregation, heartily wishing that, just this one time, the homily of the service could be skipped. Just go straight from the scripture readings to communion. Just this once ... Why let a man plead for something he couldn't have? And the bishop simply could *not* grant permission to use the church for those classes. Not after Fanny Sharp had hauled him away from the breakfast table this very morning and made him watch her friends, their Sunday-best clothes covered with long dusters and their fancy hats removed, scrub down the sanctuary as if it were infected with the plague.

"Is this really necessary?" he had asked timidly.

"Do you want people to come to church or not?" The woman's pea-sized, black eyes had drilled holes in him. *Most unattractive woman I ever met!* The bishop cast his repentant eyes at the vaulted ceiling of St. Paul's, but the moment the choir began to sing, he was filled with alarm. *What was John thinking when he chose this hymn?* The bishop groaned as he listened to the first stanza.

> Oh brother man, fold to thy heart thy brother!
> Where pity dwells, the peace of God is there;
> To worship rightly is to love each other,
> Each smile a hymn, each kindly deed a prayer.

Bishop Randall felt anything but peace! This John Neville was really quite the rebel. What to do? The bishop struggled not to wring his hands.

> For they whom Jesus loved have truly spoke:
> The holier worship which He deigns to bless
> Restores the lost, and binds the spirit broken,
> And feeds the widow and the fatherless.

Bishop Randall's indigestion-prone belly rumbled, but not as loudly as his conscience, as the organist slowed the tempo and the choir emphasized the last stanza.

> Follow with rev'rent steps the great example
> Of him whose holy work was doing good;
> So shall the wide earth seem our Father's temple,
> Each loving life a psalm of gratitude.

Poor John! The bishop tried to catch the young priest's eyes. To offer support? To beg for forgiveness? His gaze found only the back of Reverend Neville's head, for John was kneeling in front of the altar, his arms upraised and pleading. "May the words of my mouth and the meditation of my heart be acceptable in Thy sight, O Lord, my strength and my redeemer." The bishop had never felt more miserable. For the first time in his entire life, he actually hated himself. *Detach!* he ordered himself. *You're just doing your job. Unity in the church is worth any sacrifice.* But he didn't believe a word he was telling himself.

As the bishop watched Reverend Neville solemnly proceed to the pulpit, his pulse started galloping. *A lamb to the slaughter...* He began to think of other parishes where he could send the young man. St. Matthew's in Tyler? *Now that's the ticket! Even a bit of a promotion in that move.* The bishop's breathing slowed, a slight smile lifted his face, and he began to coach John silently. *Keep calm, low-key. Remember, Rome wasn't built in a day.*

"'For as the body is one and hath many members, and all the members of that one body, being many, are one body: so also is Christ.'" John Neville began his homily by rereading a portion of the day's gospel.

Bishop Randall broke out in a sweat. *Not there, John! For mercy's sake, don't go there!*

"'For by one Spirit are we all baptized into one body, whether we be Jews or Gentiles, whether we be bond or free; and have been all made to drink into one Spirit.'" Reverend Neville continued to read the day's reading, emphasizing the verses that explained the necessity of all parts of the body serving each other.

The bishop's heart pounded as he scanned the congregation. How easy it was to spot those who disapproved of the immigrants' classes being held in the church. It was equally easy to spot those who supported them, especially General Gibbes, who was glaring at him, daring him to—to what? A quiver of anxiety shook the bishop. Averting his eyes, he focused on those who had not formed an opinion. How would they react? If they sided with Fanny Sharp and her hateful gang, he couldn't possibly send John Neville to Tyler. No indeed, he'd have to think of a more liberal place.

"This scripture exhorts us to recognize that even though we have differences, we are equally God's children and a valid part of the church." John began his sermon. "It exhorts us to honor our differences, to see their usefulness and purpose in creating the whole body of Christ. We are commanded to care for one another. To suffer with each other. To rejoice in honor that comes to even one of us."

John leaned across the pulpit and changed his voice to the tone of a personal conversation. "The very next chapter—a chapter you have surely taken as the basis of your personal values, a chapter you have surely taught to your own children—emphasizes the importance of charity. 'Though I speak with the tongues of men and angels and have not charity, I am become as sounding brass or a tinkling cymbal.' The message could not be clearer: sound without substance is absolutely meaningless. Our fine words about our commitment to Jesus Christ, about following in his footsteps mean nothing if we do not *live* those words in our daily life.

"And make no mistake about it, my dear brothers and sisters in Christ. Jesus, while he was still here on earth, showed us exactly *how* He meant for us to live. He *demonstrated* the life we are called to emulate as He fed the hungry, healed the afflicted, and embraced the outcast and the forsaken. We do not have to guess what the focus of our lives should be. *We have been told*. We have been given two commandments: to love God with our hearts and souls and minds and to love each other.

"Furthermore, there can be no mystery, no confusion as to *how* we are to love each other. Jesus spelled it out for us. He could not have been clearer. 'Verily I say unto you, inasmuch as ye have done it unto one of the least of these my brethren, ye have done it unto me.' Matthew 25, verses 40–45 tell us that each time we aid the least fortunate among us, we aid our Lord. Each time we serve 'the least of these,' we serve God. He specifically exhorts us to feed the hungry, give drink to the thirsty, cloth the unclothed, visit the sick and the imprisoned. We know these exhortations, and we obey them. Too meagerly, no doubt. Still, we obey. Why then do we avert our eyes from the part of this text that quotes Jesus as saying, 'I was a stranger, and ye took me in'?"

Overcome with shame, the bishop lowered his chin to his chest and fought back tears as he begged God for His forgiveness.

John Neville broke with tradition entirely and stepped away from the pulpit to address the congregation more informally. He quoted the first stanza of the sermon hymn. "'Oh brother man, fold to thy heart thy brother! Where pity dwells, the peace of God is there;

To worship rightly is to love each other, each smile a hymn, each kindly deed a prayer.'" He paused, gazing out at his congregation. "Brothers and sisters in Christ, God has blessed us communicants of St. Paul's with a holy task, an opportunity to serve the least of our brethren. Will you join me in welcoming the immigrant population to use our building for their much-needed classes?"

"I will!" The bishop hardly recognized his own voice, but he could not deny he was rising from his chair and walking toward John Neville. "I will welcome them to St. Paul's." He turned toward the congregation. "Indeed, I will welcome them to any Episcopal church in the diocese. Furthermore, I shall encourage—no, I shall exhort all Episcopal churches in the diocese to aid the immigrants in every way *and* to welcome them to come worship with us." The bishop paused, uncertain how far to go in his remarks, but his conscience prompted him to speak on. "In a few moments, this congregation will be blessed to receive Holy Communion, but before we do, we will kneel and make our confession of sin. My personal confession will include my lack of commitment to aid the strangers among us. I implore you to examine your own conscience on this matter. If you are convicted that your previous charitable actions have been too little, confess that sin and resolve, with God's help, to change your ways. I assure you that I shall be resolving to change mine."

The bishop had planned to conduct the communion part of the service, but he felt far too close to tears to do so. In a desperate, choked whisper, he pleaded, "Please, John, if you would ..."

John nodded and turned toward the altar as the bishop made his way back to the Bishop's Chair with as much dignity as he could muster. From the corner of his eye, he saw several people get up from the pews and walk out. *So be it. I have done as God commanded me.* The tightness in his chest had disappeared. A healing peace came over him.

CHAPTER FORTY-TWO

From Sarah's vantage point on the staircase landing, she could see a unique collection of people swarming around inside the old Boyd homestead—a team previously impossible in Riverford. Polish men sawed and hammered in the main parlor, constructing and installing bookcases; across the hall from them, Czech men busily built benches and tables. In the back rooms, Riverford men led by Lee were painting trim work and hanging new wallpaper. The main hallway below her held a bevy of women, including her own mother, Jana. They were speaking different languages but understanding each other well enough as they cleaned windows and scrubbed woodwork.

Sadly, her pa and brothers were absent, or so Sarah thought, until she heard shouting outside. *"Buď opatrný!"* a familiar male voice demanded. *"Sledujte dveře!"*

"What's going on?" Lee called up to her.

"It's Pa shouting at someone to be careful and to watch the door." She turned her attention back to the door where she saw her father backing through, directing her brothers as they slowly moved a grand piano, turned on its side and without its legs, through the front door.

"Wait!" Lee yelled as he turned back to the room of workers. "I'll get you some help."

"We don't need help," Pa insisted. *"Jsme Češi!"*

"What did he say?" Lee asked Sarah.

"We are Czech!" Jana laughed as she answered his question. "In other words, they're too stubborn to accept help."

Sarah dashed down the stairs. "Get help anyway, Lee. That's Miss Mamie's piano they're moving in, and she'll die if there's a single scratch."

For the next ten minutes, Sarah hovered as near as she could get to the instrument, her hands clutched in a prayerful posture, her nerves strained. Slowly but surely, with extra help from the Polish and Riverford men, the piano was righted and held aloft while its legs were attached.

When it was secure, Sarah's pa turned to her and announced proudly, "I brought it for Mrs. Boyd to play," as if he had moved the piano single-handedly.

"He would do anything for Mrs. Boyd," Jana whispered behind Sarah.

"Where does Mrs. Boyd want it?" Pa asked.

Sarah hurried back to the foot of the staircase and pointed to her left. "I think you should place it here, in front of the staircase but over to the left."

Pa eyed her coolly. "Where does Mrs. Boyd want it?" He repeated his question. "I put it where she wants it."

Sarah swallowed hard as she struggled to ignore the rebuff. "She wants it here so she can see Signore Santoro. He will be standing on the first step when he plays."

"She told you this?"

"Yes, Pa. She asked us to put it here."

"Then that's what we do. Come, men, we lift now. All together! One, two, three."

All ethnic differences were forgotten as men raced to participate in the final placing of the piano. As soon as they backed away, Mrs. Dobrowski hurried forward with her dust cloth, and to Sarah's amazement, she leaned forward and kissed the keyboard.

"Oh, Mama!" Sarah gasped as tears sprang to her eyes.

Jana encircled her daughter in her arms. "They lost everything," she whispered. "You are giving their lives back to them."

"Not me!" Sarah exclaimed.

"Yes, you! And I'm so proud of you. So is your pa, even though he'll never say so."

"Back to work!" Lee called, but before the men could move, the front door opened, and with a flourish, Victoria and Antonio Santoro entered. Sarah was surprised that silence suddenly reigned in the main hall as the workers stared at the elegant lady and the dashing, dark-haired Antonio who didn't hesitate to wave his black cape to draw attention to himself.

Seconds later, Antonio saw Sarah and, in his usual vibrant way, raced toward her and swept her hand to his lips as he declared for all to hear, "*La mia bella, brillante signorina!* I see you again at last!" With great reverence, he kissed her hand, then held it to his chest. "Now that I'm here in Riverford, we spend all our time together. Yes?"

"No," Lee declared as he stepped forward.

Victoria laughed. "Things have changed, Antonio," she warned. "Sarah is engaged to be married."

"No! *Questa è una tragedia! Non posso sopportarlo.*"

"You'll have to bear it." Victoria turned him toward Lee. "This is Mr. Lee Logan, banker and Sarah's fiancé."

Antonio noisily drew in his breath, held it a moment as he looked Lee over, then exhaled with disdain. "You love her?" he demanded of Lee.

"I love her." Lee's voice was bold. He took Sarah's hand from Antonio's. "And don't you forget it."

"My memory is perfect." Antonio pointed to the immigrants who had returned to their various tasks. "I remember my mother scrubbing floors like these women do so I can have music lessons. I'm glad I get to play for these people at the benefit."

Victoria cast a troubled glance at Sarah. "These people, most of them, won't be here that night, Antonio."

"Of course they will! We have party for the peoples! With music and dancing."

"That might not be wise, Antonio," Lee said. "The lure for the wealthy is exclusivity. They are paying for the exclusive honor of hearing you play; they must feel they have been singled out."

Antonio looked at the swarm of workers. "Then they pay to hear someone who came from people like these people."

"And now your talent has raised you to the top of society," Lee answered.

"No! My mother raised me. She scrubbed floors until her hands bled so I could have these hands." Antonio whipped off a glove and revealed a smooth hand with manicured nails. "But I will never forget!" He turned to Sarah. "When do classes for poor *bambini* begin in this house?"

"Not until February, I'm afraid. Oh, dear." Sarah's voice became agitated as her attention was drawn to the front door. "Why is Mr. Bellows here?"

"Because I told him that Antonio would be here," Victoria answered. "After all, the arrival of a famous violinist in Riverford is front-page news in the local newspaper." She raised her hand to draw Mr. Bellows' attention, then turned to Sarah and Lee. "Just play along, you two."

Mr. Bellows, a chewed cigar hanging from his lips, strode through the workers.

When he reached them, Victoria began to make the necessary introductions. "Signore Santoro, may I present the proprietor of the *Riverford Times*, Mr. Bellows?"

Antonio narrowed his eyes as he hesitated ever so slightly before tossing the right side of his cape open and extending his hand.

"Welcome to Riverford, Signore Santoro." Mr. Bellows grasped the violinist's hand and gave it a quick shake. "We're honored to have you as our guest."

"*Grazie*, Signore Bellows." Antonio ignored the enthusiasm of Mr. Bellows' welcome as he looked over the journalist's shoulder toward the door. "But where is the *bellissima* Signora Bellows?"

"My wife?"

"Mrs. Bellows?" Sarah demanded. "She would hardly be here, Antonio. She disapproves of our entire project."

"*Impossibile!*" Antonio dismissed the idea with a flourish of his hand. "*Una donna dal gusto impeccabile? No, non ci credo.*"

"What did he say?" Mr. Bellows asked Victoria.

"He refuses to believe that a woman of Mrs. Bellows' impeccable taste would not support a library."

"She is a leader of society, no?" Antonio demanded.

"Well … uh …" Mr. Bellows cleared his throat. "Be that as it may, I'd like to interview you for the newspaper."

"I must meet her!" Antonio insisted. "We will have much in common. Where is she?"

Mr. Bellows shrugged. "Why, at home, I guess."

Antonio glared at him, then turned to Victoria. "Why have you not introduced me to this lady of culture?"

"Lady of culture?" Mr. Bellows guffawed.

"I believe she was indisposed when you were visiting three years ago," Victoria answered.

"Poor lady!" Antonio shook his head sadly. "The world is cruel to ladies of such sensibility."

Mr. Bellows looked confused. "As I was saying, Signore Santoro, I'd like to feature you on the front page of the *Riverford Times*—"

"Yes, of course." Antonio dismissed his comment. "Everywhere I go—New York, Boston, New Orleans—is always the same. My picture on the front page. I have no time for this." He turned to Victoria. "I shall call on Mrs. Bellows first thing tomorrow."

"I'm sure she'd be delighted to meet you, Antonio. Perhaps we could invite her to tea—"

"No, no! *Il signore visita sempre la signora!*"

"What did he say?" Mr. Bellows demanded.

"The gentleman always calls on the lady," Victoria translated.

"The lady?" Mr. Bellows looked from face to face. "Edith? Is he talking about Edith?"

Antonio scowled at Mr. Bellows, then offered his arm to Victoria. "*Venire! Scrivo una nota alla donna.*"

"He wants to go now and write a note to Edith," Victoria translated. "Perhaps you could interview him when he visits her," she called back.

"But, but … Is he crazy?"

Lee clapped Mr. Bellows on the shoulder. "I wouldn't argue if I were you. Crazy or not, he's the most famous visitor Riverford's ever had, and you missed the chance to interview him last time he came."

Sarah fought to reduce her grin to a sedate smile as she comforted the newspaper owner. "I'm sure Mrs. Bellows will help you gain an interview."

"The man's crazy! Edith's a nobody."

Lee chuckled. "Not after word of this gets out."

"And it will get out," Sarah assured Mr. Bellows. "You know, I suddenly remember that I have some shopping to do downtown."

CHAPTER FORTY-THREE

Christine was shocked when Nancy brought Mrs. Bellows' maid to the door of the music room. "'T's sorry to interrupt your lesson with Miss Ceci, but Ada just gotta talk to you. She got a message from Mrs. Bellows."

"An *urgent* message," Ada called from the doorway. "Mrs. Bellows say it be life and death."

"Life *or* death." Nancy's voice grew haughty as she corrected the other woman. "If you's gonna talk to the quality folk, you gotta learn to do it right."

"I don't know nothing 'bout that. I just know Mrs. Bellows beside herself, and there ain't gonna be no peace in the house 'til Mrs. Boyd say she gonna come to tea tomorrow afternoon at four o'clock."

"Well, Miz Christine ain't comin'. That Mrs. Bellows talk mean to her when she's over here, and Miz Christine ain't puttin' up with nothing like that."

As Christine rose from the piano bench, she directed Ceci, "Memorize the treble line of the sonatina. When I return, I want you to play it for me with perfect timing. Those eighth notes must be quickly played and with staccato, as the music indicates." She extended her hand to the keyboard and played a line of quick notes.

Ceci immediately applied herself to the task of repeating the phrase over and over as Christine left the room.

"Now, what is the problem?" she asked Ada.

"That Italian violin player done announced he comin' to visit Mrs. Bellows tomorrow, and she just beside herself."

"Antonio Santoro is planning to visit Mrs. Bellows?" Christine's voice betrayed her disbelief. "But why? I mean, how did this happen?"

"I don't know, Miz Boyd. Something 'bout givin' Mr. Bellows an interview. That foreigner—oh, I forgot! Mrs. Bellows say I ain't to call him that no more. Ain't proper, she say." Ada shook her head wildly. "I tell you; ever'thing done changed over there. Mrs. Bellows suddenly saying she always love violin music better than anything. She's done gone crazy, and I ain't far behind."

"I see," Christine said even though she didn't.

"Mrs. Bellows say I got to bake something Italian, but I ain't never even met an Italian."

"Just bake your delicious lemon pound cake," Christine advised. "I believe Italians favor desserts that are lemon flavored."

"That cake don't have no frostin' on it, Miz Boyd. Mrs. Bellows say we got to have heaps of frostin'"

"As a general rule, Ada, simplicity denotes sophistication."

Ada looked at Nancy. "What do that mean?"

Nancy shrugged her shoulders. "I ain't sure, but if Miz Christine say bake the lemon pound cake, that be what you better do."

Christine smiled. "I mean, Ada, that people of class do not need to put on airs to gain respect. Now, hurry home and get to work."

As Christine watched Ada rush toward the kitchen to exit the back door, she murmured. "This whole business suggests the cleverness of Victoria to me."

"My dear Mrs. Boyd." Mr. Bellows met Christine at the front door shortly before four the next afternoon and did his best to bow over his protruding paunch. "How kind of you to come help Edith through this ordeal."

"Ordeal?" Mrs. Bellows' voice was haughty as it rang through the hall. "I should hardly call it an ordeal to have the most famous violinist in the world honor me with his presence." She hurried forward and, pushing her husband aside, planted a kiss on Christine's cheek. "And of course my dearest friend in all the world would attend my little soiree."

"Now, Edith, calm yourself. You're making too much of this." Mr. Bellows poked a cigar between his teeth.

"Don't you start that filthy cigar smoking in my house!" Mrs. Bellows ripped the offending tobacco from her husband's lips. "I nearly froze to death last night leaving all the windows open so this place wouldn't smell like your newspaper office."

"I brought you some of my camellias." Christine stepped between the two as she held out a tussie mussie.

Edith ignored her offering as she demanded. "How do I look?"

"I already told you," Mr. Bellows growled. "You look like you're going to the opera. Ridiculous to wear your fanciest dress to a tea in your own house."

"Aren't you going back to your office?" Edith demanded. "You usually spend as much time away from home as you possibly can."

"If you'd look in the mirror, you'd know why I stay away. Even *you* could figure that out." He turned on Christine. "What's wrong with this Santoro guy anyway? Refuses to give me an interview for the paper until he's called on Edith. Is he crazy?"

"I've never seen any evidence of insanity in Signore Santoro." Christine kept her voice quiet. "As for the interview, we must remember that he is frequently featured in the major newspapers of the country. Perhaps an interview in the Riverford paper is not high on his list of priorities."

"And Edith is?" he demanded.

"Apparently so." Christine smiled sweetly. "I'll just find Ada and have her put these flowers in a vase."

"I's here, Miz Boyd," Ada called as she rushed in. "I baked my lemon pound cake just like you said, and Miz Hodges done sent over some small cakes with almonds on them. How you like my new uniform?" Ada held out her black cotton skirt and starched white apron. "Miz Bellows bought it for me yesterday. I ain't never had a single piece of clothes that come from a store!"

"Good Lord almighty!" Mr. Bellows exploded. "A foreign fiddle player comes to town, and you women go crazy. How much did that cost?" He pointed at Ada's new frock.

"I will not have my dear friend, Antonio, called a foreigner!" Edith exclaimed.

Mr. Bellows turned to Christine. "He *is* a foreigner, isn't he? I haven't heard a thing about Italy joining the United States, and I *am* a newsman."

"Perhaps that is what you better remember, Mr. Bellows," Christine advised coolly. "It will be quite a *coup d'etat* if you can be the *first* editor in Texas to interview Signore Santoro. Quite the *grande victoire*, wouldn't you say?"

Mr. Bellows stared at her, then, after clearing his throat loudly, exclaimed. "Exactly. Yes, indeed. That would put the *Riverford Times* on the map."

"I am sure you will gain that victory if you allow Mrs. Bellows to soften Signore Santoro's heart toward you." Christine smiled sweetly. "Perhaps you could manage to go now and reappear about five o'clock. By then, he will be quite receptive to an interview, I am certain."

"Good idea!" Mr. Bellow grabbed his hat off the coat rack, then paused to take Christine's hand. "I leave my fate in your capable hands, Mrs. Boyd." He rushed to the front door, then turned back to add. "And I assure you that my next editorial will be very complimentary toward the new library you've so graciously donated."

"And the classes for the immigrants?" Christine asked.

"Whatever you wish. *Anything* you wish."

CHAPTER FORTY-FOUR

"What a special day this is." Sarah's mother hugged her daughter as they stood on the landing of the staircase at the soon-to-be-dedicated Richard Boyd Library. "Just think! A library for all the children, no matter where their parents came from."

"And for the adults too."

"I'm so proud of you for bringing it about."

"Oh, you mustn't give me the credit," Sarah protested. "This is Christine's doing."

Her mother shook her head. "As wonderful as Mrs. Boyd is, she wouldn't have thought of this unless you had come into her life and worked so hard for your own education."

Sarah drew back slightly so she could lock eyes with her mother. "But I would never have gone to school at all if you hadn't fought for me, Mother. You're the one who defined me as a student, not a farm worker. You're the one who defied tradition and insisted that a girl deserved an education, a choice about her life."

"I had a dream, a desire for you, but I never imagined it could go as far as this. A benefit concert for a library, a famous violinist performing to raise money so poor children could learn to read. How did this happen?"

"Great trees grow from small seeds."

"Only if those seeds fall on fertile soil and have enough rain and sunshine," Jana added. "Countless seeds never spring from the soil at all or don't survive the first drought."

"Like the countless children who are born into a world that denies their worth. Most children have no one to fight for them like you fought for me, Mama."

"I didn't fight alone." Jana pointed to the front door where Christine and Victoria were entering. "Without their help, I hate to think where you—or any of our family—would be today."

"Not standing here, for sure. It takes all of us, doesn't it? All of us working together to create change, to forge a better way. If the more powerful in a society don't pick up the challenge, nothing much can be accomplished."

Jana nodded. "But first they have to see that the poor are not as different from them as they think, and that's not easy."

"Why are Christine and Victoria able to do that when so many others can't?" Sarah asked.

"Their own sufferings have created a bond with others who suffer."

"That's the thing about suffering, isn't it? It can embitter or empower you. Stop you or set a fire under you." Sarah's chest tightened, and her breath became ragged. "Oh, Mother! What if my plan doesn't work? What if the Saturday classes fail? The immigrant children will spend their lives wearily plodding up and down endless rows of cotton in blinding, deadening heat. Their lives will—"

"Stop it." Jana's voice was firm as she encircled her daughter's upper arm in her strong grasp. "Stand up straight. Hold up your chin. We don't serve a God who starts a loving project and doesn't finish it."

"And you believe that this is God's project, that providing education for all the children is God's project?"

Jana swept her hand in front of her, indicating all the rooms below them. "Could this have happened without His help? Look at the elegant women gathering below with their fancy dresses and elaborate hats, but also look at the shabbily-dressed women—the Czechs, the Poles—scurrying around the edges, doing the menial chores. They're all here working in their individual ways, but working together. And if you need ultimate proof ... your pa is outside, shovel in hand, ready to add coal to the fireplaces when needed."

"Pa is here?" Sarah was stunned at the thought. "He's actually here?"

"He is. Don't despair, Sarah. Not even in the face of your pa's stubbornness. No one's journey is complete until God calls him home. In the meantime we're here to love, to serve."

Sarah nodded. "And to grow."

Half an hour later, Sarah stood close to the front door of the old Boyd House and surveyed the results of their work thus far. In a mere month, the immigrants and the few town volunteers who had joined their cause had refinished the oak wainscoting of the main hall, papered the tall-ceilinged room, and waxed the wide pine planks of the floor. The staircase that dominated the center of the back wall gleamed in the sunshine that poured through the window on its landing. Both newel posts were flanked by the standing candelabra from St. Paul's Church that were decorated with flowing ivy and Victoria's camellias. Miss Mamie's mahogany square grand piano glowed in the candlelight. The forest-green, brocade-cushioned chairs from the Hodges Store tearoom were arranged in neat rows. Those chairs were now filled with the elite of Riverford society, those who had paid a premium price to hear Antonio perform. Sarah smiled as she spotted many obviously new and proudly worn elegant afternoon dresses. The ladies were draped in every hue of silk, velvet, and brocade, and lace adorned gowns in the most fantastical ways.

Sarah glanced to her left and then to her right and noted that the floor-to-ceiling, sliding pocket doors were open, revealing the polished wood and new wallpaper in the front rooms, as well as a crowd of more modestly dressed attendees sitting on the benches the Polish men had made. At the back of these rooms, the braver immigrant adults respectfully stood with their children. Sarah's smile widened, and her heart raced with joy. *They came! Of all the guests, these are the most important.*

Hayden Hodges walked to the first step of the staircase and addressed the crowd. "Welcome, ladies and gentlemen. This is a historic day in Riverford, one that will be remembered for decades. It's true that the calendar declares that we are a full year away from the beginning of the twentieth century, but today Riverford enters that new, shining age of promise. Few towns in Texas, indeed in the nation, can claim to have a library to educate and edify their citizenry. Thanks to the generosity of the Boyd family, Riverford is leading the way.

"As you know, this structure housed one of the founding families of Riverford for decades, providing the Boyd family members with rest after long days in the fields in the early years of this century. This home has welcomed generations of Boyd children into the world and provided them with safe haven in their growing years. It has welcomed Boyd men as they returned victorious from the war for Texas independence and as they returned exhausted from the War Between the States. Much of importance to Riverford and to Texas has occurred within these walls, but today this house has achieved its grandest hour. Today, this house provides a place for unification of all our citizens, those who have resided here for generations and those who have recently joined our community. Starting today, this house is to be Riverford's center of learning. Much of the future education will come from the books we will place in these rooms, but even more will come from the sharing of our cultures.

"Texas has always provided refuge for those needing a new beginning, whether they sought a place to make their fortunes or a place of safety from persecution. We all came here from another place. The magnificence of Texas derives directly from the fact that we have chosen to unite and share our strengths. Texas is strong because we learn from each other, because we value new ideas, because we do not fear our differences. We embrace them and grow stronger.

"Our beloved and much-missed friend, Richard Boyd, knew this truth about Texas. He spent his life holding out the hand of welcome to the newcomer. He even funded the new beginnings of countless members of our society. There could be no better place to begin our next triumph for Riverford, Texas, than within the walls that saw the birth and early years of Richard Boyd."

Sarah's pulse lurched into a racing speed when the audience spontaneously applauded. She noticed that some clapped more enthusiastically than others, but none clapped more loudly than Edith Bellows. Sarah's heart melted at the sight of the wide smiles on the faces of the immigrants, and it did not escape her notice that many of them reached for their handkerchiefs. She glanced across the room at Lee, who stood next to John Neville. He raised his fingers to his lips and sent a kiss her way.

When the applause died down, Hayden bowed to Christine and her children. "Riverford thanks you, Mrs. Richard Boyd, for your gracious gift of this structure to house our new library. We pledge to you and to the memory of your husband that we will pour our own funds and personal energy into making this institution a guiding light in the darkness of ignorance and bigotry.

"If you will kindly do the honors, Mrs. Boyd." Hayden held out his hand to Christine, but rather than standing herself, she shook her head and urged Andrew and George forward. The boys joined Hayden on the first step, and when he directed everyone's attention to the draped easel behind him, Andrew removed the cloth with a flourish and revealed the bronze plaque that proudly proclaimed the building to be the Richard Boyd Memorial Library.

As the audience applauded again, the boys started to return to their seats, but Hayden stopped them. "One moment, boys. You have one other duty." Sarah was startled when Lee and John carried a large, draped object forward and, holding it squarely between them, turned toward the crowd.

"Wait!" Juli cried out as she ran forward. "I want to do this one." The crowd burst into laughter as she hopped up and down in front of Hayden. "Can I? Can I?"

Hayden stifled his own laughter and nodded as solemnly as he could.

Juli turned to the audience and announced, "I already know what it is!" Then she turned back and, grabbing the bottom corner of the velvet cover, revealed the surprise.

The audience fell silent, and Sarah heard a soft gasp from Christine. A portrait of Richard Boyd, which Victoria had kept so carefully hidden that even Sarah didn't know she was painting it, was revealed. Sarah's eyes filled with tears as she gazed on the beloved benefactor of her family. Throughout the rooms, people reached for handkerchiefs and dabbed their eyes. As George dragged Juli back to her chair, Hayden cleared his throat and struggled for composure. Finally, he was able to speak.

"It seemed to me that the Richard Boyd Memorial Library must have a portrait of my friend, of our friend, of the man who served this town all his life. Happily, a great painter allows me to be her husband, and she was painting this magnificent likeness for Mrs. Boyd's Christmas present. I confess, I confiscated it." He turned to Christine. "Can you ever forgive me, Christine, for stealing your gift?"

Christine nodded as she rose. Eyes glistening with tears, but posture erect and composure intact, she turned to Victoria. "Thank you, Victoria. You have more than painted his face; you have captured his spirit." She turned back to the portrait and held out her hand. *"Pro honoris, pro caritas, pro Texana."*

The front row jumped to their feet as they applauded, and Sarah watched as the whole crowd rose to their feet in waves like a fan unfolding toward her. Much to her surprise, Antonio leapt to the staircase and began to fiddle the lively "Yellow Rose of Texas." The somber mood changed instantly as people began to clap, and when Antonio played the tune the second time, the crowd raised their voices in joyful tribute to the mighty state of Texas. Sarah glanced at the immigrants and noticed that, unfamiliar with the words, they continued to clap along.

Hayden finally quieted the crowd by holding up his hands. "I'm sure you've guessed that this fiddler is the famous violinist, Antonio Santoro, who has left the concert halls of Europe and New York behind to spend Christmas with us in Riverford. He has most kindly agreed to support our fund-raising efforts for the library by playing for you this afternoon."

The crowd began to applaud, but Antonio dismissed their tribute with a wave and raised his voice above the sound. "I cannot play without *la bella signora,* Christina. Without her, I am just a poor fiddle player. With her, I am *grande violinista.*" He held out a pleading hand toward Christine. *"Per favore, bella signora,* come save me."

Christine rose, walked to the piano, and seated herself.

As the romantic strains of Chopin's Nocturne in E flat Major began to drift through the house, Sarah imagined she saw countless dancers from earlier decades waltzing in each other's arms in this very hall. It took all her self-restraint to keep from running across the room to Lee's arms. When the last sweet notes drifted away, the audience sighed before breaking into applause. Sarah glanced at the side rooms and noticed that the Polish immigrants had crept forward. Their eyes were now aglow with pride as they hugged each other. *Chopin is theirs.* Sarah's own eyes misted at the thought. *Here in their new country, they find a bit of their heritage honored.* She could have hugged Christine and Antonio for beginning in this way.

"I knew Mrs. Boyd could play the piano," a lady sitting close by commented, "but I never realized ..."

"Can you believe it?" her friend asked. "She's every bit as good as he is."

"Better, in my mind," a man responded. "What a pity she's just a woman."

Sarah rolled her eyes toward heaven and prayed for patience, but Antonio jerked her attention back to the musicale as he began to play a very spirited solo. She watched in awe as members of the audience leaned forward, their eyes riveted on Antonio's flying hands. When he finished the complex, fast-paced work, he separated the bow from the violin with a flourish and held his arms up.

The audience sprang from their seats, applauding wildly.

"I could not resist." He grinned as he raised his voice over the clapping. "I must play a little something Italian."

When they had returned to their seats, Antonio added, "That was Paganini's Caprice No. 24. Now I quit showing off ... at least for a little while. La bella signora, Christina and I play the most *appassionato* piece you ever hear. It is like two glowing hearts meeting in a dark world. *Ah, amore!*"

He and Christine played a piece Sarah had never heard, and as the poignantly romantic melody painted pictures of embracing lovers in her mind, she glanced at Lee. He was staring at her, and the look in his eyes sent a tingle straight to her core. She felt herself blush, so she hurriedly glanced back at Christine and noticed tears in her eyes.

Oh! She is thinking of Richard. Sarah's heart ached for her friend, and she made a vow not to waste a single day she had with Lee.

When Antonio and Christine finished playing, the audience sat transfixed, unwilling to accept the end of such beauty. Finally, someone began clapping, and as others wiped their eyes and joined in, the sound ricocheted off the high ceiling.

"Magnificent!" a man called out.

"So moving … I can hardly breathe." A lady near Sarah fanned herself.

Antonio held up his hands to quieten them. "This beautiful music is new to you, yes? I just met this composer in New York three years ago. He loves America and believes the greatest classical American music can come from American tunes."

The audience applauded.

"In fact, he directed the New York Musical Society for two years, but during the summers he took his family on tours of America and began to write a great symphony called *New World Symphony*. Who is this man, you want to ask me? His name is Antonin Dvorak."

Sarah heard a gasp from the Czech immigrants as they recognized the Czech name.

"Yes," Antonio continued. "This great composer is Bohemian; he is Czech. And he loves America. He is inspired by America." He paused. "Next time he comes to America, we bring him to Texas. Yes? Here he will learn the best music from many countries. Here he will be most inspired!"

The crowd broke into raucous applause that only diminished when Antonio raised his violin and he and Christine began playing again.

After the concert, the crowd drifted into the back rooms where Jana led the immigrant women as they served hot spiced tea and delicious, but unusual, pastries to the crowd. Many an attendee was heard to exclaim over the delights of a fruit-centered *kolacek* or a honey-flavored *medovnik*, both made by the Czech community. And the Polish filled donut, the *paczki*, and the poppy seed cake, *mazurek,* were greeted with the same enthusiasm. Sarah and Victoria wandered through the front parlors, explaining to the ladies how the spaces would be used to create a library and pointing out the need for more bookcases, library tables, and especially books to be donated. Hayden and Lee cornered the men and talked about financing electricity and a radiator system for the building.

By far, the most encouraging words Sarah heard all afternoon came from Edith's mouth. Sarah overheard a conversation between Mr. Bellows and his wife that was decidedly one-sided as Mrs. Bellows insisted that her husband publish a glowing report of the afternoon as well as a list of items the library needed. Sarah grinned at the memory of Antonio's wooing of the cantankerous Edith. *Antonio did his work well!*

CHAPTER FORTY-FIVE

After the benefit weekend ended, Sarah returned to teaching the last three days of classes at the Riverford School before the Christmas holidays began. Like the increasingly rambunctious students, she was eager for the break from routine and ready to enjoy the beauty and joy of the season. There was much talk of gifts, but Sarah felt she had already received the gift she most wanted. The library school was a reality, and those who opposed it were helpless to stop it. Sarah was especially grateful every time she looked out at her class and saw the deepening friendship of Alison MacKenna and Stephanie Sharp. In her own way, each was a pioneer: In spite of many setbacks, Alison had started a new life in a new country; Stephanie had grown past and defied the bigotry of her mother. Their friendship was emblematic of Sarah's ultimate hope that Riverford would learn to recognize and embrace the God-given worth of every individual.

When the last student had called out "Merry Christmas!" and fled the confines of the classroom on Wednesday afternoon, Lee paid Sarah a surprise visit. "Your holiday begins now," he announced. "I've come to take my fair lady home. The temperature is dropping, and rain is falling."

"Maybe it will snow!"

Lee laughed. "Ever the optimist. We're going to have something frozen, but I'm afraid it's most likely going to be sleet. This is, after all, Texas."

Sarah leaned against her desk and closed her eyes. "Oh, but wouldn't snow be beautiful ... and romantic?"

Lee stole a quick kiss, then pulled her to her feet. "Let's get going. The north wind is beginning to whip around."

"Oh, I have to clean the blackboards." Sarah turned toward the Christmas art the children had drawn on the front board with colored chalks. Each child had contributed to the mosaic and signed her or his name.

"Why don't you leave it?"

Sarah considered. "It would be nice to come back to this Christmas cheer instead of a blank board after New Year's Day." Her shoulders drooped.

"And you're tired. Come on. You're going home and hopefully get a nap in before Victoria's dinner party."

Lee's evaluation of her level of exhaustion was correct. Sarah remained quiet throughout dinner, unable to conjure up the energy to make conversation. When the guests gathered around the fireplace, she felt herself nodding off and was most grateful when Victoria pulled her aside and suggested she go up to bed. She not only slept through the night, she hardly stirred from her room the next day. One nap flowed into another, interrupted only by the arrival of Delphie every few hours with a tray of food to tempt her. In the distance, she heard Antonio playing the violin and Victoria's occasional laughter. The downpour outside shifted from sleet to rain and back to sleet as night fell and she drifted off to sleep.

December twenty-third dawned bright; the clouds had slipped away shortly after midnight and left the dripping world to the mercy of the freezing temperatures. When Sarah rose from her bed, donned her robe, and went to the window, she found an ice-encased world, a glistening show outside her window. Every limb was coated in a crystal sheath; ice "berries" were hanging off every twig.

"Well finally!" Victoria called from the doorway as she entered Sarah's bedroom. "I was beginning to worry about you." She looked over her shoulder. "Bring the tray in, Delphie. Sleeping Beauty has awakened."

"And she must—absolutely must—go Christmas shopping," Sarah exclaimed. "Tomorrow is Christmas Eve, and I'm totally unprepared. How did this happen?"

"You have been just a bit distracted. We all have. Here." Victoria handed Sarah a cup of tea. "Sit down and eat some breakfast. You hardly touched food yesterday." She poured herself a steaming cup as Delphie added coal to the fireplace. "A certain anxious young banker came by several times yesterday, but I wouldn't let anybody awaken you. No doubt he'll be back as soon as he can abandon the bank."

"Well, I probably won't be here." Sarah lifted the cover from the rose-sprigged-china serving dish. "Oh good, eggs and bacon. I'm absolutely starving!"

"And biscuits hot out of the oven." Victoria pulled back the linen cloth keeping the bread warm. "Antonio is still asleep, of course. These Europeans! They don't eat dinner until nine o'clock and wouldn't think of going to bed before midnight." She sipped her tea. "And Antonio is worse than most since he refuses to eat before performing and is so keyed up after a performance. He says he rarely goes to bed before two o'clock, and I believe him."

Sarah studied Victoria as she buttered a biscuit. "Do you still miss the excitement of living abroad?"

"Sometimes ..." Victoria's eyes saddened as she grew reflective. "I miss the company of other artists. I miss the encouragement of a culture that appreciates art." She met Sarah's eyes. "That's why I loved our weeks in Colorado so much. They brought artistic vitality back to my life."

"And look what you've accomplished since you came home!"

"Yes. I like both of the paintings I've done this fall, but I'm especially proud of that painting of you on the mesa. I think it will gain me a place in that show in New York I want to enter. And I owe it all to you, Sarah."

Sarah grimaced. "Unfortunately, you owe the distractions of this fall to me too. I shouldn't have involved you in my struggles with the school board."

"I'd like to see you keep me out of them!" Victoria's teacup clattered as she settled it into its saucer with a vengeance. "By throwing away all these people from other countries, this town is throwing away invaluable talent. Who knows how many artists, musicians, scientists ..." Her words sputtered to an angry end as she clamped her jaws shut.

"You are the best ally I have, Victoria. You're the one who taught me to fight."

"Oh no, I'm not!" Victoria burst out laughing as she leaned toward Sarah. "You're the girl who fought her way off the farm. I just went along for the ride."

"Ha! You engineered my entire education."

"*You* refused to be a maid and stomped out of Edith Bellows' house!"

"Speaking of Edith, what on earth has come over her? She actually waved at us when Lee brought me home. She came out onto her front porch in that sleet and waved at us!"

Victoria grinned devilishly as she settled back in her chair. "Antonio has come over her."

"Amazing results."

"And something we should all learn from, I think. Antonio treated her like a lady; he made her feel valuable, and she rose to his definition of her. Best of all, Antonio's behavior redefined Mr. Bellows' view of his wife's worth."

"Does this mean she's going to support us in our fight for the immigrant children's education?"

"She's going to support the library, but I suspect we'll find that she remains silent about the classes."

"Silence would be a welcome change. I'll take it!" Sarah declared.

"Yes, one less leader in the opposition. That's a victory."

"Maybe we should send Antonio to call on Fanny Sharp and Louise Proper."

Victoria laughed as she rose and reached for the breakfast tray. "I doubt they have the same vulnerability to male charm that Edith does. Now, you get dressed, young lady. We have shopping to do. Antonio is spending the afternoon at Christine's house. Supposedly they're just having tea, but I think he's got some kind of surprise up his sleeve."

"Whatever it is, it won't outdo his conversion of Edith Bellows!"

CHAPTER FORTY-SIX

As the gaslights were turned down in historic St. Paul's Church on Christmas Eve and the glow of candlelight softened the parishioners' faces, Antonio slipped to the front of the sanctuary and lifted the bow of his violin. The hauntingly beautiful strains of "Lo, How a Rose E'er Blooming" filled the air. Sarah scanned the faces near her and hoped that the song, which retold the most important story in history, was softening even the hardest hearts. Lee slipped his hand around hers. How Sarah yearned to lean into him and feel the strength of his arm around her! The weeks of December had been crushingly busy as she taught her classes, then gave every other waking hour to the effort to provide future education for the immigrant children. There had been such opposition from many in the town! Sarah had felt like she was swimming upstream in the dark, but now that the library was a reality, she had substantial hope. She bowed her head as a prayer of gratitude flowed through her mind.

"'Lo, how a Rose e'er blooming from tender stem hath sprung!'"

Sarah started at the accent of the girl's voice that unexpectedly rang out from the back of the church. Was she imagining things? Could it be?

"'Of Jesse's lineage coming as seers of old have sung.'"

Unable to resist, Sarah, like many in the congregation, twisted around and stared up the aisle. There she saw Alison MacKenna, her auburn hair flowing round her fair face, holding a lighted taper. "How beautiful!" Sarah's immediate thought escaped her lips as the girl continued to sing.

"'It came a blossom bright, amid the cold of winter, when half spent was the night.'"

Sarah saw a movement in the shadows behind Alison. When Piotr Dobrowski, carrying a lighted taper, stepped forward, she gasped. In a clear tenor voice with a decidedly Polish accent, Piotr sang the second verse.

Isaiah 'twas foretold it, the Rose I have in mind.
With Mary we behold it, the Virgin Mother kind.
To show God's love aright, she bore to us a Savior, when half spent was the night.

Sarah watched in wonder as Alison and Piotr parted and revealed Stephanie Sharp, who stepped between them carrying a third lighted taper. Together they sang the final verse.

O Flower, whose fragrance tender with sweetness fills the air,
Dispel in glorious splendor the darkness everywhere.
True man, yet very God, from sin and death now save us, and share our ev'ry load.

Joy surged through Sarah. She might be battling the town, but clearly her students had embraced the higher ground. There they stood—Scottish Alison and Polish Piotr forming a string of solidarity, and the vital link was Stephanie Sharp.

"Why, that's Fanny Sharp's daughter!" Sarah heard a woman's shocked voice behind her.

Yes! Yes, it is! She wanted to shout the words.

Antonio began to play "Silent Night," and Sarah followed the lead of the rest of the congregation, turned, and knelt. Her eyes fell on the carved wooden images of the Holy Family, the nativity scene Victoria and Hayden had brought back from Italy. She contemplated the difficulties Mary had endured to follow God's calling. She remembered the selfless support Joseph had given. *Such faith! Such sacrifice!* She felt her face lift in a grateful smile as she focused on Mary's expression, on the adoration she displayed as she gazed down at her newborn Son.

Still kneeling, the congregation began to sing, ever so reverently, the words of "Silent Night." Sarah's heart sang, even though her throat was too tight to utter a word. Slowly her emotions gentled, she found her voice, and managed to join in the final "Sleep in heavenly peace." As the last words faded away, the congregation was stilled, kneeling together in spite of their differences. Sarah prayed that every adult present was reevaluating his or her recent words, actions, or reactions. *Oh Lord! Change their hearts.*

The acolytes came forward and extinguished the candles on the altar. Silent still, the congregation began to file out. Sarah tried to rise to her feet, but Lee pulled her down to sit on the pew.

"Let's stay a while," he whispered.

"I should go thank the children."

"Just wait. The children will come to you."

"I can hardly believe ... have you ever heard such beautiful voices?"

"Never."

"And the message. 'Dispel in glorious splendor the darkness everywhere.' How perfect. And to think, the three of them singing together ..."

Before she could say more, the three children plus Alban slipped down the aisle to hug her and wish her a merry Christmas.

"Thank you. God bless you," was all she managed to whisper before they were gone again.

Lee insisted she sit awhile, and together they watched as the acolytes returned to snuff the candles in each window niche. Only the standing candelabra at the front sides remained lit as John and Lavinia walked down the center aisle, hand in hand.

"How did you like your Christmas present, Sarah?" Lavinia's eyes shone with happy tears.

"Nothing could have meant more to me. I'm quite overcome. But who has arranged this?" She looked at John.

"Not I," he hastened to insist. "Antonio and Christine."

"Of course." Sarah nodded. "The surprise."

John grinned at her. "You've only seen the ribbon, my friend. Just you wait." He handed a candle snuffer to Lee. "I'll trust you to extinguish the remaining candles. There's no hurry."

Lavinia leaned over and kissed Sarah on the forehead. "Merry Christmas, Sarah."

"The most blessed Christmas ever," John added before taking Lavinia's hand and leading her away.

"And the same to you," Sarah softly called after them.

She turned to Lee. "I can't think of words beautiful enough—"

"Next Christmas we will kneel here as husband and wife." His lips met hers and lingered.

She pulled back so she could smile up at him. "As husband and wife ... and as what else, I wonder."

"Banker and teacher." His voice was firm.

"I wonder ..."

"I don't. I know you'll be teaching one way or the other. And I know we'll be celebrating our first Christmas together." He pulled a small, satin-covered box from his pocket. "And you'll be wearing this, starting now. I promised myself I'd wait until Christmas Day to give it to you, and I have. It's way past midnight. Open it, my darling."

When Sarah opened the hinged box, diamonds glistened up at her.

"It was my grandmother's engagement ring," Lee said as he took the ring from the box. "And now it's yours." He slid the ring onto her finger. "I hope it's not too old-fashioned a setting for such a modern lady."

Sarah held out her hand so the candlelight could catch the sparkling stones. "We modern ladies are standing on the shoulders of the women who came before us. That's what Victoria says, and she's absolutely right." She kissed the ring. "I am blessed to be allowed to stand on your grandmother's shoulders in our marriage." A worry flitted through her mind. "You're not sorry we postponed our marriage?"

"No. When we stand in this church and take our vows, I want us to be free to focus on our relationship. I want us to build something that will bring us joy for a lifetime."

Sarah relaxed against his broad chest as she watched the candles flicker. "For this one moment, my world is perfect."

"I wish I could make it stay that way for you, but I know I can't. Life will present us with ups and downs, but whatever comes, we'll live it together. Always together."